Out of A Darkening Sky

Norma Jolliffe

Out of A Darkening Sky
Copyright © 2019 by Norma Jolliffe

All rights reserved. No part of this publication may be reproduced, distributed, or transmitted in any form or by any means, including photocopying, recording, or other electronic or mechanical methods, without the prior written permission of the author, except in the case of brief quotations embodied in critical reviews and certain other non-commercial uses permitted by copyright law.

tellwell

Tellwell Talent
www.tellwell.ca

ISBN
978-0-2288-2146-5 (Hardcover)
978-0-2288-2147-2 (Paperback)
978-0-2288-2148-9 (eBook)

Chapter 1

She stood outside the small, noisy train station, one shoulder hunched against the falling rain, wondering why she had come this far to get wet, when she could have easily done the same thing at home. There were noises all around her, the traffic, the rattle of trains on tracks, doors slamming, soft drink cans rattling down metal shuts. And the smells; diesel fumes, perfume and aftershave, rotting fruit, but most of all the hot scent of machine produced instant coffee, that was making her mouth water. Then there were the voices that were everywhere, sometimes drowning out the sound of rain on the metal roof above her. Voices that were greeting new arrivals with joy and voices bidding tearful farewells, mostly spoken in varying British accents, a few with the familiar tones of India. Her own accent she knew would mistake her for an American, even though she was a West Coast Canadian.

It was early fall, but she and her mother had hoped that the weather might still be pleasant. She wiped the rain from the end of her nose and glared at her mother's bent back as she spoke through the open window of a taxi. A taxi that would take them to the old, stately home that was their bed and breakfast for the next two weeks. The prices were better at this time of year and her mother had longed for her birthplace for many years.

She turned her head to look at the wet green around her. They were two hours north of London, after a long flight. She wished she had been able to persuade her mother to stay over at least one night in London to recover from jet lag. But her dear, impatient mother had wanted to go directly to Leicestershire. And now, here they were in Whipford, where her mother had spent the first years of her life.

"Riana! Riana, come along! I've found us a taxi!"

Riana Ingram smiled, amused in spite of herself and the misery of the rain. Since her arrival in Great Britain, her mother's accent had increased with each mile away from the airport. She lifted her head and turned smiling, toward the older woman. A thin, hunched man was lifting their luggage into a small, mud-coloured car and Clare Wigmore was hurrying him along with an impatient wave of her hand. Riana left the dubious shelter of the overhanging station roof and skirted her way around other's luggage, boxes and animal crates, going to where her mother waited. Clare looked up at her daughter with no little expression of impatience.

"Riana, where have you been? I've been calling you."

Riana sighed, "I know. I heard you. But I'm tired, Mom. I just want to go to bed."

Clare smiled as Riana approached, "I know, dear, but it's best to finish the day here as if we woke up here this morning."

She paused to peer into her daughter's face with concern, "Are you feeling alright? If you really need to rest, then you must."

Riana reached out and touched Clare's sleeve, giving her a light caress.

"I'm fine. You promised to not baby me. And I think you're right, we should finish this day properly. We did discuss this before we left home." she peeked over her mother's shoulder, "Is this man able to take us all the way to Riverton Abbey?"

The man looked around the upraised trunk hood, his pale eyes in his wizened face twinkled with no little humour.

"Yes, M'um. I takes this road daily." He said mildly.

Riana felt heat in her cheeks, "I'm sorry to have doubted you."

He gave a little chuckle, "You Americans all think my little motor will let them down. It's fifteen years I've had it and it has never let me down. I takes care of her and she takes care of me."

He stowed the last bag and closed the hood before opening the back door of the car. It squeaked a little, enough for Clare to give it a doubting glance. Riana moved ahead of her to the back seat and sat down, more than a little surprised by the spotless upholstery. Clare followed immediately, giving Riana a rueful smile as the man slid behind the steering wheel. The engine started easily and there was no sound of grinding gears as he shifted the car into motion.

"How long does it take to get to Riverton Abbey?" Clare asked, leaning forward to clutch the back of the front seat.

"No more'n thirty minutes in this weather, Mu'um. It's faster when the weather is fine. You'll like the Abbey, it's on the National Register, you know. It has a manager what knows what's what and as fine a man as you wish to meet. And the cook is American or so I've heard"

The driver turned out to be a most informative guide. As they drove through narrow, tree-line roads, he pointed out the ruins of an old castle, describing it's history and the history of the area. When they passed through a village, with old building mingling with new, modern houses, he pointed out the best places to eat and the shops that gave the best value for money. Riana like the charming stone walls that seemed to delineate every plot of land, and the pretty front yards of the houses. From time to time, he named some of the flora that edged the road.

"What about Riverton Abbey itself?" Riana asked when he paused for breath.

He stopped the car to let a flock of sheep and their shepherd pass before them.

"It's not so old as some around here, but it has a proud history. It dates back to the time of Charles the Second. The land was given as a reward for duty in the Dutch Wars and it's been in the same family ever since."

He stopped talking as he negotiated a particularly rough and twisty part of the road, and Riana looked out the rain-streaked window. She was used to the intense greens of Coastal vegetation, but here it was even greener. There was none of the New World wild growth here. The modern housing of the village faded, giving way to some small, neat cottages with brightly blooming gardens that broke up the monotony of the road. She felt the tension in her spine relax, for somehow it was beginning to feel comfortable here. She glanced over at her mother and saw the small smile of pleasure on Clare's face. Clare was home.

The car slowed and Riana's attention was drawn away from her mother. They were turning left of the main road, going between black-painted iron fences that led up to two concrete octagonal shaped pillars that were nearly twelve feet tall and six feet around, made to look like elongated buildings. Tall iron gates stood open, and on each pillar was a black shield with the words "Riverton Abbey" printed in plain, yellow letters. There was a decided bump after they drove between the pillars, and the quality of the road surface lessened, becoming rougher.

"The road to Riverton Abbey." The driver told them unnecessarily.

Gradually the road curved, edged by a wire and wood fence that held in the fall coloured trees that edged a leaf covered lawn. The curve of the road ended abruptly, and an arching concrete bridge, covered with lichen and guarded on either side by huge willow trees suddenly rising up before them. A wide river flowed under the bridge, and on it floated two white swans

The road continued to curve after the bridge and the fencing ended. In the misty distance, almost hidden by big, old trees, they could see the roofline of a large, dark building, with chimneys that rose into the grey skyline. The sun poke out weakly as the curving road ended in a straight, tree-lined avenue, lighting the windows of the building and throwing shadows across the road and lawn.

The driver slowed, allowing his passengers to study the sprawling lawns, the little church and the old, dark headstones of the small graveyard. Then the pavement widened again, changing into a parking lot, where three cars were parked. Riana had to crane her neck upward to see what was going to be their home for two weeks. It presented a rather plain, flat front, with an ornately decorated entry, set in the last quarter of the facade, jutting out several feet, with an arching porticoleading to the tall, glass and wood main doors, through the high arching entry. On either side were huge pineapple shaped urns fill with tall grass and ferns. Jarringly modern light posts stood by the red granite pillars, their bottoms hidden by bright masses of geraniums.

"There be forty-five windows on the front of this house. Those tall, Gothic windows above the door is the picture gallery. It's one of the finest in the country."

"When I was a little girl, my mother worked here as an upstairs maid." Clare was unable to control the awe in her voice, "She never brought me here, but she spoke of it often."

The driver's head twisted in astonishment, but he kept his eyes on the road.

"You be from Whipford, M'um?"

"Yes!" Clare seemed equally astonished by this, "I was born here, but I left many, many years ago. In 1962. My husband and I moved to Canada, a few months before our first son was born."

"Who is your family then? You'll be visiting with them?"

"Unfortunately, I was an only child. My last relative, my aunt Mamie died four years ago."

"Mamie Pickett?"

Clare laughed, "Yes. Did you know her?"

"I most assuredly did. Our back gardens joined. I miss our chats over the wall. You were Clare Pickett and you married Daniel

Wigmore. Sad family those Wigmores. You did right moving from here. Did you have better luck in Canada?"

"Oh, much better." She paused as said almost to herself "I'd forgotten that small villages never forget."

"Mother?' Riana broke in, her mind whirling with curiosity, "What's that all about?"

Clare patted her knee, "I'll tell you later. I suppose it's time you knew. Oh! Here we are! I'm so excited to be here after all these years."

But Riana was no longer paying attention to her mother. The sun had vanished as quickly as it had come, and once again, the light dimmed. Her focus now was on a figure that was standing in a grove of trees passed the little footbridge that arched over the river on the far side of the lawn. It was a man in a very tall top hat, who was leaning with hands crossed on the top of a thin, black cane. His features were hidden in the shadow of his had brim, but there was a sense of strength in the tall body. A long, grey coat fell to his calves and flapped around the tops of his high shiny black boots. As the breeze teased the opening of his coat, she was able to glimpse pale coloured pants, tucked into the boots, a brighter vest and a dark jacket. There was a hint of a white shirt with a high collar and a white sort of tie. Her eyes stung from her unblinking stare and when she finally blinked and looked back, he was gone. She opened her mouth to ask the driver about the man, but by then the car had curved into the parking area and stopped at the front door.

Without waiting for the driver to open the door, Clare scrambled out of the car, almost falling in her eagerness. She had spent her youth wondering and dreaming about this house and now she was here. At one time, as a teenager, she had fantasized about marrying the young lord of the manor, until she had seen him. A thin, gangling youth with spots and a shambling manner. And he was three years her junior. She turned to beckon Riana from the car, turning without seeing if her daughter was following, and met the taxi driver, who now held a bag in each hand, at the step. Riana traipsed behind her mother at a more leisurely pace.

Once inside, she stopped in awe, unaware that her mother was doing the very thing ten feet in front of her. The main room, whatever it had been before, was now the front office. Her eyes followed the line of the curving marble stairs up to a balcony that lined half the entry, and with Arabic-styled arches and red granite columns, overlooked the floor below, which had the same arches and columns, holding up the balcony, but on a much, much, larger scale. Clare began moving again, her heels loud on the pallid marble floor. Couches and chairs in red brocade were scattered about, some clustered with coffee and lamp tables. Under the curve of the staircase, was the front desk, long and high in dark wood, glaringly out of place in the room. A man came forward to relieve the taxi driver of the luggage.

"Mrs.. Wigmore? Mrs.. Ingram? Welcome to Riverton Abbey. We will show you to your rooms directly you have checked in."

"But how did you know?" Clare sputtered.

He gave them a smile, and it was then that Riana saw the discreet nameplate pinned to his jacket, announcing he was the general manager. Before she had a chance to speak, the driver waved back at his late charges.

"Mrs.. Wigmore be the wife of Daniel Wigmore. D'you remember him, Arthur?" he announced with a sly smile.

The man looked stunned, "Clare? Clare Pickett? I'm Arthur McGrath, Dan's best mate in school."

Clare held out a shaking hand, delight brightening her face, "Arthur? My goodness! I never expected to see you here! You always said you were going to travel the world. Did you?"

"I did that. For more years than I care to remember. I was very ill in India when I met Lord Ranleigh, who offered me a job here. It was about the time he opened it to the public and needed someone he could trust to run the place. I've been here nearly ten years. It is exceedingly good to see you, Clare. How's Dan?"

Clare's face went blank for a moment as it always did at the mention of her husband, "He was killed in a plane crash three years ago." she half-turned to Riana, "This is my daughter Riana Ingram. Riana, this is an old school friend, Arthur McGrath."

Riana held out her hand and after a brief hesitation, he took it, "I am very pleased to meet you, Mrs.. Ingram. I have a son, Bron who must be a year or two older than you. He is in London at present, but he comes here from time to time. You might enjoy his company?"

Riana swallowed the rebuke that formed in her throat. There was no reason to offend this man, nor share her miseries with him.

"That might be nice." She murmured, then forced a smile, "And why is the manager greeting us?"

He gave a small chuckle, "The desk staff is at tea, so you must be patient and let me check you in."

"Of course."

As he led them to the front desk, Riana's head swivelled, taking in the details, from the heavily carved cornices and doorways. Never before had she seen such an elaborately carved ceiling, nor a chimney piece that was nearly large enough to stand in. The light beige tiles on the floor were so closely fitted it was hard to tell where one ended and another began. Her eyes were following the graceful lines of the floral draperies that fell from the bottom of the cornices, when the manager's voice interrupted her study.

"If I can have you sign in, Mrs.. Ingram?"

He was holding out a pen to her over the top of the desk and she was only half-aware of her mother thanking and paying the driver. She returned to Riana's side just as she was finishing.

"It is such a delight to see you again, Clare. Please be my guest for dinner this evening. I eat in what was the Breakfast room, it's a charming place. More comfortable than the formal dining room where the guests take their meals. And you as well, Mrs.. Ingram."

"Thank-you, Arthur. We would be delighted."

He clapped his hand together in satisfaction, "Splendid! Dinner is at eight o'clock. Lord Ranleigh likes to keep what he calls civilized hours."

"Is Lord Ranleigh at home?" Clare asked breathlessly, briefly recalling her childish fantasy.

"Not at present. He's in banking in London, so is seldom in residence. The young Lord Jared is home most weekends. He's in show business." He made a disgusted face, "Please allow me to show you to your rooms."

From somewhere a young man in his late teens, wearing a gold-braided burgundy jacket, appeared and silently gathered their luggage.

"There's no lift, I'm afraid." Arthur apologised, "Lord Ranleigh wanted to leave the Abbey as close to original as possible."

Riana stood in the middle of her bedroom in stunned silence, nearly tripping over her carry-on as she wandered into it. Never before had she had a room with such opulence. Tall and wide leaded glass windows let in the dull grey light, but the yellow-gold of the walls made the room seem cheerier than the weather might allow. Her bed was half-testered, the canopy and spread embroidered cream satin. There was a portrait of a man in Elizabethan dress over the white marble of the fireplace that was edged with green and gold tiles. Beside the fireplace was a cozy wing chair in tonal stripes of cream with a handy little table beside it. There was a small dressing table between the tall windows, skirted with the same striped cream fabric and a white and gold desk with a matching low-backed chair, also in striped cream close to the bed. The floor was covered with a sky blue carpet that was soft underfoot and gold-framed pictures were scattered in charming arrangements on the walls.

She went to a half-open door and discovered a small bathroom with a deep, old-fashioned tub and a small shower in one corner. The single, narrow window was set to high on the wall, she knew she would never reach it and thick yellow towels hung from a bar below it. A pretty basket of toiletries sat on the marble countertop along with a dainty floral arrangement of dried flowers. Returning to the bedroom again, she took a deep breath of contentment. Yes, she would be quite happy here for the next two weeks.

Clare's room across the wide, carpeted hallway was far different. It too, was in shades of yellow, but the walls were papered with a tiny floral print. The window was much smaller with only a single chair under it. The bed, however, was full testered, it's hanging and bed skirt a bright floral pattern, the spread pale yellow damask. The plain fireplace had a plain marble surround and a gold framed mirror above it. There was a comfortable easy chair, a round table and a pretty crewel work screen and matching hearthrug. Clair was sitting in the easy chair, exhaustion deepening the lines in her face.

"You're the one who should be exhausted, Riana. Not me." She complained in a teasing voice.

Riana smiled and touched her mother's shoulder, "Well, you're the old lady, remember? I'm fine Mother. Must be this good, British air. We have a while before dinner, so take it easy."

"I will, but you must, too. You're the one that's sick. You have to take care."

"There's so much to see and do. If it wasn't raining, I'd go for a walk, just to see the grounds. Maybe I'll just walk the hallways to see what there is to see. Isn't this place fabulous? Can you imagine living here? And the cost of upkeep. No wonder the rates are high. Thank-you, Mother, for bringing me here. It's going to be a wonderful trip, I just know it."

Clare felt tears sting her throat as she looked at her only daughter. She swallowed them, knowing how much Riana hated pity and tears.

She gave what felt like a shaky smile, "This is something I've always wanted to do. I wanted both you and your brothers to see where your father and I grew up. I'm just sorry Jake and Brian couldn't come."

Riana gave her a gentle smile, "They don't like to be reminded that I am no longer healthy enough to climb trees and fences. It's alright. They were never interested in coming back, anyway, even 'tho they were both born here."

Clare touched Riana's wrist, "Be sure to dress warmly, these old buildings are always drafty. You will come back for me in an hour?"

"Sure thing. And I'll bet I'll have a lot to tell you."

Riana returned to her room and took a heavy cardigan from her luggage. As she pulled it on, she went to the window and looked out across the lawn at the line of trees a fair distance from the house. The sky had darKened even more since their arrival, so she was only barely able to make out the figure that stood under the spreading shelter of a tree whose leaves were turning yellow and orange. It was the same man she had seen from the car. He was dressed the same, this time holding the cane in one hand, tilted negligently away from him, his other hand holding back the edge of his long coat, resting on his hip. His head was slanted upward, looking toward the house. Riana stepped back from the window, feeling as if he was looking directly at her. When she glanced back a moment later, he was gone.

"That's odd." she said aloud as she buttoned her cardigan.

She began her exploration of the house by going down her own corridor, pausing to look at each great painting on the walls and examining a piece of Wedgewood or some of the porcelain pieces that decorated chests and tables. At the end of the corridor was a set of narrow stairs that went steeply upward. She began to ascend the steps with the now-familiar throbbing n her head began and she backed down carefully. In only a few minutes, if she did not take her medication, she would be stiff with pain. As she retraced her steps, walking slowly, placing her feet cautiously, she hoped she would get to her pills in just in time, for her episodes of pain often frightened her mother.

She medicated herself in time. She lay back on the cool, slick satin of her bedspread with her eyes closed, waiting for the threatening pain to disappear. For a time there was no thought in her head, lately a new experience for her and the quiet of the room helped. She dozed without realizing until a knock on the door woke her. Groggily, she went to the door and opened it to find Clara standing in the hall, her brow wrinkled with concern.

"I overslept. Riana, dear are you alright? You look pale." she gasped softly, as she recalled Riana's condition, "Are you in pain? Have you taken your medication?"

"I'm fine." Riana croaked, "I took a pill and fell asleep. Blame it on jet lag." she gave a tiny grin, "Neither one of us could control ourselves, it seems. Are you ready for dinner? Come in, and I'll change. I've been in these clothes far too long. I hope we can find our way." she called back over her shoulder.

Clare closed the door behind her and sat down by the fireplace, "Didn't you notice those small, discreet plaques on the walls pointing the way?" she spoke louder over the sound of running water, "We'll just follow those."

Arthur McGrath met them at the bottom of the elegant, marble staircase. With him was a much younger and taller man, dressed in an extravagant white shirt, rich navy brocade vest and sharply creased navy pant. This man had a mass of blond hair and round blue eyes framed with thick, dark lashes. His elegant, sculpted mouth widened with a warm smile as they approached. With her hand on the mahogany banister, her new bead-trimmed jacket and matching pants, Riana felt like a princess nearing a prince. She returned his smile with what she hoped was a royal smile.

"Mrs.. Wigmore, Mrs.. Ingram, please meet Lord Jared Thorpe, heir to Riverton Abbey."

Well, not a prince but a Lord, Riana thought. Close enough. Jared took the hand that Clare held out.

"Mrs.. Wigmore. Mrs.. Ingram." his wonderful, deep voice had the ring of good breeding.

He smiled at again at Riana, but made no attempt to shake her hand.

"The heir to Riverton Abbey." Clare said with delight, "I can remember when your father was the heir. How is he doing now?"

"Splendidly. He very much enjoys his work with the Bank and hates to leave it. You knew my father?"

"Good heavens no!" Clare said with a charming laugh, "Only to see him. We hardly travelled in the same circles. My husband and I left here before our first son was born."

There was a silence, but his welcoming smile did not quaver. "You are one of the Whipford Wigmores? My Goodness, I thought there were no more left. So, Mrs.. Ingram, my I conclude that you too, were once a Wigmore?"

"That's right. What is the big deal?" she tilted her head a little, "That's the second time today that there has been a negative comment about the Wigmore name."

Jared glanced quickly at Clare who immediately dropped her eyes to the floor.

"Didn't you know that our families have been oddly linked? There is something of a curse on the Wigmore name. It's a good story."

He took Clare's hand and tucked it into his elbow in an unconscious, elegant manner and turned them all away from the hall.

"Let's go to the Breakfast Room, shall we? The hall is rather too chilly when the weather is like this."

Riana moved in step with Arthur following her mother and escort. The comment intrigued her.

"Curse? What kind of curse? A good, old-fashioned British curse? Isn't that just a bit melodramatic? How did it all come about?"

He did not answer her until they were in the small, oval Breakfast room. Graceful yellow tied back draperies decorated the leaded glass windows that all but reached the floor. Riana was curious about what was beyond them, then lost the thought. Arthur held out a chair for her and Jared did the same for her mother. Jared sat down directly across from Riana and gave her a cheeky, teasing smile.

"The story goes back to the beginning of the nineteenth century, about the time of the Napoleonic Wars. It seems one of your Wigmore ancestors killed an Irish guest in a duel. Why a guest of Riverton Abbey would be fighting with a townsman, or more likely, a farmer, I've never been able to find out. In any case, the man cursed his murderer with his dying breath, declaring the Wigmores of Whipford would have no prosperity until one of them righted the wrong. Well," he took a deep, dramatic breath, "he neglected to say just what wrong had to be righted. More than a few Wigmores have attempted to do just that, only to fail. Lack of proper information, you see. And as well, it seems that this Irish guest now haunts Riverton Abbey, for reasons of his own, I suppose. Is that why you're here, Mrs.. Wigmore? Or is that why you are here, Mrs.. Ingram, since you are Wigmore blood."

He was being cheeky at this point and Riana returned with a mock smile that he acknowledged with a wink. But Clare did not see this quick exchange.

"We're here in holiday." Clare told him stiffly, "I never put much credence in that old myth. My late husband did and that is why we moved to Canada. And prospered." she finished defiantly.

"And I, of course, knew nothing about it until I came here. So am I now expected to try to right the wrong? Aren't there any Wigmores at all left here to do the job? Not even one?"

He shook his head and gave a quick look at Arthur, "No. It didn't take long for them to realize Whipford is not the place for them. From time to time a descent returns, but leaves within the space of a few years."

"Nice tale for the Canadian tourists."

Riana looked at her mother but was prevented from speaking by the appearance of a waiter. He was dressed in a white shirt, striped vest and wore a huge grey apron that covered him from chest to nearly his ankles. He looked at Arthur in silent question.

"Would you like a cocktail to begin?" Arthur asked the assembled table.

Before Clare could speak, Riana answered for both of them, "The medication I take does not allow it, but my mother would love a small sherry. For myself, just plain water, thank-you."

The men also ordered cocktails as Riana set out by her spoon, the array of pills she had to take with food. Jared rested his arm on the table as he bent toward her.

"You're ill?"

"Not when I take these." she replied with a smile, "Are you a real Lord?"

"I'm the oldest son of an Earl. But yes, I am. Why are you avoiding my question, Mrs.. Ingram?"

Her smile widened, "I answered your question. And please call me Riana."

"Riana. Lovely name, that. Welsh, isn't it? How does your husband feel about your being so far away from him?"

For the first time, Jared felt the deep penetrating gaze of Riana's deep green eyes. It was almost as if she were the witch for whom she had been named. It disconcerted him, a feeling he did not like.

"My husband is dead." she informed him bluntly, ignoring the grimace that always came over Clare's face when she announced her marital status so bluntly.

He pulled away from her a little, "I beg your pardon. I didn't know."

Her smile released him, "Of course you didn't. It has been three years. And no, I do not have any children."

The twinkle in her eye now relaxed him. She reached across the table and touched her fingertips lightly to his shirtsleeve.

"I'm sorry. I can be kind of blunt, sometimes. I speak without thinking."

"Don't be sorry." he assured her "It is all a part of getting to know each other."

The drinks arrived and the conversation stalled a moment. He tasted his and nodded his acceptance to the waiter. Then he looked back at his guests.

"I was thinking that if you don't have too much planned for tomorrow, I can take you," there was a slight hesitation, "and your mother on a drive around the countryside. I can show you things most tourists in this area don't see."

Clare sipped her sherry, "Do take Riana. I think I will spend tomorrow visiting old friends who have kept in touch. And I am a little tired from the trip. Riana has so much more energy than I do."

That settled it. Riana cast aside any doubts about leaving her mother and gratefully accepted the offer. Then the meal came, exceptionally delicious, given the British reputation for bad food. The conversation over the meal became light hearted as Clare and Arthur began sharing their childhood memories of Whipford. Jared's contribution to the conversation was the telling of amusing tales of his career as a television producer.

When the meal ended all of them made their way back into the hall and paused at the bottom of the staircase. Arthur excused himself to return to his job and Jared laid a light hand on Riana's shoulder.

"Can I show you the house before you retire?"

Clare had take two steps upward and now she stopped and turned.

"I think Riana should go to bed. It's been a very long day for both of us. And thank-you for the meal, it was lovely. But exhaustion and good food has taken it's toll, I'm afraid."

Riana could almost see him bow, yet he did not. Riana glared at her mother as Jared answered.

"Of course. How thoughtless of me. Can I meet you right here tomorrow morning at nine o'clock?"

"I'll be here. And thank-you for the offer."

Chapter 2

As it turned out, there was not to be a drive around the countryside. When Riana's breakfast arrived in her room the next morning, there was a note from Jared. A crisis at work called him back to London. He was very sorry, but promised to take her out as soon as he returned. Riana smiled and put the note on the table beside her, relieved that she didn't have to spend the day with a stranger. She wanted to spend as much time with her mother as she was able.

The rain of yesterday was gone, replaced by a glorious sunny day. Riana joined her mother and together they walked around the grounds closest to the house, going through one of the big window-doors in the dining room, strolling form a time along the arch-shaded gallery before crossing across the lawn toward the balustrade and the steps that led to the lower lawn. They did not talk, but enjoyed the warm sunshine, the spicy autumn fragrance of the air and the beauty of the blooming fall flowers. Clare brought along her camera and took pictures of Riana sitting on the balustrade, standing on the wide steps, with the rather plain back of the house in the background. Riana posed patiently, for she understood her mother's need to make as many memories as possible.

It was Clare, once again, who tired first.

"Sweetheart, I must go inside. I'm pooped. Why don't you come in too, you need to rest."

Riana stepped down another step and glanced over at the willow trees in the distance.

"You go in, Mom. I'm not in the least tired. I'll just go for a walk. I feel full of energy today, and this place seems made for walking, so I'm going to take advantage of it."

"You won't go far?" Clare asked anxiously.

"I'll go as far as I'm able. Don't worry, I won't push myself. I know better than that." she made a shooing motion, "Go inside, I'll be fine. I've made it this far without doing damage to myself. And I'm sure there are lots of people around if I need help. Which I won't. I'll come and get you for lunch and we can decide what to do this afternoon."

"You won't overdo?"

"No. I promise."

Riana went up the stairs after her mother and leaned on the concrete railing, watching her mother return to the big house. There was a peace here she had not experienced before and she wanted to enjoy it. She lifted her face to the sun and smiled at it's warmth. Slowly she turned her head toward the echoing screech of a peacock and saw, standing in the distance in the shade of the willow trees, over the arching foot bridge, the man from the day before. He was dressed the same, leaning on his cane, his free hand beckoning to her. She looked behind her, thinking for a moment that maybe he was signalling someone else, but there was no one.

She took one step down, tilting her head, thinking he must be an employee, dressed in period costume. His hand continued to wave her forward so she carefully made her way down the remainder of the steps and across the lawn. Her hand slid on the railing of the wooden footbridge and when she reached the middle of it, he turned and began walking away from her, waving his hand behind him to urge her to follow him. She had to run a little to keep up with his long-legged stride as he moved quickly toward the crumbling remains of a high stone wall. He had to bend a little to get through the arched opening and for a moment, she lost sight of him. She stopped in the opening, peering around.

"Hello! I'm coming, but what do you want?"

He had stopped under another tree, waiting only long enough for her to see him then continued onward, assuming she still followed. After ducking under thick, low hanging branches, she found herself in a patch of woods. It was wild and untended, unlike the rest of Riverton Abbey and she caught a flash of his coat as he strode ahead of her. His stride slowed and within moments she was almost close enough to touch him.

"Please!" she managed to gasp, "You're going too fast. Can you slow down a little?"

He stopped abruptly and turned toward her. She controlled the stunned gasp that nearly opened her mouth, for he was the best looking man she had ever seen. He was tall and broad-shouldered, something that had always been apparent, his coat fitting him like a second skin. He raised a gloved hand to remove the tall hat and revealed dark, curling hair that was brushed close to his face. The high white points of his shirt collar did not hide the firm, square jaw, but accented the wide, firm mouth, that was generous in it's width. His straight, perfect nose was accented by deep-set hazel eyes, under heavy, arching brows. He raised these brows now as he looked down at her.

"You are finally come." he said in a voice so deep and rumbling that she felt her toes curl, "I have long waited for you."

Irish. She easily recognized his accent, for it was one she had always loved.

"For me? You've always waited for me? Why? I don't know you, do I? And who are you, anyway?"

He smiled, showing her his white, even teeth and teasing dimples. With heels together, he gave her a slow bow from his waist and then replaced the hat back on his head.

"I am Kieran Gilmartin, third Baron of Donaghmore, at your service."

Riana took a small step back, "Baron? Well isn't this wonderful. An Earl's son last night and a Baron this morning. I sure didn't imagine this when I left home. What are you doing here, dressed like that? Is there some kind of Regency revival going on that I haven't heard about yet?"

His eyes watched her steadily as she spoke, his mouth curving slightly as she spoke.

"I have been waiting for you."

"Me? Why?"

"So many questions." he said almost to himself, "You are a Wigmore, are you not?"

"I was before I got married. Why?"

"Because it is you who must help me."

"Help you do what?" she was beginning to feel a little uneasy.

He placed one hand over the other on the elaborate gold top of his cane and tipped the top half of his body toward her. She smelled a sharp, sweet scent from him that was very pleasant. If he was trying to intimidate her, he failed, for she stood her ground, staring back at him without so much as blinking.

"Find peace. Come with me."

He shifted his cane and began to turn away from her, but she caught at his sleeve. He halted to quickly it took her off-guard and she found herself closer than she wanted. He looked down at her hand and a smile spread slowly across his face, showing her again the long dimples that framed his mouth.

"You can touch me." he said in a low, amazed voice.

"Of course I can. Why shouldn't I?"

With the cane held between two fingers, he touched the back of her hand with the backs of those same fingers. His glove was soft and cool on her skin.

"You are the one. I have long waited for you."

The last words came out with something like a relieved sigh. Riana was fast losing patience with this man she was beginning to suspect was out of his mind. Still the strong beauty of his face held her. Nobody this good looking would be crazy, she was sure of it. At least she hoped she was sure.

"I'm the one what?" she heard the tone of rising fear in her own voice.

Instead of answering, he tucked her hand into his elbow and with a nod of his head, began walking again, making her walk with him. When he felt her falter and drag back, he stopped.

He shifted his cane again, poking the tip of it into the damp ground.

"You have nothing to fear from me. I could never hurt you. All that I ask is that you come with me into the woods. It's just a short distance. When you wish to return to the Abbey, I will not stop you. In fact, I shall escort you so that you do not lose your way."

Riana looked back toward the house, but was able to see only the top floor and the chimneys over the high, moss-covered walls. She looked at the man again.

"Why should I believe you?"

His chuckled rumbled in his chest, "I've not set out to ravish you, if that is your fear. I merely have something I wish you to see. Will you come with me?"

Riana shrugged one shoulder, believing yet not wanting to, this man with the deep, Irish voice.

"Okay then. As long as it isn't far."

"It isn't."

"Lead on, then."

As they began to walk, he lightly brushed his fingers over the back of her hand, sending delicious shivers down her spine. Shivers she had not felt in a very long time.

"You are unwell."

It was not a question, but a statement. A statement she could no more avoid or lie about than she could voluntarily stop breathing. He had sensed the essence of it.

"I am dying. I have a brain tumour. My doctors have given me less than three months to live."

His fingers shifted to give her hand a commiserating squeeze and she felt the cold metal on the top of his cane.

"Doctors can be wrong you know. So why are you come to England?"

"My mother was born here, and my father. She wanted to show me her home. We had planned to come a few years ago, but I was never able to find the time."

"So you have come to please your mother?"

"Yes. It's the least I can do. And my doctor said I could, if I continued my medication as prescribed."

"Ah, yes, so that is why."

"Why what?"

She went over on her ankle, but he caught her enough to keep her upright. He stopped abruptly. Riana looked around at the small opening in the forest. At one end was a small stone cairn on which was a small plaque that she was unable to read at this distance. There was something about this place that raised a wave of apprehension in her.

"Here we are." he announced, looking down at her.

"What is this place?" she heard the tremor in her voice.

He stood a little straighter and took a deep breath.

"Once this was a place of peace for me. Now it is a place of great sadness."

He held up a hand as she opened her mouth to question him again. The black cane did not waver in his grip.

"All I ask is that you walk to the centre of the glade alone. I will wait here for you and return you from whence I found you."

His colourful, old-fashioned language was starting to make it's way into her consciousness. She shrugged.

"Sure, I can do that. Is that all you want?"

He looked up over her head, his eyes focussing on the cairn, "That is all. And I thank you for it."

Reluctantly, she slid her hand from the warmth of his elbow and with a little hitch in her step, began walking through the short, coarse grass toward the middle of the sunlit glade. Curiosity filled her for the first few feet of her walk before a heaviness began pressing down on her. There was a buzzing in her ears and her throat went dry. She glanced back at the tall man and saw to her alarm that he was fading, his head and shoulders bent in an attitude of sorrow. She tried to stop walking and found she was unable, as if something was forcing one foot to move in front of the other.

Riana could not stop and now the clearing itself was fading into a silvery mist. She knew from recent experience that she was fainting and there was no way to stop herself. The ringing in her ears increased as her vision lessened until at last there was oblivion.

"Wake up, Miss. Wake up!"

Riana heard the male voice through the pain that thudded in her head. She wished he would stop talking so loudly, that his voice would vanish. If she kept her eyes closed maybe everything would go away. Light fingers stroked her cheek, the mere sound of flesh on flesh caused another wave of hurt; pain that had been unknown to her before. Was this a new symptom of her disease? She pushed at the hand, only to have her own caught in a light grip. Reluctantly, she opened her eyes to look up at the face that blocked out the sun. She recognised him instantly.

"You! What happened? You said I only had to walk a little way and I could go back. Did I faint?"

Lord Donaghmore frowned as he looked down at her. It was obvious to her, even in her state of pain, that he had no idea what she was talking about.

"I did not see you come, Miss. I looked up and there you lay. I have a little water in my bottle, shall I fetch it for you?"

He helped her into a sitting position, and even that small motion was enough to send waves of nausea from her stomach into her head, that joined the pulses of pain already there. She opened her mouth, but was incapable of speech as she swallowed to keep down her breakfast. The grey, hissing mist gathered again and once more she fainted.

Kieran Gilmartin looked down at the woman in his arms and tightened his grip around her. She felt warm and pliant, but the bare surface of her skin was chilled. Perhaps it was because of the odd clothing she wore. What woman would be out of doors attired thus? Not even in the privacy of her own bed chamber. Still, there was something alluring about her still, pale face. Was it the way her long dark lashes brushed her pale cheeks, or the tempting fullness of her mouth? He felt heartily ashamed of his thoughts as his eyes drifted down to the bare tanned legs and to the place where the neck of the odd garment, so similar to his own winter underclothing, gaped in a revealing fashion. He rose, lifting her easily in his arms. He looked above the treetops toward Riverton Abbey, deciding to take her there immediately, even knowing her clothing would cause no little shock among those living there.

She did not weigh a great deal and he was strong from many years working with his horses. Her head rested lightly on his shoulder and the movement of air caused by his walking made strands of her short, red-gold hair to fly up into his face, a few attaching themselves to the corner of his mouth. He smiled down at her, feeling a sudden, unexplained possessiveness.

A servant met him as he came through the opening in the wall. Another followed close on his heels. The first reached out to take his burden, but he shouldered him away.

"Lady Thorpe saw you from a window and bid me to assist you, Lord Donaghmore."

"Good. Go and have a place prepared for this lady. She has taKen very ill. And have my man go into the glade for my paints and easel. I'll follow you into the house."

"Very good sir."

The servant signalled to the one behind him and each of them hurried away in opposite directions. By the time Lord Donaghmore and his burden reached the house, a bedroom on the first floor had been found and he was taKen to it. His hostess, Daria, the Countess of Ranleigh, was waiting at the bedside as he deposited his burden. The jumping of the muscles in his arms told him of his exertion.

They looked down at her silently, Kieran feeling oddly embarrassed by the woman's odd state of dress. She was wearing what could only be men's shortened drawers and the odd, tight shirt appeared to have no opening at all. He felt heat in his cheeks as he could not help reading the words across her chest, "Victoria, BC" in elaborate script, under a garland of flowers. On her feet were shoes that were mostly leather straps that tied around her ankle.

"Oh dear, Kieran, where ever did you find her? And why is she dressed so oddly?"

"Her attire I can't explain. But I found her in this state in the glade where I paint. She is very chilled."

"Well, leave us and we will attend to her. I have called Smith and we shall have her as right as rain in no time. You go along. I'll call you if there are any improvements. Go along now."

He backed away from the bed reluctantly, feeling an odd possessiveness for the strange woman lying there.

"Out!" Daria said with a teasing smile and a waving motion of her hands.

Riana woke to darkness. She felt the coolness of a cloth on her forehead and discovered that her headache was gone. Slowly, she opened her eyes and looked up at the patterned fabric above her.

It was not the ceiling, as it moved slightly with air current. There was a dim, flickering light in the room and turning her head she saw a single candle guttering in a brass holder on the bedside table. Then she remembered. She was in Riverton Abbey and the power must have gone off. Yet, it didn't smell the same. It didn't have the antiseptic, cleaning liquid hotel smell about it. The smell was clean, but unfamiliar.

"So yer awake then, Miss."

A broad, rosy-cheeked woman lumbered into Riana's line of vision. Riana looked up at her, neither recognising her nor understanding why she wore the odd, frilly cap one her head. None of the chambermaids she had encountered wore anything like it.

"What happened?" her voice came out in a dry croak.

The woman poured water into a glass and gently lifted Riana so she could drink. She drank greedily for the water tasted fresh and sweet.

"Lord Donaghmore brung you in this mornin'. I was beginnin' to fear you was not coming 'round. But here you are. Are you hungry?"

Riana swallowed feeling moisture in her throat, "Yes. A little."

"Then I'll ring and have some broth brought to ye. T'would not be good for yu to have heavy food on top of an upset like this. And some tea. We'll have you up and about in no time." she gave Riana a gentle smile "Will you be a'right on yur own?"

Riana needed to be alone to think. Who was Lord Donaghmore? She dropped her head back on the raised pillow. Oh, yes. The man by the trees. The Baron of Donaghmore. The same man? The man she had been seeing in the distance since she arrived. Probably. She gave the maid a quick nod and was soon alone in the room.

Using her elbows, Riana levered herself into a semi-reclining position. She was just beginning to settle herself when the man of her thoughts entered the room almost as soon as the woman left it. She struggled and found herself hampered by long billowing sleeves and a skirt. She was wearing a nightgown not her own, for she would never wear something with so much fabric. His light hand on her shoulder held her back to the pillows.

"Do not try to get up." that deep rumbling voice again, "Rest and gather your strength. You look much improved from when I first brought you here."

"Who are you?" were the first words out of her mouth.

He straightened and gave her a bow as good and as neat as the first he had given her. This time he had removed his long coat and tall hat. He was still oddly dressed in a high collared shirt, whose sharp tips brushed his cheeks, a white tie that was folded and tied in an elaborate knot under his chin and a dark, wine-coloured jacket that was tightly buttoned across his broad chest, showing a couple of inches of a striped satin vest below. He wore pale gray pants with a buttoned flap rather than the usual zippered fly. White ruffles showed below the flared cuff of his sleeve.

"Allow me to present myself. I am Kieran Gilmartin, third Baron of Donaghmore.

"You aren't British." she said in an accusing voice.

"Indeed I am not. I am a visitor here. I'm from Ireland."

"So why are you dressed like that?"

He looked down at himself with confusion, "Like what?"

"Like you're in costume. Are you in costuMr.e?"

"Most assuredly not!" he sounded very offended, "This is the height of fashion."

"Sir!" a female voice broke in "It is most improper for you to be here. She is in her bed, for heaven's sake. "

There was a different smile on his face as he turned to greet the newcomer. By peeking around the man's magnificent frame, Riana was able to see a woman in her early thirties, close to her own age, entering the room, followed by a thin, nervous girl. The man clasped his hands behind his back and Riana saw the heavy gold ring he wore on the little finger of his left hand. He gave the woman a slight bow from the waist.

"Lady Ranleigh." he murmured, and Riana heard the smile in his voice, "I know it is improper, but I had to see how fared my lost soul. She is much improved, I am happy to say. Enough to give me a mild dressing down. But as yet, I have been unable to ascertain her name."

He moved aside to let the woman come to the bedside. She bent over Riana with a smile, then glanced back at the man as she waved the girl forward.

"Kieran, as long as you are here, make yourself useful. Would you raise her further to as sitting position so she can take some tea and broth."

Riana remembered the scent of him as he leaned down and gently lifted her to a sitting position. Lady Ranleigh stuffed thick pillows behind her so that she sat back into a cloud-like softness. She looked from the man to the woman.

"My name is Riana Ingram." she told them, "Mrs.. Ingram."

"Can we contact your husband, Mrs.. Ingram?" came the soft question, "Are you visiting in the district?"

Riana thought a moment, her eyes glancing quickly over the high-waisted, printed gown the woman was wearing. It resembled fashions from the '60's.

"My husband died three years ago. And I suppose I am a visitor."

"Where are you stopping?"

"Riverton Abbey, I thought."

The two at her bedside cast quick glances at each other. The man stepped back into the shadows, almost colliding with the girl who held a tray that trembled in her hands.

"I will leave you now. You are not yet recovered." he gave another sharp bow and spun on his heel to walk into the darkness.

The girl placed the tray on the table and backed into the shadows as Riana strained to follow the man's departure. Daria sat on the edge of the bed and spooned some of the broth out of the bowl. With a hand under Riana's chin, she brought the spoon to her mouth. Obedient as a child, Riana opened her mouth for the warm, flavourful soup. She spoke with a smile as she dipped the spoon again.

"This is Riverton Abbey, Mrs.. Ingram, and as this is my house, I would know if you were a guest here. And I know you are not."

There was only kindness in the pale brown eyes that regarded her. With the salty tasted of the broth still in her mouth, Riana was in a panic. Where was she? This *was* Riverton Abbey, but why had it changed? Why had the people changed? What should she do? Was some kind of terrible trick being played on her? Or was this one of those reconstructions she had heard so much about? Or was this an unexpected symptom of her brain tumour? The spoon was in her mouth again and this time she savoured it. She could not remember tasting anything quite so good.

"You are ill, Mrs.. Ingram?"

That much was true, but how to explain?

"Yes, I am." she could think of nothing further to add to the statement.

"Well, perhaps that explains your confusion. Do you recall how you came to be in the glade?"

Amnesia! That's what she would fake for the time being. It prevented any unnecessary explanations.......at least until she knew where she was and what was going on.

"I don't know. The last thing I remember is going for a walk and feeling sick. Then I woke up here. Thank-you for taking me in."

Daria fussed with the spoon and the bowl, "Nonsense, I could do nothing less. You do not know here you were staying?"

Daria put the spoon at Riana's mouth again, "I could not begin to describe them." she gave a tiny shudder, "But in time we will find out about you, I am certain. There must be somebody in the district looking for you, I should think. In the meantime, you will stay here at Riverton Abbey until we are able to locate your people."

For a time, the two of them focused on the eating of the broth, the only sounds in the room were the clatter of the spoon on the bowl and the crackling of the fire. When the broth was nearly finished, Riana felt exhaustion sweep over her. It became difficult to keep her eyes open. She was relaxed and compliant, wanting only to snuggle into the amazing softness of the bed and pull the covers up around her ears. Still, she finished the broth and had a few sips of the cooling tea. Finally, Daria rose to her feet and gently removed the pillow from behind Riana's back.

"I think you must rest now, you are barely able to keep your eyes open. A good night's sleep will be just the thing for you. I'll leave Susan here to attend you in case you wake in the night." she looked back at the girl who still stood in the shadows, "I'll have Mary relieve you in the morning."

"Very good, Mu'um."

Riana was able to see the quick, bobbing curtsey in the dim light. She tried to muster a smile, but the warmth of the food inside her made her eyes close firmly this time and she surrendered to sleep.

She felt the sun warm on her face when she woke once more. For a moment she lay still, enjoying the comfort of the bed and the quiet room. Faint sounds from outside drifted into her consciousness; a man calling out an order, the rattle-scrape of wheels on stone, a horse whinnying, a rooster crowing. She almost smiled before recalling where she was. Gasping aloud, she half-raised herself in the bed. Oh God, what was she going to do? How long was she going to be able to fake amnesia? And just what had she gotten herself into?

"Miss? Are you ill? Can I fetch you something?"

Riana peered up into the anxious, pale face that hovered over her. This was Susan from last night. The girl's hands fluttered over the bed covers as Riana hauled herself into a semi-sitting position. She managed a wobbly smile.

"I'm fine. I want to get out of bed."

As she struggled with the heavy covers a quick, sharp pain between her eyes reminded her that she had no medication. She was long passed due for it. She accepted Susan's help getting to her feet wondering why she was feeling so well. She should be screaming in pain. Well, take favours as they come. Susan put an arm around her waist and helped her to the chair by the low-burning fire.

"Lady Ranleigh sent some clothes for you if you feel well enough to dress, Miss. I'm trainin' to be a proper lady's maid, so I can help you."

Riana fought with the yards of nightgown fabric as she sat down. She looked up at the girl, seeing the dark rings under her eyes, thinking she looked undernourished and nervous. She needed better nutrition. And sleep.

"Have you been here all night?"

"Yes, Mu'um. Mary will take over for me later, once you have dressed."

"Well, I'll get dressed now."

Susan frowned doubtfully, "It is very early, Mu'um. Shall I fetch you some chocolate and rolls?"

"I don't think I'm hungry. What time is it anyway?"

Susan looked at the little china clock on the mantle, "Just gone on half past eight."

Riana gasped, "So late? I'm usually up by six-thirty. Must be all this good British air. I do feel kind of odd, maybe I should walk around a bit."

There was some dizziness when she stood, but Susan quickly grasped her around the waist, holding her upright until the dizziness passed. Holding her lightly, she helped Riana cross the room to the dressing table by the window and let Riana drop into the dainty chair. Without speaking, she began to unbutton the tiny white buttons down the front of the nightgown. Riana caught her hand.

"I can undress myself, you know." Riana informed her, still trying to brush away the busy hands.

Susan's eyes were unusually piercing, "But t'would not be proper, would it then?"

Riana was surprised by her own lack of will, "I suppose you're right."

Susan left her then to go to one of the bedside tables, from which she pulled out a china washbasin which she took to the fireplace and lifted a copper kettle from the side of the hearth. After pouring water into the basin, she returned to Riana and placed the basin on the dressing table. With brisk efficiency, she pulled the nightgown over Riana's head before dragging on a long, off-white sack-like thing then proceeded to wash her in warm, scented water. After drying her with a thick towel, she then put a kind of dress over the sack that was fitted to just below her breasts and laced it tightly in back.

Riana closed her eyes, not wanting to be part of this elaborate dressing ritual. She was mortified by the attention, yet decided that if this was the norm, she must along with it. She must go along until she knew just what was happening and why. She felt the dress go over her head, and without thought she cooperated. Gently, Susan seated her on the backless, padded seat and began brushing her hair. It felt so good that she could not help but relax. She felt Susan's fingers in her hair, brushing and parting and curling. Finally, the maid picked up what seemed to be a scrap of sheer cloth and lace. This she settled on Riana's head, adjusting it carefully. Then she stepped back.

"There." she announced with no little satisfaction.

She helped Riana rise from the seat and turned her to face a pier glass mirror. Riana hardly recognized herself. It was her own face to be sure, but framed with curls that were edged by a pretty white cap on her head. She was wearing a long yellow dress that had a lace trimmed scoop neckline, a high, sashed waist and had a Grecian scroll pattern worked down the front in black and light blue. The long sleeves were edged in lace topped by lace-edged puffs.

"You do need your stocking and shoes." Susan said from somewhere behind her.

Riana stepped back from the dressing table. There were more than shoes and stockings missing she realized. She was wearing no underwear, other than the chemise and corset. She was embarrassed by the mere thought of it. She turned to look at the maid who was holding a pair of ballet-like slippers by their ribbons in one hand and stockings in another.

"What about underwear?"

"Underwear, Mu'um? That I've done already. Your shift and petticoats. If you sit down again, I will put these on you."

So, Riana decided, not undies. At least not the type she was used to. Obediently she sat down and watched as Susan rolled the stockings up her legs. Once these were on, she silently signalled for Riana to stand. Around the top of the stockings, she tied embroidered satin garters, then slipped on the off-white slippers and wound the ribbons around her ankles.

Lifting the hem of her dress a little, Riana inspected her feet. The shoes flattered them and were more comfortable than she expected them to be. Raising her eyes, she saw herself in the long cheval mirror and smiled at her reflection, liking what she saw. It was so different from her usual style of jeans and slacks and shorts when the weather was hot. She felt pretty and feminine, something she had never before aspired. Even her wedding gown had been plain and she had worn no veil. She looked over at Susan who was smiling, proud of her handiwork.

"What now?"

"Shall I take you down to the breakfast room, Mu'um? It's a little early, but I expect breakfast will be ready. Lord Ranleigh and Lord Donaghmore breakfast early."

"Thank-you. I'm starving. Lead the way."

There was only one person in the breakfast room and that was Lord Donaghmore. He was wearing a Royal blue quilted satin robe that fell almost to his ankles. Under it was a white shirt without a tie, a long pale blue waistcoat and long navy breeches. He stood when she entered the room, still clutching a damask napkin in his hand. He seemed oddly disconcerted by her appearance, but had the presence of mind to give her a neat, sharp bow.

"You slept well, I trust?" he asked in a low, deep voice.

"Very well, thank-you. I've never slept in such a comfortable bed."

He gave her another, smaller bow, "Will you allow me to get you some breakfast? Would you like coffee or chocolate?"

Kieran pulled out a chair for her, close to where he had been sitting. His breakfast was still sitting on his plate and the cup beside it still steaming.

She side-stepped the chair, "I can get my own, thanks. Coffee or chocolate? Both are full of caffeine, but I think I'll have the chocolate."

"Please allow me."

Without waiting for an answer, he swept around the table, his long satin robe whispering behind him. Expertly, he poured dark liquid into a lovely porcelain cup. His mouth curled with amusement as he placed the cup on the table, looking at her over his shoulder.

"The chocolate here is very good. As is the breakfast."

He did not take his chair immediately, nor to her amazement, did he so much as glance at his own cooling breakfast. His large hand curved lazily over the back of his chair as he shifted his body toward her.

"Please sit down and finish your breakfast." she told him, "You don't want it to get cold."

Only when she moved away from the table to go to the long, bow-fronted sideboard did he finally sit down. The array of silver chafing dishes with lids and little candles was a little overwhelming. The scent that rose from them made her mouth water. She picked up a plate, glancing first at the plates of sliced cheese and fruit that sat apart from the heat. Behind her she heard the scrape of cutlery on china indicating that the man had resumed eating his meal.

She lifted silver lids, eggs smelling of spice, sausage looking rather greasy and chunks of meat that smell like bacon. The potatoes were fried with onions and too much pepper from the smell of them. Another held a dark liquid with darker lumps floating in it. She bent closer to sniff. Prunes! She jerked her head away. A silver filigree basket of rolls and sliced bread sat at the end of the collection, smelling warm and fresh.

She shifted her plate and took some sliced apples and peaches, with eggs, well-drained prunes and two of the irresistible rolls. There was butter in a small, square dish, unused with a pretty pattern pressed into the top of it. She took only a little, reluctant to spoil the pattern. With a small smile at her silent companion, she slid into her own chair.

Nervously, she shifted her cutlery, wondering at the numbers of it for such a simple meal. She was unable to look at the man across from her, so she picked up her cup and sipped the chocolate. It was delicious, sweet and tasting of vanilla, so unlike the rather gritty-tasting, machine produced hot chocolate she had known. With firm concentration, she placed the cup on it's saucer and took up her fork. Blindly, she chose a piece of apple, delighted at it's crunchy and sweet texture. She rolled the chewed fruit around in her mouth, savouring the flavour.

"It is to your taste, Madame?"

The voice broke into her enjoyment and she raised her eyes to look at him. His eyes were on her, studying her closely. Slowly, she lowered her fork to the side of her plate to return his look. For a time, neither of them spoke until he broke the silence.

"Have you recovered your memory?"

Memory! Riana swallowed the last of the apple so quickly she nearly choked on it. She recovered quickly. Yes, until she knew what was going on, she had to pretend amnesia.

"No, I haven't, not even a glimmer. Isn't that funny? I don't think I've bumped my head or anything. But I still can't remember where I am or what I'm doing here."

"You have an odd accent. Perhaps American? There was nothing to identify you. You were wearing odd clothing, with only 'Victoria, BC' on it, but there was nothing in the small pockets that would tell us who you are."

Riana picked up her fork and stirred her eggs on her plate. It was, she decided after a moment, that what was going on was a result of her tumour. Her doctor had spoken of odd delusions that might be a symptom. If that was the case, her best bet would be to simply go along with it. After all, what was the harm? They were delusions, anyway. She scooped eggs on to her fork.

"I'm afraid I don't know. Do you know if anyone is looking for me? I might have a family that is missing me."

He gave her a tiny smile, "A very great loss indeed. But I am certain Lord Ranleigh will put out inquires in the neighbourhood to see if anybody is missing you."

Riana looked into the dark blue eyes that regarded her and knew she could become lost in them, given half a chance. The man himself was enough to keep her in this odd place, not once considering the costs. She looked at him with serious eyes.

"Thank-you. That would be very nice."

He gave her yet another of his tiny, tight smiles, "Oh, do not thank me. Not yet, at least."

As he lifted his cup to his lips, another voice broke into their silent regard of one another.

"Thunder an' turf, Donaghmore! Why did you allow me to get so bosky last night? Did I make a cake of meself?"

They both turned to see a thin man of medium height standing, fully dressed, in the doorway holding the tips of the fingers of his left hand to his forehead. Kieran rose, lightly pressing his hand to Riana's shoulder as she made to rise as well. There was a slight, exasperated smile on the Irish lord's face as he gave a small tip of his waist.

"I was not with you last night, Ranleigh. I was concerned about the lady I found in the glade yesterday. You were drinking with your brother and Wigmore last night. I suggest that you stay out of your lady's way this morning, you know how little she likes Wigmore. I should think she is far from pleased with you this morning."

Riana was stunned by the mention of her family name. Would she get to meet one of her ancestors? The prospect made her feel slightly dizzy. Then she recalled Jared Thorpe's remark about town people not mixing with nobility. But heavy drinkers were not usually so particular about their company.

The man came into the room and raised what appeared to be a magnifying glass tied with a ribbon on a stick, and turned it in Riana's direction.

"Ah, so this is the foundling then? Eh, what? And what are you doing up at this ungodly hour of the morning?"

Kieran stepped away from the table, "Please allow me to introduce Mrs.. Riana Ingram. Unfortunately, she remembers little about herself. Perhaps it would be a good idea to inquire in the neighbourhood to find out if anyone is missing her. Mrs.. Ingram, I present to you, Lord Ashley Thorpe, the Earl of Ranleigh, owner of Riverton Abbey."

Lord Ranleigh came closer and stood before her, looking somewhat expectantly. Riana could see nothing in his face of Jared Thorpe, only deep lines of dissipation and eyes reddened by the excesses of the night before. There was an odour about him that was sour and unpleasant. Reluctantly, she held out a hand to him.

"I am pleased to meet you." she told him.

"Ah, American. Shouldn't be too difficult to learn if an American is missing." he bowed from the waist and touched the backs of her fingers with his lips, "I will begin the search immediately."

Almost negligently, he dropped Riana's hand and went to the sideboard to pour himself some coffee. Casting a lazy leg of a chair at the head of the table, he sat down, grimacing at the hot tasted of the coffee.

"Must forgo our ride this morning, Donaghmore. I'm fagged to death and my estate manager has been after me to go over the accounts with him and I promised today was the day. Although I know I will make a mull of it."

"Then I suggest you put some food in your stomach. Some bread and eggs. It will make you feel better." Riana could not help speaking, for she had no patience with drunks.

Lord Ranleigh gave her a look of surprised shock, "Perhaps you are right, Madame, perhaps you are right. But I never take food in the morning, me pudding-house won't take it."

Riana opened her mouth to say more, but Kieran broke in hastily.

"It is just as well, Ranleigh. I was planning to finish Daria's portrait this morning. And I will be needing you tomorrow. Mrs.. Ingram, may I take you for a turn about the garden later in the day? There are very fine grounds here that I know you will enjoy."

Riana glanced at her host, but he appeared to have lost interest in them. He stared morosely into the depths of his cup as he leaned lazily back in his chair. She smiled at the man who was watching her so intently.

"Yes, thanks. I'd like that."

"Good." he picked up his fork, "Then I shall find you later."

Chapter 3

Riana returned to her room with the aid of the servants that seemed to be everywhere. As her feet whispered along the polished wooden floors, she reflected on the cost of keeping all these servants. They were polite and most appeared to be undernourished, the women moving about on specific tasks, but most of the men seemed to be standing around in green and white livery.

As she opened the door to her room, another girl rose from a stool by the fireplace. She gave Riana a slight bob. She was older than Riana, plumper, with rosy cheeks. Riana closed the door gently, for she was feeling the beginnings of a head ache.

"Who are you?"

"Mary, mu'um. Can I fetch you anything? The other ladies are still abed."

Riana touched her forehead lightly, "Something for a headache. If there is such a thing here."

Instantly Mary was at Riana's side, putting an arm around her shoulders and leading her toward the now-made bed.

"I will fetch some laudanum straight away. You should have a lie down, I shan't be long."

When Mary returned, Riana was lying on the bed with her eyes closed. She opened them and sat up as Mary put a small bottle and a spoon on the bedside table.

Riana did not sit up, "Tell me about the Wigmores, Mary. I heard Lord Ranleigh speak about one of them at breakfast."

Mary gave her a strange look, "Terrible lot, them. The Squire lives at Winslow Hall. And a poor master he is, too, what with his beatings and the like. Mr.. Edward Wigmore spends a great deal of time with Lord Ranleigh. Nothing good will come of it, I say." she uncorked the bottle "Now, mu'um, you take this."

The laudanum was bitter and she thought she might have taKen too much, for she fell asleep fairly quickly, having hardly a chance to digest this new information about those who might be her ancestors. It was hard to reconcile what Mary had said to the kind man who had been her father. But her thoughts got no further as darkness and strange dreams overtook her.

She was shaKen awake. Blearily, she looked up into Susan's anxious face.

"Are you aright, mu'um? You was sleeping like the dead."

"I'm fine. What time is it?"

"Nearly two o'clock, mu'um. Lord Donaghmore is waiting in the passage for you."

Riana sprung off the bed, her headache gone. She had forgotten that he had suggested a walk outside. Her hands went to her hair, but Susan only smiled.

"You must change into a walking gown."

"Change? Why? I'm perfectly alright the way I am."

"Oh no, Mu'um. You must change. Lady Ranleigh has sent some gowns for you to wear until your people are found."

A few minutes later, in a pale green gown of what Susan said was kerseymere and a jacket that ended above the waist called a Spencer, Riana was ready to meet the waiting Lord Donaghmore. She tugged at the sleeve that ended over the knuckles of her gloved hand and twisted her neck against the wide ribbons that tied a lace-trimmed straw hat on her head, before taking a deep breath and opening the door.

He rose from a chair placed close to the door, and he too, had changed clothes. He was wearing a double-breasted green coat with an M-notched collar and turned back cuffs, a red waistcoat that showed only inches at his waist and above the collar of his coat. Beige breeches were thrust into long black leather boots that reached his knees. His white shirt and stock were immaculate. He gave her a short, stiff bow, one hand holding a black walking stick and the other a tall, black hat.

"Madame? You are ready?"

"I am. But if I had known how much effort went into a simple walk, I think I might have stayed in."

He gave her a slight smile that barely curved his mouth, yet showed the beginnings of long dimples in his cheeks. His looks fascinated her. She knew, however, that it was more than just that, for she had known many good looking men in her life. Her husband had been one, but he had never made her hold her breath as this one did. She wondered at the difference.

Kieran held out his arm to her and when she hesitated, uncertain of what he wanted, he gently took her hand and curved it into his elbow. Slowly, they made their way along the boards of the rather dark passage. There was silence between them and Riana tried to find something to say to him.

"You're an artist?"

"It is a hobby of mine. I raise horses in Ireland, but my cousin, Daria, Countess of Ranleigh wrote and asked me to come here and paint portraits of her and her family. I am very fond of Daria, so I agreed."

"Can I see your work sometime?"

He stopped so suddenly that she walked a pace or two ahead of him. Turning, she saw he was smiling at her. A full smile that revealed completely the long, deep dimples in his tanned cheeks.

The smile was dazzling. No man should have a smile like that, came the hysterical thought in her head.

"Shall I take you there now? I have just finished Daria's and it is still in the gallery."

It was her turn to smile, "Oh, would you? I'd like that."

He closed the space between them, covering the hand that still curved into his elbow.

"Come along, then."

Kieran mad a slight turning to the left and because her hand was still on his am, she had little choice but to go with him. He took her along wide hallways, some lit by the sun through tall windows, some dark and smelling a little damp. Finally, they passed through a wide, arching doorway finished in dark wood carved with fruits and nuts. The sunlight here was almost blinding as it bounced off white-painted walls. Riana hesitated a little until her eyes became used to the light. On the bright walls hung portraits in heavy, elaborate frames, their subjects in clothing from several periods of history.

At the far end of the room, an easel was set up with a small table beside it, covered in a grey cloth. On the grey cloth was a pot of brushes, surrounded by other small pots. Riana did not know where to look, where to settle her eyes, her head felt as if it should be on a swivel. Her face turned from the painted faces that hung on the walls to the green beyond the windows.

"These are all the Ranleigh ancestors. Most of them not as good as they should be. But then, some of my ancestors have been blackguards. Here is the first Earl. Tradition has it that he was a smuggler. It was true that he killed a number of men for reasons of his own. And this is the present Earl's father. Died in a duel over a lightskirt, when Ranleigh was only three years old."

His gloved hand tightened around her own as he steered her toward the waiting easel. It was uncovered and set so that it was in full light, without glare or direct sun. Instantly, Riana recognized her hostess. She was seated in a low back chair with her hands in her lap. An elaborate shawl in bright jewel colours was wrapped around her right arm, the other end of the shawl was draped over the back of the chair. She wore a white satin gown, trimmed at the high waist and neck with delicate, pointed lace. In her dark hair was a wreath of tiny white flowers. Beside her, leaning against her knee was a boy in navy velvet, whose arm was crooked into her lap near her hands. There was mischief in the dark brown eyes.

"It's beautiful! I'd know her anywhere. You are very talented. And this is just a hobby for you? You should take it up as a living."

He gave a polite laugh, "If I did that, then I should neglect my horses. And they are a source of income. Besides, I have not the patience to deal with those who want their portraits made. I paint as I please, and whom I please. This was done as a favour to Daria."

"Who's the little boy?"

"The heir. Little Shelby, the terror. His father indulges him entirely too much." he turned away from the painting and with his free hand tipped Riana's face into the sunlight, "I should like to paint you."

"Why?" the word was out of her mouth before she thought.

"Because I believe you would be a good subject. I would do this for my own pleasure."

Riana did not know how to answer and was spared by catching sight of yet another portrait propped against the wall, half-hidden by the draperies. She stepped back from his disturbing grasp, her fingers barely touching his elbow.

"What's that?"

His eyes followed the direction of her pointing finger. "That? It's a portrait of Ranleigh. I've done most of it from memory, but I need him to sit for his face and hands."

Sure enough, the background of a long, tree-edged field on which deer grazed had already been painted and the faceless figure of a man in a blue striped coat trimmed with gold braid, a gold trimmed white waistcoat with white lace at the neck and wrists. The white breeches ended and the knees and white stockings with a fancy raised pattern accented the buckled black pumps. In one hand was a bicorn hat edged with light feathers. His other hand was sketched in hanging lazily from the arm of the chair in which he sat.

"That will be Ranleigh. He wanted to be portrayed in Court Dress, although the Regent has forbidden him to come to Court. I had a servant who was close to him in size to be the model for me. He has better legs than Ranleigh, I think."

He went to the picture and pulled a corner of the drapery over it. Straightening, he rested his hand on the deep windowsill beside him. His dark blue eyes were fixed on her face.

"Will you sit for me?"

Riana watched him, unable to look away from the eyes that seemed to pierce her soul. She swallowed, the motion causing her finally to break the silence that had developed between them. She glanced over his shoulder through the window then back at his face, feeling less trapped now, by his gaze.

"I suppose so. But I don't know how still I can be. When?"

Kieran reached over and grasped her hand, catching too, the one that had been resting on his own arm. His fingers were warm on hers, even through both of their gloves.

"Shall we try for tomorrow? I must decide on a place for you. Now, "he slid his hand around hers to tuck it back into his elbow, "we must continue our walk. You are looking pale and the fresh air is just the thing for you. Mary told me you had a headache. Are you well, now?"

"I'm fine. She gave me some laudanum and it did the trick."

"You must not take it too often, for it is addicting." he cautioned her.

Kieran took Riana down a set of stairs that was narrow and plain, apologizing that is was the servant's stairs, but that it was the closest to the outside. The door that he opened had raised panels and a latch that he had to lift. He pushed it open and put his hat on his head before taking her into a gravelled yard that was surrounded on three sides by the high, windowed walls of the house. The fourth wall was nearly solid, with a high and wide archway. Through the arch, she could see long rolling lawns edged by trees bright with fall foliage.

A walkway led away from the house, toward a small lake visible in the distance. As they walked, a loud, childish yell drew their attention to a copse of trees nearby, just as a young boy ran from it toward them. He flung himself a Kieran who tossed him high into the air.

"You little devil!" Kieran laughed at the child, "You have escaped your nanny again, haven't you?" he set the child back on the ground, "Now, little Lord, please meet your mother's guest. Lord Shelby Thorp, please meet Mrs.. Ingram."

There was almost an instant change in the boy. He bowed from the waist, extending one short, chubby leg. Riana was unable to keep the smile from her face. She dipped a little curtsey, similar to the ones the maids had made to her. It was far more awkward than theirs and a little off-balance.

"Madame." he said in a high, childish voice.

"Lord Shelby."

"Lord Thorpe." Kieran corrected quietly.

The boy was studying Riana with undisguised curiosity, "Are you visiting my Mamma?"

She smiled down at him, "Yes, I am. She is helping me until I regain my memory."

He held up a hand to her, "May I take a turn around the garden with you?"

Riana glanced up at the big man beside her and took the offered, chubby brown hand. Walking stick in hand, Kieran touched his fingers to the curled brim of his tall hat. With a sharp, quick bow, he silently indicated that Riana and the boy precede him. They walked along the path, the gravel crunching audibly under their feet. None of them spoke for a long time, Riana had been quietly relishing the feel of the small damp hand in hers, sorry that he had never had time to have a child of her own. It was Kieran who finally broke the not unpleasant silence.

"How are your riding lessons coming along, Master Shelby? Do you like the pony I brought you from Ireland?"

"Very well, sir. But I like Papa's horse ever so much."

As Riana was still being amazed by the child's grasp of vocabulary, Kieran's voice broke out in a delighted laugh.

"Your Papa paid dearly for that horse. He is, at least, a good judge of horseflesh. But I do not think you are quite ready for an Irish stallion. Do you ride, Mrs.. Ingram?"

The question caught her unaware, "No. At least I don't think so." she amended quickly.

"Then someday soon, we shall have to find out, won't we?"

She opened her mouth to answer, but the call of a young, female voice interrupted her.

"Master Shelby! Master Shelby! I have been looking all over for you, I have. And here I find you with your father's guests. Shame on you! Shame on you for forgetting yer manners!"

Riana's grip tightened on the small hand and Kieran's hand came to rest on the narrow, childish shoulder. It was he who spoke to the red-faced girl who was hurrying toward them.

"It is of no consequence, Nan. Master Shelby has been a perfect gentleman. It is my opinion that children can learn a good deal by not being shut away in the nursery all day. They must prepare for society at an early age."

Without so much as a glance at Riana, the nurse took the boy's hand from hers and gave his arm a sharp tug. Riana winced at the action.

"He's a nice little boy."

"But disobedient. Come along, now, it's time for your tea."

Standing side by side, Riana and Kieran watched as the child was led away from them. As the two disappeared through a door, he again offered his arm to her.

"Shall we continue?"

She smiled and went along with him. As they walked, she revelled in the peace that surrounded her. Only the sounds of birds and busy people reached her ears, none of the high speed sounds associated with the future. She curled her fingers into the arm that supported her.

"Can you tell me about the Wigmores? Mary mentioned them this morning."

They did not stop walking, but she felt his curious gaze on her.

"The Wigmores? The Squire, Regis Wigmore, in Ashley's words, draws the bustle much too freely and dips rather too deeply."

"What?" Riana laughed, "I have no idea what you just said."

Looking up, she saw that he was smiling as well, but he continued to look straight ahead.

"It means that he spends too much money and he drinks too much. Not too different from Ashley himself, I might add. But where Ashley is harmless, if too cocksure of himself, Wigmore is of a more vicious bent. I cannot like him, I'm afraid. Why are you asking about him? Do you think you know him?"

She swallowed nervously, "When Lord Ranleigh mentioned the name at breakfast this morning, I thought it sounded familiar. Do you think I might be related?"

"Lord! I should hope not! You seem nothing like him and the family. But I will make inquiries if that will ease your mind."

She did not know how to answer him, so said nothing. They walked in companionable silence for a few minutes more, then she spoke again.

"Do you miss Ireland?"

"I miss it like the very devil. I miss my own house, my own people and my horses. At least I have my own horse here with me as well as the two Ranleigh bought. And he treats horseflesh well, else I should never have sold them to him, no matter our connections. I am anxious to return to Donaghmore."

He stopped abruptly and turned to her, gripping the hand that still rested in the crook of his elbow.

"But I will stay long enough to paint your portrait."

"And what will you do with it, once it is finished?" she asked, tipping her head to one side.

Those piercing eyes were on her again, watching and studying, "Why, I shall take it back home with me. It will be my property after all. Perhaps you will one day go to Ireland to visit it?"

"If my circumstances will allow it, I suppose. Are you inviting me?"

"Of course I am. I should very much like you to see my home. Will you come to Donaghmore, Mrs. Ingram?"

Would she? She decided then and there she would crawl on hands and knees for him if he asked it of her. He must have seen the answer in her face, for he stepped closer to her, so close that she felt his warm breath on her face. As she looked up at him, her lips parted, she wanted him to kiss her, wanted with an unexpected passion.

"Donaghmore! Lord Donaghmore! I've been looking all over for you. And here you are with Mrs.. Ingram. Are you much improved, my dear?"

Both turned to see Daria, Countess of Ranleigh hurrying toward them. She was wearing a dark brown spencer over a mustard coloured print gown, but no hat nor gloves. She came to an abrupt stop before them, her bright eyes going from one to the other with undisguised amusement.

"Are you well, Mrs.. Ingram? I must say your colour is much improved. Mary said she dosed you with laudanum for a headache. Is it gone now?" she put her hand on the elbow of Riana's free arm.

"I am feeling very well now, thank-you. I don't know how I will ever be able to thank you for all you've done for me."

"Nonsense and I will hear of more it. I came out to remind Donaghmore of the Assembly we must attend tomorrow night in the village, and since you are much improved, perhaps you will wish to attend as well. It is a simple country dance, but I believe you will enjoy yourself none the less. I will find something for you to wear that has not yet been seen here."

Riana smiled, "Thank-you. I would like that. And maybe I might find someone who knows me."

"Yes," Daria nodded, "I had thought that."

Daria looked up at her handsome cousin, "Are you enjoying your stroll?"

"Yes, cousin. And Mrs.. Ingram has agreed to pose for me. I am trying to find the right setting for her. What do you think?"

"Why not the glade where you found her? It is a pretty place and you do paint there often." she turned a cheeky smile on Riana, "More, I think, to escape my husband who tends to blather on far too much. And Kieran tends to silence. Have you not noticed that about him?"

Riana looked up at the man and smiled into his face. His lips curved into a tiny, returning smile. Something that did not go unnoticed by his cousin.

"Yes, I have noticed that about him. But I am much the same."

"Yesss." Daria agreed slowly.

Again, the look from one to the other and another secret smile, "I must return to the house now. I saw you both walking and remembered I had not mentioned the Assembly to you. I have found that if I do not do something as it occurs to me, then I forget it completely. Enjoy the remainder of your walk."

Standing together, still joined at his elbow, they watched Daria return to the house as they had watched her son earlier. As she disappeared around the corner, in a single motion they began walking again.

"Shall we begin the portrait tomorrow? I can take you to the glade right now and we can choose the perfect place for you. And I can decide just how I want you to pose."

"We can do that. Is it far?"

"Just across the lawn and over that small bridge." his gloved hand pointed for her, "There is a wall over there, the last remaining part of the original Abbey. King Henry the eighth had it razed to the ground during his purge of the Churches and gave the land to one of his officers as a reward for service in one of his wars with France."

Riana looked at the bridge and remembered following him over it. She turned her eyes to the ground ahead of them as she recalled the circumstances, how he appeared to know her. Shiny black boots walked across her vision, but she did not need that reminder that he was so close to her.

"Lord Donaghmore, have we met before? Somehow, I think I know you. Is that possible?"

He took several steps before answering her, "I should have remembered if we had. You are not a woman to forget. From whence came this idea?"

She lifted a shoulder in a small shrug, "I don't know. It just felt like I had."

He swung his walking stick ahead of him, barely missing the toe of his boot, "It is odd, you know, for you have never felt like a stranger to me."

Riana gave a little, nervous laugh, "Oh well, maybe we knew one another in a different lifetime."

There was a slight start in him, "You study Hindu philosophies? Reincarnation is one of their beliefs. Take care with whom you speak about it, for you will be considered the worst kind of bluestocking."

"Many cultures believe in reincarnation. More, I think, than don't."

"And you? Do you believe in it?"

She was silent for a time, deciding how best to answer a question in a time period nearly two hundred years before her own.

"Yes, I do. It makes sense to me. I mean, everything in nature seems to recycle, why not our so-called souls?"

"Recycle? That is a very interesting term." he broke off to walk without words again, "But a good one. Yes, recycle souls. I admit I do like the idea."

He stopped to look down at her, a faint smile barely curving his straight, generous mouth, "Are you a bluestocking, Mrs.. Ingram?"

She recalled the term from somewhere, but did not quite know just what it meant. He must have seen her confusion, so hastened to enlighten her.

"Are you a learned woman?"

"I have studied a lot, yes. I like to read anything I can get my hands on. Usually I am reading two books at a time. One fiction and one non-fiction."

His smile widened briefly and he continued walking, "You are a remarkable woman, Mrs.. Ingram. I hope your husband appreciates you."

"My husband is dead. And yes, he did appreciate me."

His voice was low when he spoke again, "You recall this much? That you are a widow? Daria did say that you told her you were a widow. Is there nothing else that stirs your memory?"

They were walking over the bridge now and she could see a crumbling brick wall ahead of them at the edge of a sunlit glade. There were more trees than she had seen before and a small gazebo was situated close to the treeline in the distance. The gazebo was covered with vines that were now coloured by autumn. She felt a ringing in her ears and a mist began to cloud her eyes. Her fingers tightened on his arm.

"There." he was saying, "I will paint you in the gazebo. The colours of the leaves will be a perfect background for you."

He looked down at her with alarm as he felt her sway beside him, "Mrs.. Ingram, are you unwell?"

She stepped backward two paces and immediately felt better, "I just felt a little dizzy. Maybe I should go back to the house."

"But of course. Shall I carry you?"

She laughed nervously, "Absolutely not. I can get there on my own."

Together they turned and made their way back to the house, to a door at the top of a double set of outside stairs. It was not the main door, but neither was it as plain as the servant's door. Inside the small entry, a servant in livery came to relieve them Kieran of his hat and walking stick.

"So shall we make plans to begin working tomorrow morning about eleven o'clock? I ride with Ashley in the morning, so will be busy for a time. I think you will need the rest, in any case. It is obvious to me that you are not yet recovered." he gave another bow, "I will see you at dinner then. Roberts, see that Mrs.. Ingram is escorted to her room. Good afternoon, Mrs.. Ingram."

"Riana. My first name is Riana." she informed him in a voice that was much smaller than she had intended.

He smiled and dipped his head, "Riana."

She liked the way her name sounded on his tongue. She watched the motion of his broad back as he walked away from her and she missed his presence almost instantly. She wanted to chase after him and throw her arms around him, but knew his strong sense of dignity prevented her from embarrassing them both. She turned to the servant who had greeted them. With a silent nod of his head and an outstretched hand, he indicated the direction she was to go.

There was another change of clothes for dinner. This time the gown was white satin with an embroidery of oak leaves at the high waist, around the neck and short, puffed sleeves, with a wider embroidered band at the hem. The sleeves also had silky green tassels hanging from the banded cuff. On her feet were white kid slippers and plain white stockings. Silk flowers were entwined in her hair, after much fussing from Susan who muttered under her breath at the short length of Riana's hair.

Susan show her the way to the drawing room and Kieran was waiting by the door for her. From the numbers of people in the room, Riana knew there were more than a few house guests and that she was the last to arrive. Three women besides Daria were seated on various sofas and chairs scattered about the cavernous room, men were standing in a corner near the fireplace talking quietly. Kieran deposited Riana with Daria and crossed the room to join the men.

Daria pulled Riana down to sit on the sofa beside her. She smiled, her hand still on Riana's arm.

"You are looking much better. The walk this afternoon must have been just the thing for you. Please allow me to introduce you to my other guests. This is Mrs.. Agnes Peasland and her daughter Miss Agnes Peasland. And over there, with the book, is my youngest sister, Baroness Lynch of Templedown. Generva. That is her husband over there in the wine-coloured coat. Ladies, please meet my guest, Mrs.. Riana Ingram."

Mrs.. Peasland was a plump woman in her mid-forties who wore high purple feathers in her hair and a gown of purple satin that made her look pale and sickly. She waved a fan languidly before her face as she regarded Riana with cold, blue eyes.

"You are from Town, Mrs.. Ingram?" she inquired, steel in her mild tone.

Daria answered quickly, "I'm afraid Mrs.. Ingram has been ill. She does not remember much about herself except for her name and that she is a widow."

The blue eyes drifted toward Lord Donaghmore. He was standing in profile to them and it was a profile that none of them could help but admire. It was clean and sharp, accented by his long sideburns. He laughed suddenly, unconsciously, showing strong white teeth.

"A widow? Hmmmm. How convenient."

Agnes Peasland giggled, the sound contrived and piercing. Baroness Lynch looked up from her book, her eyes going first at the woman who laughed, then to her sister and finally Riana. She raised he finely arched brows.

"Mrs.. Ingram. You are with us this evening. I am glad indeed to see you awake. My dear Daria tells me that you felt well enough for a turn about the garden. I must say, your colour is much improved from when they brought you in yesterday." she looked at the other two women, "She was quite done in. Quite senseless. One could not help but feel a great deal of pity for her."

Rising to her feet, she laid the book on the table beside her and went across the room to sit on the sofa beside Riana. She took Riana's hand and smoothed the back of it with her cool fingers. She smiled at her sister and only Riana saw the quick wink Daria darted at her.

"Lord Donaghmore found her in the glade where he was painting and he brought her straight to us." Daria explained, and Riana heard a tone of censure, "We did worry for her for several hours, as nothing seemed to bring her 'round, not even smelling salts." she put an arm around Riana's shoulders, "But she recovered very well and it is indeed a pleasure to have her with us. Kieran is very much taken with her. As are we all."

Mrs.. Peasland opened her mouth to speak again, but was interrupted by a footman who opened the tall, wide doors.

"Dinner is served." he announced solemnly.

Dinner indeed. First there was a shuffle of guests behind Lord and Lady Ranleigh, so they would enter the dining room in order of precedence. Baron and Baroness Lynch behind her sister and Generva smiled back as Kieran caught Riana's hand, to follow them. The Peaslands came up to the rear, with their daughter Agnes between them. Riana felt awkward and out of place.

Riana sat carefully in the chair Kieran held out for her and looked at the display of china, cutlery and glasswear spread before her. She looked around the room with curiosity, for she knew she had passed through it before, in a different time, and it had changed a great deal. Now it was lit by candles, which flattered everyone, and there were more pictures on the walls now. There was a single, long table now, rather than the small, more intimate ones that had been scattered about. Heavy gold damask draperies were pulled across the tall windows, keeping out the drafts, she suspected, but it gave the room a cosier feel.

And then the food began. Riana learned the names of the dishes that were presented by listening to the voices around her. The amount of food served, was, in her eyes, obscenely bountiful. First came a bisque of fish, then chine of mutton, that she found too rough and too strong tasting, then fried smelts, olives of veal with ragu, stewed mushrooms, buttered peas, artichoke pie and lemon torte, ending in a selection of fruit and cheeses. She had closely watched the others, trying to copy them, as she tried to keep a conversation with Mr.. Peasland and Kieran, who sat on either side of her.

She knew she made mistakes. She handled her cutlery differently, although she did manage to use the right pieces at the right time. There was so much wine and no bread at all. She felt the narrow eyes of Agnes Peasland on her during the entire meal. And saw how often those same eyes drifted toward Kieran, who seemed hardly to notice her. And she knew that each of her mistakes was being categorized for future reference. How long, she wondered, would her amnesia act work? And that thought was followed by an even more horrifying thought. How long would she have to keep up her act? Would she ever return to where she belonged? Or was all of this just a result of the tumour in her brain?

At last, the meal was over. Everyone rose and Kieran offered his arm to her to take her back to the drawing room. There was more interaction between the sexes this time. A table was set up and a card game begun with Lord Ranleigh, Baron Lynch, Mr.. And Mrs.. Peasland. Generva picked up her abandoned book and Agnes took up a chair close to Kieran who was seated at a writing desk. Daria pulled Riana down beside her on the sofa. She patted the hand that lay limply in Riana's lap.

"This must all be terribly confusing for you. But it is fortunate that my cousin Donaghmore knew what he was about when he took you out of doors." she smiled in the direction of her cousin who had taKen up a quill and was now writing, "But then, he was ever the most sensible of me, without any of the artist's temperament. I suppose it is because he spends so much of his time with his horses. It tends to keep one's feet planted firmly on the ground, does it not?"

Riana looked at the broad back, clothed in a dark grey coat and admired the movement of muscles as he wrote. He dipped his pen into a bottle of ink, and she silently thanked the creators of ball point pens. What a nuisance it must be to have to dip your pen every five words or so.

"I suppose so." she replied after a pause of several heartbeats, "I wouldn't have guessed that he was an artist if I hadn't seen the portrait he had painted of you. It's wonderful! It captures both of you so well."

"Yes!" Daria sighed with satisfied delight, "My cousin has great talent, although he is very sparing of it's use. He does portraits but rarely. He is far happier painting horses."

Before Riana was able to reply to that statement, Agnes Peasland's voice rang out, all but echoing in the large room.

"Sir! What are you doing, scribbling away so studiously?"

Riana saw the stiffening in Lord Donaghmore's spine. Carefully, he laid aside his pen and half-turned to the rest of the room. His blue eyes flickered over the woman who had spoken yet were carefully blank.

"I am writing to my brother in Ireland. He has the charge of my stable while I am away and I write to inquire about it."

Agnes gave a coy, teasing laugh, "You are not writing, then, to lighten the heart of one of your conquests, then?"

Riana felt his eyes brush her lightly before he turned back to his letter, "There is no need of that, Madam."

Generva spoke this time, barely taking her eyes from her book, "My cousin does not make conquests. He is far too much the gentleman for that and too busy."

Agnes looked a bit taken aback and Daria smile wickedly at Riana, knowing that because of the way they were seated, Agnes would not see the smile. The mild tone of her sister's voice had not hidden the steel of her words and Riana sensed this was a contest of long standing. They were protecting their cousin, yet Agnes Peasland had no idea what they were doing.

Mrs.. Peasland, on the other hand, understood, even as she concentrated on the cards in her hand. She put a card on the table and looked toward Riana. All evening she had sensed the competition.

"Do you play, Mrs.. Ingram?" she asked suddenly.

"Cards? No I'm afraid I don't. I can't distinguish one card from another."

Riana met the steely, formidable gaze. The thin lips widened into a cold smile.

"I do not mean cards, Mrs.. Ingram. Do you play the pianoforte? My Agnes is most accomplished."

Riana almost smiled with her own triumph. Could she play? She had won several prizes in her teens and early twenties, playing in local and provincial music festivals. Caution held her back from speaking immediately, for there was still the amnesia aspect, and she had already admitted that she remembered she could not play cards. The lie had to be maintained. She pretended to consider.

"I don't really know. It feels as if I should. May I test myself?"

Daria's hand tightened around hers and she smiled with encouragement.

"By all means, Riana dear."

"I hope I don't make a mess of things, if I really don't know how to play. Will you forgive me if I mess it up?"

Daria laughed, "Of course, my dear! How could we not, given the state of your memory? And I shall applaud merrily if you do not."

Generva set her book aside as Riana got slowly to her feet, smiling positively as Riana made her way to the pianoforte. But before she reached the instrument, Agnes, who was closer, jumped up and flounced herself down before the keyboard.

"Let me first play. I know I can play. You shall have next turn, Mrs.. Ingram."

Shock stilled Generva's face and she reached out to grasp Riana's hand to pull her down to sit in the chair beside her. She leaned close to Riana and spoke in a voice so low as to be nearly inaudible.

"I hope she makes a cake of herself."

Agnes nearly did. She had chosen one of Hayden's 'Emperor Quartets', slurring and hitting wrong notes. Riana could not help wincing at the missed and wrong notes. When thankfully, it was finished, she went immediately into another piece. It was a tune, this time, unfamiliar to Riana, but from the expression on Generva's face, well known to the rest. Agnes had a voice that was slightly flat, yet not unpleasant to Riana's twentieth century ears. To the others, however, as she glanced quickly around at those in her line of sight, it was painful. The song itself was long, the lyrics overly sentimental and rather silly, telling of lost love. She heard Generva's audible sigh when the song ended, and the sigh was closely followed by Daria's voice.

"You must allow Mrs.. Ingram her chance, Agnes. If she finds she is unable to play, then we will welcome another performance from you."

Riana felt a hard brush of Agnes' hand as they passed near the piano and felt it was deliberate. It surprised her and she rubbed at the spot as she sat down to study the instrument before her. It was nothing like she had ever seen before. A solid rectangular mahogany case with lighter inlaid wood, with a small keyboard that took up three quarters of the width, with beautiful painted flowers surrounding the manufacturer's name which was unfamiliar to her. She felt around for the pedals as she looked at the hand-written music sheets. Lightly, she rested her fingers on the cool, ivory keys, lightly experimenting with the tones of the two pedals under her feet. It would do. She continued her testing of the keys and pedals until she was satisfied.

Kieran had turned from his letter and watched her, his arm hooked over the back of his chair. He gave her a small, encouraging nod and settled himself in his rather awkward position. The imp of competition pinched at the corner of Riana's mind and she went into the complicated arrangement of Mozart's Sonata in F. Her attention was focused on the keys, her brain effortlessly remembering the complex array of notes, so she was not able to see the delight on some faces and the dismayed expression on others. Her fingers were a little stiff, but they obeyed her will, although making the tune a trifle slower than she might have wanted.

When the turn ended, she dropped her hands into her lap, her eyes still on the keyboard. The instrument was tinnier than she liked, but well-tuned for all that. There was a long silence until the first hand clapped with deliberated slowness. Looking up, she saw it was Kieran, a wide smile lighting his face. Others quickly followed and above it, Lord Ranleigh's voice all but shouting.

"Bravo, Mrs.. Ingram! Bravo! Well done, my dear."

There were other smiles, if those of Mrs.. Peasland and her daughter were more than a little strained. Their determined politeness showed their determined disapproval. Mr.. Peasland, however, had his attention divided between his cards and the glass of wine at his elbow.

"Encore, Riana dear." Daria called out, "Encore, if you please."

Riana's mind was a whirl of possibilities, then that imp in her brain settled on something and she slid closer to the keyboard. Almost without conscious thought of her own, the fingers of one hand began playing the Beatles' 'Long and Winding Road' and she wished she had Paul McCartney's plaintive voice to add to the beauty of the song. She peeked quickly at her small audience, taking satisfaction in their confusion. When the piece was over, she rose to her feet, ignoring the applause from the others.

"A most unusual melody." she heard Mrs.. Peasland comment, "Rather simplistic in arrangement, do you not agree, Agnes?"

"Yes, Mamma. But I do not recognize it at all. What was it, Mrs.. Ingram?"

Riana took her place beside Daria, who reached out to give her a congratulating hug.

"I'm afraid I don't know. It was just something that came into my head. I'm sure it must have a name."

She felt eyes on her and looking up, she saw Kieran watching her with a wide smile of pride on his face. He nodded quickly in congratulation and turned back to his letter.

"Will you favour us with another piece?" Baron Lynch asked her.

Riana panicked, knowing she had already gone too far. She did not want to push her luck. She touched her fingertips to her temple and gave Daria a small, apologetic smile.

"I'm afraid I'm getting a headache. May I be excused?"

"The very thing, Mrs.. Ingram." Lord Donaghmore rose to his feet, "Please allow me to escort you to your room."

"Lord Donaghmore!" Mrs.. Peasland burst out, "That is hardly proper!"

He had already come across the floor to stand before Riana. He had begun to bow, but halted to look at the older woman.

"Ordinarily I would agree with you, but Mrs.. Ingram's circumstances permits a little flexibility. Having found her, I feel more than a little responsible for her. In any case, she is a widow."

"And therefore a woman without the protection of her husband."

"In that case, to a certain degree of decorum, I claim the duty of a casual replacement."

He finished his bow and held out his hand toward her. Afraid of making a glaring social error, Riana first looked at Daria in silent question. Daria squeezed her arm and nodded in assent. Riana held out her arm and allowed him to help her to her feet.

With nods to the others in the room, they made their way to the door and went out.

"Thank-you for the excuse to leave." Kieran said to her when they had not gone ten feet from the door, "I hate those dull social evenings. Playing cards for the most part bores me and there is not enough silence for me to read. I do not know how Generva does it."

"You will have to go back."

She felt, rather than heard him chuckle, "Yes, for appearance sake I must, but I will not stay long and will take myself to my own bed."

His hand curved over hers where it rested in his elbow. It was warm and strangely, it comforted her. Together, they walked along the chilly maze of corridors, Kieran telling her of his past visits to Riverton Abbey, his anecdotes told with dry humour. Too soon, they reached her door and reluctantly, she slid her hand from him. He caught her fingers and held them.

"I was most impressed with your skill at the pianoforte, Mrs.. Ingram. I hope you will honour us with more in the future."

"Thank-you, Lord Donaghmore. I just might do that. It seems like a long time since I've played."

He was watching her face so intently that she felt a little uncomfortable under his gaze. She gave him a stiff smile that seemed to tear at the corners of her moth. She had been watching his face, so did not see his hand rise until it rested on her cheek. She gasped softly, but did not move away from the caressing fingers. He bent his head closer to her and she smelled the faint hint of wine on his breath.

"You are an extraordinary woman, Mrs.. Ingram. I have never before known your like."

There was a long silence as she kept her eyes on his face, "Thank-you Lord Donaghmore, but I am really ordinary."

His face was closer, his head blocking out everything in her line of vision, his voice low and rumbling.

"Not so ordinary, Riana. And I should like it very much if you would call me Kieran. Just to hear my name from your lips."

She was stunned to silence, unable to respond. A second later, his lips on hers prevented any reply. She knew she stopped breathing, knew she must breathe, but the unexpected joy that swept through her at his touch prevented any thought but that of his mouth on hers. The kiss felt as if it went on forever, she felt his hands pull her closer and raised her own to the hardness of his chest. After an eternity, he lifted his head to look down at her with burning, glittering eyes.

"Do not forget our sitting tomorrow."

He touched her hair lightly and tugged loose one of the silk flowers. Without a backward glance, he walked quickly away from her down the passage.

Chapter 4

The sweet smell of chocolate woke Riana and opening her eyes, she looked first at the ceramic clock on the mantle. Immediately, she jerked upright.

"My God! It's ten-thirty!" she gasped out.

There was movement to the left of her and turning her head, she saw Susan coming toward her carrying a tray.

"Good mornin', Mu'um." she said cheerily.

"Why did you let me sleep so late? I'm usually out of bed by seven o'clock."

Before answering, Susan set the tray on the table by the fireplace and then came forward to the bed, lifting a light cotton garment off the chair as she came. She shook out it's folds, holding it out for Riana.

"If you will pardon me, mu'um, I thought that since you have trouble rememberin' I might help you out. If you is to be in p'lite society, you must know the proper forms. I would not have you a figure of fun to the others. If you will excuse me."

Riana slid off the bed and let Susan help he into the light, embroidered robe. Susan tied the ribbons with swift efficiency.

"I would be grateful for any and all help you can give me. Don't think I didn't notice the looks I got at dinner last night. I guess by these standards, my table manners are not up to much. But that doesn't explain why you let me sleep so late."

Susan let Riana sit down to her breakfast of cheese, rolls, fruit and steaming chocolate. She opened the large linen napkin onto Riana's lap.

"Ladies do not rise until eleven o'clock and they break their fast in the privacy of their bedrooms. Only gentlemen take breakfast in the breakfast room, it is their time of the day alone. A lady never descends until twelve o'clock. Oh, and that reminds me. Lord Donaghmore said to tell you that he will meet you in the entry at twelve o'clock, so you can begin your portrait. Lady Ranleigh has sent the proper clothes for that. Special, they are."

"Why?"

Susan busied herself behind Riana and answered in a distracted manner.

"Wanted something special, he did. Most certainly not suitable for this time of the year."

"What?" Riana chuckled, "A mini skirt and a tube top?"

There was a long silence, "Mu'um?"

Oh, oh! Caught again! When would she learn to keep her mouth shut?

"Oh, nothing. Is it shocking?"

"Certainly not, mu'um. Lady Ranleigh would never be so. It is just not quite right for the autumn."

Riana closed her eyes to savour the warm roll and sweet, fresh butter. After swallowing, she sipped the chocolate, holding it carefully on her tongue for as long as she dared.

"So what is it that shocks you?"

"This."

Riana turned in her chair to look at the things Susan was holding out. There was a satin gown of white with a scalloped net overskirt embroidered in pale yellow. The net was also on the bodice and puffed sleeves, and there was a stiffly starched lace standing collar. Even her eyes knew this was an evening gown.

Draped over Susan's arm was a lovely shawl of a slightly darker shade of yellow, fringed with an even deeper yellow, and her hand held a deep brimmed bonnet the same yellow as the shawl's fringe.

"Isn't that kind of dressy for noon?"

"Indeed it is, mu'um, but Lord Donaghmore would not be gainsaid. He went through Lady Ranleigh's wardrobe himself and she objected saying this gown is sadly out of date."

"But it's lovely."

"Indeed, mu'um."

Riana made a face, "Susan, when we're alone, please call me Riana. I don't like being called 'mu'um', it makes me feel like an old lady."

"Oh no! That just wouldn't be proper." Susan looked horrified.

"Well, in this room, with just the two of us, 'mu'um' isn't proper and I won't answer to it."

A bare hint of a smile curved Susan's mouth and she carefully set the hat on the dressing table.

"If you say so, m.....Riana. My, what an odd name."

"It's Welsh. It's a witch's name, I think." she saw Susan was busying herself with gloves, "Oh Susan, not gloves too?"

Susan held them up, they were pale yellow, "Evening gloves." she said mournfully.

Riana was in the main entry hall just as the big case clock struck twelve. She was on time, but Lord Donaghmore was not. Sighing with impatience, she tugged at the shawl, the operation of which she had not quite managed and sat down on one of the silk damask chairs. She fidgeted with the bonnet in her hands, wondering why she carried it if Susan had been instructed to style her hair with ribbons and tiny yellow roses. She felt the movement of the trailing ribbons every time she turned her head.

Ten minutes late, Lord Donaghmore joined her, carrying a thick blanket under one arm. He was casually dressed in dark breeches, black boots and a loose, paint spattered grey smock. He gave her a bow more suited to a more formal manner of dress.

"Please excuse my tardiness, Mrs.. Ingram. I am set up and ready for you, but there is a chill in the air today, so I thought a blanket might warm you from time to time. Are you ready?" he studied her critically, "Good. Yes, yellow in an excellent choice for you. I am pleased that your maid followed my instructions implicitly. You look very well, indeed. Come along. The light is good only for a few hours."

He held his free arm to her and she placed her hand on it, feeling a little glimmer of pride that it was rapidly becoming easier and easier to do this. His skin was warm under her hand and she could feel the movement of muscle as they walked.

They walked in no great hurry, but neither did they dally. Riana recognized the direction she had taken when she followed the strange man and ended up in this time and place. It had not changed a great deal, the wall looking only a little less aged.

"Do you read, Mrs.. Ingram?" he asked as they passed through the opening of the wall.

"Haven't we had this discussion before? I do read. You know that."

"But you did not quite say what exactly it was. Poetry? Do you like Byron? Scott?"

"I think I've read 'The Lady of the Lake' in school." she just hoped her timing was right.

"Ah yes. One of his newer efforts. I must confess, I do not care for his work. I prefer Byron's imagery. And novels?"

Riana racked her brain. She always confused Charlotte Bronte and Jane Austin. It was a few moments of frantic brain searching before she answered.

"'Sense and Sensibility'?" she queried hesitantly.

She felt him chuckle beside her, "Yes. I has had some ladies of my acquaintance all aflutter. I must confess that I have not read it myself. Perhaps some day, but I greatly doubt it."

"When you are completely bored?"

He looked down at her and their eyes met. Both were recalling the kiss from the night before. Kieran stopped suddenly and turned to her, twisting his arm so that her hand slid down to be caught in his. He held it almost too tightly.

"If I were a true gentleman, I should apologize for last night." a wry smile twisted his perfect lips, "But in general, the Irish are not considered gentlemen, so I suppose I can consider myself free of those restraints. But I did, however, take advantage of both you and my cousin's hospitality."

Riana found herself leaning closer to him, "But you were not alone in it, were you? And heaven knows I didn't resist."

He laughed suddenly, the joyful sound of it echoing in the cool air. Deliberately, he began walking again, putting her hand back in his elbow.

"You are an unusual woman, Mrs.. Ingram."

She slowed enough to pull him back, "Please call me Riana. I prefer it."

There was only the faintest hint of a smile, "You know it is not proper. But then you would not be half so interesting if you were. I will call you Riana, if you will call me Kieran. Only when we are alone, mind you, for it would not do to shock some of the visitors of Ranleigh Abbey."

They circled the glade until they came to the vine-covered gazebo. Inside an easel had been set up, with an unsteady table that held jars of paints, brushes and a paint-covered palette. In one of the corners of the hexagonal structure was a plain wooden chair with a cane seat.

Kieran put his hands on Riana's shoulders and steered her toward the chair, but instead of seating her on it, he leaned her against it, making one of her gloved hands clasp the top of the ladder back and the other clutching the ribbons of her hat. Fastidiously he arranged and re-arranged her shawl to suit him, and fussed with the cuff and ties on her over-the-elbow gloves.

He tipped and turned her head, often standing back to study the results, before beginning again. At last, with a soft, satisfied snort, he was ready. He backed to his easel and without taking his eyes from her, picked up a charcoal and began rapidly sketching.

The only sound was the scratching of the charcoal on the canvas and the occasional sound of birds. Boredom made Riana's ears strain for other sounds. She heard a dog barking and the mooing of a cow. People spoke in shouts far away and the breeze rustled the drying autumn leaves around her. She felt herself relax, the peace here was so unexpected. She closed her eyes, unable to keep the smile from her lips.

"Open your eyes and stop smiling!" came the curt command.

Startled, Riana opened her eyes to see Kieran had taKen up a paintbrush and was rapidly applying paint. She was astonished by his speed.

"Do you always paint that fast?"

He made several strokes before he answered, "Not always. I suppose I am inspired. Are you chilled? We can stop until you are warmed."

"Not yet. I'll tell you when I am. How long do you think this will take?"

He peered around the canvas at her, his brows drawn together in annoyance.

"Not as long as most I have done, but a few days at least. I hope this weather will hold. We have been having unusually fine weather for this time of year, so I hope to be able to at least have the background complete before the weather turns bad. Now stand still and stop talking."

His concentration was such that she did not tell him she was cold until she was shivering from it. He looked at her with not little aggravation and set down his brush. Without speaking he unfolded the blanket and put it around her shoulders, pulling her close to him to use some of his body heat. He was very warm, for sweat dotted his forehead even in the cool air. She huddled closer to him, needing to be warm.

"You foolish woman," he murmured softly, "I should have stopped much sooner if only you had spoken. It will not do to have you ill just when I am about to reach a crucial point, now would it? Tomorrow, I will have Smith send out some tea. I am sorry I did not think about it until now."

At some point he had unbuttoned the top buttons of his smock, revealing the hair at his throat. She wanted to reach out and stroke it, wanted to press her face to it. Gasping, she straightened away from him a little. His arm tightened around her and he looked at her with alarm.

"You are unwell?" he asked quickly.

Wordlessly, she shook her head. She couldn't very well tell him that she was feeling more than a little lascivious. That would be too much of a shock for this man who prided himself on being a gentleman. And she didn't want him to think any less of her. Well, at least, she was much warmer than she had been.

"Do you wish to take a seat?"

"No, I'm fine. Is your light going to hold out much longer?"

He squinted up at the sky, "Not long. A quarter of an hour, perhaps. But we can go indoors if you are too chilled."

She shook her head, suddenly wanting away from him. He was too disturbing when he was so close to her that she could smell his soap.

"I can stay out until you can't work anymore. I won't drop dead of cold or exhaustion in that short time."

He stroked his fingers down her cheek and at that moment if he had asked any more of her she would have gladly done it. She studied his back as he returned to his paints, trying to imagine it naked on a bed beside her. Her fingers gripped the chair back so tightly that the wood dug painfully into the palm of her hand and she welcomed it's distraction.

Just as he promised, he painted only for fifteen more minutes, then he carefully put first her shawl, then the blanket around her shoulders. She warmed almost immediately and dropped to the chair to watch him fastidiously clean his brushes. When he finished he held out a rather grimy hand to her, but she took it, mindful of the gloves she still wore.

"Don't you have to put that away?" she asked him, trying to see what he had already painted.

He dropped a light cloth over it, "My man knows what to do. He will fetch it presently. For now, I must get you to the house before you catch a chill."

He was tired. Glancing up at the profile that was sharp against the blue sky, she saw the lines of weariness around his eyes. She let her eyes follow the line of his stubbled jaw and wanted to smooth away his exhaustion. She did not speak, not simply because she was not the chattering type, but because she did not want to burden him further. She did long to be in the house, snuggling close to the warmth of a blazing fire.

Kieran was intensely aware of the woman at his side. He felt her stumble as she hurried to keep up with his long strides and slowed his pace to accommodate her. The light breeze made the scent of her drift across is nostrils and from the corner of his eye he could see a silly yellow silk rose bobbing in the swirl of her hair. He controlled a smile that threatened to shape his mouth, the smile that might tell her that he knew her place was with him.

As they reached the wall, he could control himself no longer. With a quick glance toward the house, he caught her elbow and pulled her away from the open glade, leading her under the low hanging branches of a huge old chestnut tree, pressing her back against the rough bark of the trunk. Her green eyes widened with surprise and her mouth opened with shock and he did not even try to resist. Bending his head, he let his mouth briefly brush hers and it was enough to strike him to his soul. He needed to explain, did not want her to think he was an animal.

"I have been wanting to do this all afternoon." he told her in a low, rumbling voice, "I think I have been waiting for your all my life."

Riana went limp as he put his arms around her and pressed her to him. For the first time in her life, the smell of turpentine was exciting. She tipped back her head to look up at him and welcomed the mouth that claimed hers once again. This time she was more than willing, she joined him, heart and soul, sliding her arms around his back to hold him as tightly as he was holding her.

His mouth slid across her face, leaving a trail of tiny, light kisses and when he reached her ear, his teeth caught her lobe tenderly.

"Riana! Riana my heart." his voice rasped in her ear, "Stay with me forever."

As the words soaked through the delightful, exciting warmth he had created inside her, she knew that he asked the impossible. She did not know how she had arrived in this time and she did not know when she would next leave. She did not want to have him hurt if she left as oddly as she had arrived. But only one more kiss, she told herself. And she did not want to be the one to break the delight they shared. She felt his hand move up her waist toward her breast and was shocked that in this time he was so bold. It was enough. She pushed him back with all the strength she was able to muster and he did not resist. There was an appalled, shocked expression on his face as he stood back from her. He ran his hand through his already rumpled hair.

"Lud, Riana! I do not know what came over me. I've treated you like some light skirt at Covent Garden. Please accept my apology."

"I won't because I enjoyed it as much as you........"

"Riana! I will not hear it. You are a lady and I......."

This time Riana interrupted him. She gathered her dignity, her shawl and her blanket around her as she stared up at him.

"Lord Donaghmore, sometimes you can be a real jerk!" she burst out.

She did not see him open his mouth for she ran from him, twisting around him and ducking under the low branches of the sheltering tree. Without thinking, she tore across the centre of the glade, in her misery hardly noticing that her head began pounding and her vision blurred. She was unaware that she was stumbling into darkness.

"Mrs.. Ingram! Mrs.. Ingram! Are you alright? Wake up! Tom, run to the house and ring the doctor. It seems out guest has had an accident."

Riana opened her eyes and looked up into Jared Thorpe's anxious face. For a moment she did not recall just who he was, then slowly, her mind adjusted. So she was back in her own time and her head was pounding, indicating she was passed due for her medication. She tried to raise her arm, but it fell back, so her wrist lay on her forehead like some heroine in an old bad play. Jared raised her shoulders off the grass.

"Mrs.. Ingram? Shall I carry you back to the house?"

"Of course not! I can walk on my own."

She struggled to sit up and he grasped her elbow to help raise her to her feet. Pain raced through her head so that she swayed from it. She felt the man's arm around her waist and smelled the scent of his cologne....Polo, she decided.

"I don't believe you can walk, Mrs.. Ingram. I will have to carry you."

Riana wanted the sound of his voice to stop for it echoed in her head, bouncing off the back of her skull. She let him lift her off her feet and clung to the hard muscles of his shoulder as he strode forward. She wished his pace was smoother, for every step he made was torture. Still, she took comfort in his strength.

"Helen, open Mrs.. Ingram's door. She is ill. Make sure Tom has called the doctor. And let Mrs.. Wigmore know we are bringing in her daughter."

Riana blacked out, coming around again as she lay on her bed. Her mother hovered over her and Jared sat on the edge of the bed beside her, holding her hand his face tight and anxious. He smiled when her eyes opened, and the charm of it delighted her. She smiled back in spite of her pain.

"You're back with us. Good. Can I fetch you anything?"

"Her medication." Clare said quickly, "She should have taKen it long ago. She's usually very good about it. How could you be so foolish as to forget, Riana?"

Jared straightened his spine, "You're ill?"

Riana glared at her mother, who glared back and moved to get the bottles of pills that sat on the dressing table.

"I'm fine. I just have these migraine headaches from time to time. I'll be fine in a couple of hours."

"What were you doing out there?" he queried, tightening his grip on her hand.

"Just walking. It's quiet out there."

Slowly, she slid her hand from his.

Clare came to the bed with a glass of water, two brown pills and one yellow cupped in her palm. Jared reached up and took the water then held his hand out for the pills. He held the pills out to her and obediently, she took them and as obediently drank the water. She smiled as she laid her head back on the pillow.

"You will make someone a wonderful nurse. I didn't expect this kind of treatment when we booked our stay here."

He chuckled and she liked the sound of it.

"I don't do this for everyone. Only women unconscious on my lawn. Are you sure you will be alright?"

"Of course. Give me a little while. And I'll see you at dinner tonight."

He rose reluctantly from the bed and seemed to tower over her, "It's a date, then, if I may join you. I'll have the chef make you something special." he touched her cheek, "I will see you later then. Take care of yourself."

Riana watched him leave then looked up at her mother who was still glaring down at her. She gave her mother an innocent shrug.

"Why didn't you tell him? A migraine! For heaven's sake, Riana!"

"Tell him what? That I'm dying and have him pity me? No thanks! What purpose would it serve to tell him, anyway? In two weeks we'll be gone and I won't see him again."

Clare smiled and pulled the bedspread over her daughter, "Did you see the way he was looking at you? He's more than a little interested, you know."

Riana rolled over to her side and hugged the spread around her ears. "Well, it won't do him much good, will it?"

As sleep began to overtake her, she felt her mother's hand on her shoulder, lightly squeezing.

Her mother's training was deeply ingrained, she thought as she smiled at herself in the mirror. She dressed for dinner. Had always dressed up when going out for dinner, no pants and shirts for her. She smoothed her hand down the front of her aqua silk shantung dress and decided that her sleep had been just what she needed. She both felt and looked better. Picking up a plastic pill bottle, she gave it a light shake before opening it. Time for yet another one. She accomplished this with an efficiency quickly learned.

There was a few minutes before Clare came to take her to dinner, so she sat in the chair by the fireplace and rested her chin in her hand. Her eyes strayed about the room and it was several minutes before she realized that this was the same room she occupied in that other.....what should she call it? Life? Delusion? Fantasy? For fantasy it was. She had been still wearing the shorts and t-shirt that she knew had been taken from her. Had that man ever existed? She felt that he must have. He was too real to have been imaginary. Or did her diseased brain conjure him as a balm to her soul? She sighed and held her breath, wanting to be back with him, back in that time where life was more complicated, yet easier.

As they entered the dining room, Riana hesitated briefly in the doorway, seeing in her mind's eye how it had once been. Now it was filled with people sitting at a number of small tables. She liked the wallpaper that was in the room now, but not the garish colour on the delicate mouldings. Across the room at a table near the window, Jared rose to his feet, smiling as he caught their eyes. Clare had to nudge Riana into motion. He held out his hand to them as they approached.

"Good evening, ladies. You're both looking lovely this evening. Riana, you seemed to have recovered admirably. You are feeling better?"

"I'm much better, thank-you. I just needed a little quiet."

As she spoke, he pulled out their chairs, but his eyes were on Riana as she waited for her mother to sit first. When they were all seated, a waiter appeared beside Jared who barely glanced up at him.

"Shall we start with a cocktail?"

Riana looked up at the waiter, "I don't drink, but I would like a glass of tomato juice."

Jared gave a quick nod then ordered for both himself and for Clare.

"I hope you will forgive me, but I have taken the liberty of having something special prepared for us this evening. Thank-you, Brian, you can bring the starters after you have brought the drinks."

Riana glanced at the departing back of the waiter, thinking how much is long, ankle-length apron resembled those she had seen in that other time. Or maybe she had reflected in that time, the clothes she had seen here. She gave herself a mental pinch.

"Your business in London was over quickly." she smiled a Jared.

"Yes. Funnily enough by the time I got to my office here, the client trouble I was having was easily solved. It was mostly financial and a quick trip to Whipford was enough to settle things. In show business it seems that everything is an emergency. People tend to panic before sitting down to think things through logically."

Riana looked at the smooth, handsome face and felt amusement that this man would be talking logic. In her experience, extremely handsome men were not usually blessed with brains as well. This one was the exception. He was watching her, his eyes intense and his hand resting close to hers on the tablecloth.

"Do you have a job, Riana?"

She gave a short nod, "I'm self-employed. I make dolls." she watched, as she always did, for a reaction.

He first looked confused then embarrassed by his confusion. It was one of the most common reactions.

"Dolls?" he echoed.

Her smile was sunny and teasing, "I make porcelain dolls. Limited edition dolls. And I sell them all over the world. I even do some custom-made dolls."

Clare spoke up then, as she sometimes did if she thought her daughter's chosen profession was about to be ridiculed.

"I have always been surprised at what a good living can be made from dolls. Riana has her own house, paid for and a condo in Whistler for skiing in the winter. Her husband quit his job to become her business manager. And he was quite good at it too."

"You make dolls." he repeated thoughtfully, "We have limited edition dolls in our gift shop. Would one of yours be in there?"

"Possibly. I don't always know where they go."

"Shall we go and see?"

The waiter was placing their drinks on the table, "Right now?" she blurted.

"Certainly. Why not? It it's not far."

Riana glanced at her mother who was sipping her drink with an air of false indifference. The look on Clare's face convinced her.

"Sure, why not?"

Jared rose, holding his hand out to her as she pushed away from the table. The gesture was so familiar that Riana caught her breath, seeing for a split second another face. She avoided the hand with a smile. Jared's hand smoothly changed direction as he indicated the direction she was to go.

Distance must be relative to him, Riana decided as they walked through the cool corridors. Near the back of the house, Jared pulled a ring of keys from his pocket and unlocked a pair of French doors. He left her standing in the doorway as he made his way around one wall. A second later, light flooded the big room. It was a bright, well-laid-out gift shop, containing all the usual trinkets snapped up by tourists; guide books to the Abbey, British candies, Cadbury's chocolate, books on British history, plastic snow globes with the Abbey inside. On the far wall, however, close to the glass fronted counter that held the till was a big glass case that held several dolls. Jared waved her inside.

"Over here. Take a look and see if you know anyone."

She could see even at the distance and she began walking forward.

"You have two of mine. Imagine that! It's kind of a coincidence, wouldn't you say?"

There was Angelica, a maiden from the Middle Ages with her small hat over her crispinette and fillet, her golden hair long and her long trailing skirts and sleeves trimmed with brown fur. Jared opened the case and twisted the small cardboard that was attached to the doll's wrist by a thin gold cord.

"Made by Riana Ingram. Why yes, this is you. I believe you have lost some weight since this photo was taken."

Riana laughed, "Yes, thank goodness."

He was still holding the doll, but she smoothed the dark red velvet gown and tugged the tiny sleeves that were buttoned to the elbow. It was like greeting an old friend, for she had produced Angelica more than ten years ago. She looked along the glass shelves and found Sarafina, one of her series of fairy dolls.

"Why here's Sarafina. My fairy princess. A fairy?" she tipped her head in question, "I do have other historical dolls, you know. Wouldn't they be more appropriate?"

"You have more historical dolls? We shall have to bring more of them in, then. As for the fairy, we have a Fairy Festival here in June that culminates on Mid-summer's night. We sell a lot of fairy items then."

He had to bend close to peer at the tall, willowy doll who's limbs were exaggerated and delicate. Her short, summer green dress sparkled with glitter and her large, glitter-veined wings were all but invisible, her reddish hair a tumbling mass of curls. On the back of one elongated hand rested a tiny lady bird, her eyes distant, her expression unreadable.

"I prefer this one." Jared said in awe, "It's so different from the rest. She's almost sexy."

Riana chuckled, "And why can't fairies be sexy? They have to reproduce somehow, don't they? You don't have her partner, Gaylord. They usually go as a set."

This time Jared burst out laughing, "Gaylord? Where ever did you come up with a name like that?"

Riana was not offended, for sometimes she had given her dolls rather outlandish names.

"At the risk of sounding like a complete looney tune, the dolls usually name themselves sometime during their design. And I think Gaylord is a perfectly good fairy name. I suppose so, anyway, never having met a real fairy."

With a wicked smile, Jared quirked a meaningful eyebrow at her and she knew just what he meant.

"Not that kind of fairy!"

Laughing, she gave him a little, friendly nudge of his elbow. He caught her hand and held it tightly between them, there was hesitation in his eyes, so carefully, she pulled her hand away from his.

"I will send you one of my catalogues when I get home so you can see my selection of fairies and historical figures."

Jared moved behind the long, dark burgundy counter and dipped down behind it. She heard a rustling of shifting paper as he spoke.

"We probably have one here. We get all sorts of catalogues all the time. Hold on. Here it is. Fancy that."

He rose above the counter, holding aloft a rather battered and old copy of one of her catalogues. Twisting his hand, he read the brief biography on the back, his eyes skimming quickly.

"Hmmm. So you live in Vancouver. I've been there two or three times. It's a lovely city. But you were born in the Rocky Mountains. You're married to Ken and you live in a character home in Point Grey. No children, but you do have a dog."

"A Norwegian Elkhound named Thora. My husband and my father were killed in a plane crash three years ago." there was a defensive tone in her voice.

Jared reached over the counter and touched his fingers to her cheek "I am sorry, Riana. I did not mean to cause you pain."

Smiling, she stood back from the warm fingers, "I accepted his death a long time ago. But I do miss his advice. And I do miss having him to talk to."

"You can re-marry, you know."

"No," she sighed "I don't think so."

He frowned, "Why not? You don't like men?"

Her sudden, tinkling laugh delighted him, "Oh, I adore men. I'm just not ready to marry one of them in the near future." she stopped and tilted her head, "Can we go back to the dining room, now?"

"Not just yet. I want to see what other fairies you produce."

Riana watched him as he flipped through the glossy pages until he found the section of fairies. He put the catalogue on the counter, smoothing the middle flat.

"So this is Gaylord. I can see why he was sold without his partner. Somewhere there's a lascivious old lady with him as a center piece in her lounge, drooling over him."

Riana bent over the counter, "I modelled him on Fabio, but I didn't like his hair on his shoulders so I put it up."

He ran a finger over the picture, "Fabio after he'd spent several weeks on a torture rack, I should imagine. But I like his hair. Aren't there some American Indians that put their hair up like this?"

"Actually, I copied the hairstyle from the Lone Ranger's sidekick, Tonto. Or Jay Silverheels version of Tonto."

Silently, he studied each of the sets of dolls. His brows were drawn together in concentration as he followed his moving finger. After a time, he looked up at her with a faint smile.

"Mrs.. Ingram, I do believe you have made another sale. Tomorrow I will talk to the store's manager and we will order some of these in time for next year's festival. Are most of them still available?"

She leaned on the counter again, "Molly and Coddle have been sold out. I have limited firings of all my dolls. I removed Fire and Ice on my own because I didn't really like them. But yes, most of the rest of them are." she looked up at him, "Do you think we could go back now? My mother has been alone long enough, I think."

He looked a little embarrassed, "Please forgive me. Yes, let's return to the dining room. I hope she hasn't given up on us."

Riana laughed, "Oh, she used to waiting. My father and brothers are late for everything. She'll still be there."

Clare was half-finished her drink and was beginning on the shrimp balls and Swiss cheese twists. She swallowed her mouthful and smiled up at them as they returned.

"These are fabulous!" she looked at Jared, "Did you see any of your creations?"

"Angelica and Serafina."

"No Gaylord?" she asked, her eyes still on Jared, "He was always my favourite. In fact, Riana created him for me after I'd admired Fabio in a TV commercial. Too bad about his hair, 'tho. I liked it long and flowing."

"But it didn't suit him, Mother. And you agreed with me."

"True enough." she reached for another cheese twist.

The meal progressed at a leisurely pace, after Riana took her mealtime medication, the conversation flowing from the hotel business, show business and it's peculiarities, to childhoods, movies and favourite places visited. Jared expressed an interest in Riana's doll business as the food came and went around them. ChicKen Okra soup followed the appetizer and the main course was game hens with spinach sage stuffing, white turnips stuffed with peas, minted vegetables and a puree of potatoes and cauliflower. Dessert was vermouth glazed pears served with a frozen rum cream. As they were served their coffee, Riana leaned back in her comfortable chair.

"That was the best meal I think I've ever eaten." she breathed.

Jared gave her a thankful smile, "We try to overcome the British reputation for bad food here. Our chef is American. He learned to cook in New Orleans and he likes to produce things not on the menu."

"Well, please tell him how much we appreciate his efforts."

He touched the back of her hand quickly and lightly, "I will do that."

Clare's eyes went from one of them to the other and she smothered a tiny yawn with the back of her hand.

"If you two will please excuse me, I think I will go to bed. It's all this fresh air, I think." she held up a hand as Jared rose to his feet, "Please no. You just stay here. I'm sure you will find interesting things to talk about. Good night Riana, please don't stay up too late, you know how I worry about you."

"G'night, Mom. Sleep well."

"Oh, I do here, oddly enough. Let me take your medication back with me. It'll be one less thing for you to worry about."

They watched her as she shoved the pill bottles into her voluminous purse, then wove her way out of the room, neither spoke. When she was gone, Jared pushed aside his empty cup and put his napkin on the table.

"I have something I should very much like you to see. I had wanted to show this to you this morning. Are you ready now?"

"Yes, I suppose I am. You won't get me lost, will you?"

He laughed, "Riana, I have lived in this house my entire life and I know it intimately. But if you're worried, perhaps we can leave a trail of breadcrumbs. Don't worry, I can't take you to any dungeons, for we don't have any. My intentions, I assure you, are strictly honourable." he stood behind her chair, his hands on the back of it, "Shall we go?"

Side by side and not touching, they made their way through the cooling corridors. Riana suppressed a shudder and wished for one on the lovely shawls she had seen in that other......what should she call it? Life? Time? Fantasy? He must have felt the tiny motion.

"Are you alright?" he asked, bending his head toward her.

"Fine. Someone just walked over my grave, I think."

Jared jerked to a stop, looking down at her, his face drawn, "Don't say that. It's a terrible expression."

She met his disturbed gaze steadily, "You're right. It is." then to break the tension between them, "So where exactly are you taking me?"

He tapped her shoulder lightly and crooked a beckoning finger. His smile was wonderful and mischievous as he began walking forward. Willingly, she traipsed after him. It was another long walk through unfamiliar, dim corridors until they stopped before a set of white painted double doors. Jared reached out and flung one of them open. The room beyond was dark and as he had earlier, he disappeared briefly before light flooded into the room and spilled out into the dim hallway.

"Right here. Come in. I think you will like this and if I'm lucky, it might inspire you. It's the gallery and seldom open to the public. Some of the paintings in here are rather valuable. We have a Joshua Reynolds, a George Romney painting of Emma Hamilton and a Constable painting of Riverton Abbey."

"Wow!" she breathed, impressed.

Riana followed him inside, halting dead in the middle of the gallery floor. Her heart pounded in her throat, for no matter who she had tried to convince herself that she had been dreaming or deluding herself, she had been in this room before. It was different now, the walls painted white and track lighting installed to accent the paintings on the walls, more paintings now that before. She had stopped breathing and when Jared caught her hand, she inhaled noisily, bringing air into her starving lungs.

"Riana?" he bent close to her with concern.

She gave her head a small shake, "I'm alright. I just never expected to come here."

"It's one of my favourite places. This is my family over several generations. I used to come here a great deal when I was younger and searching for some meaning in my life." he waved his hand, "And it was here all the time. My I introduce you to my family?"

Riana was charmed by the question. She lightly squeezed the hand that still held hers.

"I would love that."

Slowly he led her by the hand around the room, "Here is the first Earl. He was a crony of Henry the Eighth, and not as nice as he should have been. Next is his son Henry. Guess who he was named for? This is the painting by Constable that the fourth Earl commissioned before Constable made a name for himself. This is the fourth Earl."

Riana looked up at it with some trepidation and curiosity. This was the man she had met. This stern-faced, unyielding looking man who seemed so different from the man she had met.

"This is the fourth Earl?" she asked, hoping he had made a mistake.

"This is Lord Ashley. A bad sort, I'm afraid. He did his best to lose his and our inheritance."

Riana was studying the painting and glanced at the spot near the window where she had last seen it and recalled what Kieran had said about it. Obviously, he finally sat to have his face and hands painted. She peered closer to see a signature, but found nothing more than a single 'K'.

"Who painted this?" her voice was carefully neutral.

Jared's smile widened, "Oh, there is a history with this one. Want to hear it?"

"Oh yes."

"You recall my comment about Wigmores coming back here. Well, the artist was the one who cursed them. He was the Baron of Donaghmore; a Baron is rather low in the Peerage and he was an Irish Baron, which rated him even lower. In any case, he was a talented artist, as you can see. There's a couple of his landscapes around the house as well. It appears that the Baron wasn't all he should be either, for your ancestor accused him of seducing another of your relatives, a cousin or niece or something and the Baron challenged him to a duel. And lost. With his dying breath, he cursed all the Wigmores and none of them ever prospered after that. Although why a Baron should be challenging one of the villagers is a question I have never had answered."

He touched her elbow to move her along, "And this is Ashley's wife. Daria, Countess of Ranleigh. Lovely, isn't she? With the heir, Shelby. Looks like a little devil, doesn't he? It was he who propped up the family fortunes. He got involved in a number of ventures, not the least was selling guns to the American South during the Civil War. He was quite old when he did that. This was painted when he was in his thirties."

There was little trace of the child she had met in the cynical expression on the haughty face. The man wore a brown tweed tail coat, buttoned tightly across his narrow chest, lighter brown trousers and a rust-coloured tie. His hair was over his ears, long side whiskers reached down almost to his jaw. Next to this was a painting of a plump, unhappy-looking woman in a yellow evening gown that had too many ruffles and sleeves too short for her plump arms. Her dark blond hair was dressed with ringlets, ribbons and flowers.

"Lady Catherine. She had ten children, eight of whom outlived her. And she outlived him, for revenge, I expect. We have her diaries and she was not a happy woman. Neither was he a nice man."

"I envy your knowing your family history. I knew nothing about mine, my father wouldn't talk about it. My mother talks about hers, but not his. I've learned more from you than from them."

"Maybe now you know why." he gave her a teasing smile, "You are a cursed family. And here in Britain, we take our curses very seriously."

They moved down the row to the two last portraits. One was a man wearing a ruffled shirt and bright colours of the late sixties, standing, holding the leash of a Russian Wolfhound.

"That's my father. He knew the Beatles, you know, although he was a good deal older. And he still does business with the Stones. His connections enabled me to get into the business as well, but I got my job on my own merit." he finished quickly.

She was impressed, "Have you ever met them?"

"Of course. As a child. Sorry to say, I don't remember anything. There are just a few photographs in my father's private study. I'll show them to you another time. And this is my mother and me. As you can see, tradition dictates the Earl is presented alone and his heir is painted with his mother."

Riana looked at the child wearing a floral printed shirt with a stiff, high collar and dress pants. He was seated on a high stool close to a thin woman in a blue evening gown with a beaded bodice and midnight blue satin skirt. Her hair was piled in bubbles on her head and her eyes darkly rimmed, but they were kind eyes as she appeared to glance anxiously at her son who had the expression of the devil in him.

"I'll bet you were a handful. Your mother is beautiful."

"She was. She died in a car crash when I was fourteen. Funnily enough, my father never re-married, because according to my Auntie Helen, he was the devil with the ladies. The swinging sixties and all that."

"So yours will be the next one up there."

"I suppose so. But it's a long way off. My father is in exceedingly good health and I'm in no hurry to take over. I'm much too fond of him."

"You're an only child?"

"Lord no!" he laughed, "I've an older sister, Marianne. She married a farmer and is raising sheep and children in the North. On seeing her now, one would never know that she was once presented at Court. But she's happy and that's all one can ask. Our father likes her husband and is over the moon being a granddad."

Riana kept her eyes on the portrait, "You're very lucky, you know."

Jared slid his arm around her shoulders and steered her back toward the doors. He watched her face intently as they retraced their steps, and she looked up at the painted faces of his ancestors. He was pleased by what he saw in her expression.

Chapter 5

Riana woke to rain tapping angrily on her window. Frowning, she pulled her arms from the covers and stretched lazily. A smile spread over her face as she replayed in her mind, pictures of the night before. There was a feeling of guilt mixed with the happiness she was feeling.

After the walk along the gallery, Jared had taken her to the private areas of the house, not she realized, to his bedroom, but to a pleasantly shabby sitting room was well lived in and comfortable. As she entered, she was drawn to a tall, wide secretary desk that gleamed in the dull lamplight. Reaching out, she touched the smooth wood.

"This is lovely. I've never seen anything like this before out of a museum."

Jared was pouring himself a drink, "You have good taste. It was bought by the fourth Countess, Daria, early in her marriage. Some think she brought it with her when she married and it's supposed to have a secret compartment, but nobody has ever found it. And believe me, I have looked. But I think it is expected that all these old pieces of furniture are supposed to have secret compartments. Can I offer you anything to drink? I know you don't drink alcohol, but a Coke or something?"

She swung to face him, "A Coke would be great, thank-you."

He took a can from a small fridge disguised as a piece of furniture and poured it into a cut crystal tumbler. He carried it over to her and watched her sip it. Once her throat and mouth were moistened, she looked at him over the rim of the glass.

"So, do you commute to work every day?"

He looked shocked, "It's fifty miles! No, I live in a town house near Pall Mall. Another ancestral possession."

"Fifty miles isn't so far." she commented mildly.

He chuckled, "I recall something a friend of my father's once said. In North America a hundred years is a long time. In Britain a hundred miles is a gret distance. He was from Texas, I believe."

His intense scrutiny was beginning to make Riana uncomfortable. Smiling, she moved away from him, bending to study a painting on the wall. She heard her heart pound in her ears as she recognized the 'K' signature on the bottom of the landscape. A whiff of his cologne alerted her to his presence as he moved to see what had caught her attention.

"Oh, that's where it is. This was done by the famous Lord Donaghmore. It's the glade beyond the wall where I found you this afternoon. It's little changed from that time, you'll find. I never go there myself. I feel too uncomfortable there, as do several others. Odd, that."

"Was he so bad, then?"

She regretted the question as soon as the words were out of her mouth, but she was compelled to know more about him. It was bad enough that he died in a duel and for the first time she felt the now familiar sharp pain of loss.

"Apparently so. But he could paint, couldn't he? He was supposed to have been dark and wild-eyed. Typically Irish."

"Typically Irish?" she echoed, "What does that mean?"

"A drinker and a carouser. And, obviously, a devil with the ladies. But it's all gossip." he hesitated a moment, "And Daria's diary....most ladies in my family kept diaries....has the pages from that particular time, torn out. By whom we don't know, but they're gone."

"Have you read any of these diaries?"

"A couple of them. Daria's was too difficult. She had bad handwriting. And some of them are quite interesting, despite the emphasis on ordinary household things. Every once in a while historical figure pop up. My mother's was particularly interesting. She makes some fairly cynical comments on people still living. Especially Keith Richard and Brian Jones. I'll show it to you sometime."

"I'd like that, if it's not too personal."

His laugh echoed against the high ceiling of the room, "Some of it is quite personal. It took me a very long time to look my father in the eye after I read it. I was sixteen and I didn't think my father even knew some of those things existed, let alone that he actually did them. And my mother!"

"Well, maybe not hers, then."

"Oh, do, Riana. The others I've read are almost as explicit, if couched in prissy terms. Come, sit down and relax."

The cording around the cushions of the silk damask sofa was frayed and the seats comfortably sunken. She sank into the softness and he sat beside her draping his arm along the sofa back behind her. For a time, they watched the flames flicker in the Adams fireplace. Jared spoke first.

"Have you planned any excursions while you are here?"

"A couple of bus trips that leave from here. Mother did all that before we left home. I'd kind of like to rent a car for a couple of days and just drive around, even 'tho you drive on the wrong side of the road. We're going to spend a few days in London...."

"Cancel whatever reservations you have and stay in the townhouse." he interrupted. "It's close to everything." he bared his teeth in a smile, "Even by British standards."

"Oh, we couldn't do that! It's taking advantage. And isn't that taking being a good host just a little too far? You don't want total strangers in your house."

The grin faded slowly as he moved closer to her, "I can't think of you as a stranger and I want you in my house. The better to keep an eye on you." he lifted one eyebrow, "In fact, I insist. It's very comfortable and I have an excellent cook who is vastly underused, as she so often reminds me. I want to show you and your mother the best city in the world."

"But you hardly know us. We could both be criminals for all you know."

He gave a dry, unamused chuckle, "Criminals would hardly come to Whipford bearing the Wigmore name. That would be foolish beyond belief. Please do stay there, Riana. I should like it very much."

"I don't...."

Whatever she had been about to say was stopped by his mouth on hers. The hand holding the glass swept out to one side and the other curled deliciously in her lap. Lord Jared did know how to kiss, his mouth light, yet demanding her attention. She closed her eyes involuntarily, savouring the feel of it, the back of her mind telling her she had missed kissing for far too long. His eyes, when he slowly drew away from her were dark, the expression on his face compelling.

"You haven't been kissed nearly enough." his voice was warm and husky.

"I've been a widow for three years. And I don't fool around for the sake of it. I'm much too busy." she replied, unblinking.

A small smile quirked at the corners of his mouth, "A woman of character. There are few enough of you."

"Maybe you weren't looking in the right places." she challenged him.

Jared threw back his head and laughed heartily, "Well, when you work in show business, even doing what I do, you don't always meet those kinds of people. And," he leaned closer again, "none like you."

She wanted him to kiss her again and as if reading her mind, he continued to lean closer so that he set both of their drink glasses on the battered coffee table. He slid his hands around her shoulders to bring her closer to him and she joined his kiss with an enthusiasm that both shocked her and delighted him. She felt him smiling against her mouth as her own hands reached to his head to hold him firmly in place. He went no further than kissing, but he did that so well she did not mind as much as she thought she might. There were no words between them above the sighing and the occasional hungry moan. The gentleman that he was, he later sat back, grasping her hand, holding on his belt buckle, leaving their two grasped hands there comfortably while they talked as new friends. He walked her back to her room; a good thing since she would have gotten lost, and gave her a thrilling kiss good-night.

Now, sitting up in her bed the next morning, she blushed at her own actions.

"You've been a widow too long, Riana." she told herself, "You've missed having a man kiss you, that's all. You're horny. That and probably the medication." she looked up at the beautiful plastered ceiling, "But God, what are you thinking? What rotten timing."

But deep within herself, she knew none of it was true. She was attracted to Jared in a much different way than she had been with Ken and certainly different than with Lord Donaghmore, that man of her fantasy. For fantasy he must be. Sighing, she threw back the bed clothes a smile curving he lips. But what a fantasy!

"Smarten up, Riana!" she said aloud, "If he ever existed, he's been dead a long time. Jared is here and now, he likes me and he's a damned good kisser. You don't have much time left, to enjoy what you can while you can."

In bare feet, she padded across the carpet and the cool wood of the floor. She glimpsed herself in the dressing table mirror and poked her tongue out at herself. She was, she decided, taking herself much too seriously, something she had done for far too many years. It was time for a little fun in what was left of her life. At least that was what she was going to tell her mother after informing Clare that their plans were changing and they were going to a Pall Mall townhouse for the next few days.

It was still quite early and she went to the window to look out to check the weather. Dark clouds dulled the early morning, but the rain was now little more than a drizzle. She was about to turn away from the window when movement caught her eye, drawing her back. There he was again, standing where he stood before, dressed the same way, leaning on his slim, dark walking stick. His free, gloved hand beckoned her. She did not think twice before hurrying to dress and rushing outside to the cold autumn air.

She pulled her long, heavy cardigan tight around her as she stumbled across the wet grass, feeling the damp through her sneakers. As she hurried toward him, he put one hand atop the other on the head of his cane, but made no other move. His head was tipped slightly forward so she was unable to see his face, hidden as it was by the curled brim of his tall hat. She saw no one as she rushed toward the waiting figure, nobody who might try to stop her.

She was breathing heavily as she came to a halt before him and he raised his head to smile at her. For a second, she caught her breath, caught again by the beauty of his smile. No man should have a smile like that. It wasn't fair. He did not speak, but held out a gloved hand to her.

"Kieran." she said aloud in a trembling voice.

"It is time again, Riana. Are you ready?"

"Yes. Please!" she replied without hesitation.

Riana put her hand in his and together they turned toward the arching footbridge and the wet, misty glade beyond it. She knew now what to expect and after a few steps she held back slightly.

He turned to her, jabbing his stick lightly into the wet lawn, understanding her hesitation.

"I know this is physically difficult for you. It continues to be your choice, Riana. To go or not."

"Will things be the same way if I don't go?"

As she asked the question, she felt distanced from her surroundings and those that she knew in the Abbey behind her. She did not, however, look back at the building. Kieran did give a fleeting look at it, his thick brows drawing together in a slight frown.

"You have already changed things, but I cannot tell you how much."

"Cannot or will not?"

He gave a short, unamused chuckle, "Cannot. I must not influence you."

Sighing loudly with irritation, she began walking with purpose, "You have already influenced me."

"No Riana. I have not. My other self has, but not I."

She tugged on the warm hand that held hers, "I don't understand."

"I am but your guide, and I am here because it is necessary that my great mistake be rectified. I have greatly wronged your family."

"You sure as hell have!" she snapped at him, and continued toward the bridge.

He kept pace with her, or she with him, she wasn't certain which the truth was. They were not close enough to touch, and neither spoke as he guided them across the narrow bridge. She shivered, pulling her cardigan closer, beginning to hear the ringing in her ears, and feeling the churning in her stomach. The grey mist formed before her eyes, veiling the trees ahead of her. Her knees collapsed and he made no move to help her, instead standing back, hands atop his walking stick, sorrow in the face that faded and disappeared.

Chapter 6

Riana opened her eyes and looked up. Early morning sun brightened the ceiling, reflecting brilliance into the room. Turning her head on the pillow she smiled with happiness. She was back! Somewhere in the house was Kieran. Joy warmed her; she had returned to him once again. The rustle of cloth warned her that she was not alone in the room and as that realization came to her, Susan came into focus as she bent anxiously over her.

"Mrs.. Ingram! Yer awake. I must tell the Countess."

Riana reached up and caught Susan's sleeve, "Not yet, please, Susan. How long have I been here like this?"

"Since yesterday afternoon. Lord Donaghmore brung you back. Frantic, he was. Only the Countess was able to get him to his own bed." She gave a sly, knowing smile, "The Countess and a footman. He was like a mad man."

Riana closed her eyes, recalling his kiss, her reaction to it and the consequent words that had passed between them. She thought of the evening with Jared and how it had made her happy. Susan was frowning with consternation.

"Shall I give you more laudanum? Are you feeling poorly?"

"No laudanum. It's addicting. And, oddly enough, I feel wonderful. What time is it?"

"It is half past eleven, nearly time for nuncheon. Shall I fetch you a tray?"

Susan pronounced the word oddly, making it sound like ''noonshine'.

Riana flung back the bedclothes, "No, I will have lunch. I'm starving."

Susan smiled and nodded, pleased that the woman she served was no hot house flower.

"I will fetch you clothes and wash water."

An infuriating amount of time later, Riana was dressed in a pale pink Indian muslin gown with a high collar edged in lace with lace-edged elbow length sleeves, and pale fawn coloured leather shoes that tied at the instep, and was on her way down to the morning room, following the stiff back of a footman. Her stomach rumbled hungrily and by the sudden movement of the man's head, she realized he had heard.

There were three women in the morning room when Riana got there; Daria, her sister Generva and a much older woman, whose face was creased in almost permanent lines of amusement. All of them looked up as she entered through the door the footman had opened for her. Daria was the first to react, half-rising from her chair with a smile of delight.

"Riana, dearest! How wonderful to see you out of your bed. Are you much improved? Yes, there is colour in your cheeks. We were all deathly afraid when Donaghmore brought you in senseless. I fear that you are more ill than you realize. Or, could you be in an.......interesting condition?"

It took Riana a moment to realize just what Daria was asking. The question was discreet, yet the other women understood for their eyes brightened expectantly. She slowly shook her head.

"No. I'm pretty sure I'm not."

The two other women raised eyebrows at Riana's choice of words, but Daria was not perturbed by them. She gave Riana a warm smile as she sat down again, using her hand to indicate

Riana seat herself in the single remaining chair. It was then that Daria introduced the older woman.

"Riana, please meet our Aunt Francis Willowby. She is come here last evening from Sussex for a visit and we are most pleased to have her. Aunt Fanny, this is Mrs.. Ingram. I have spoken to you about her. She is our guest."

Aunt Fanny regarded Riana with a stern eye, studying her from the top of her head to where her body went under the table. After a long spell, her face softened and she smiled.

"I am very pleased to meet you, my dear." she said at last, smiling.

"And I am pleased to meet you, too, Mrs.. Willowby."

The woman gave a gravelly, amused laugh, "Oh, it is Miss Willowby. I never did have much patience for the idiocy of men."

Looking around, remembering another visit in another time, decided she liked the informality of the room. A few moments later, a plate was placed before her and food served. She had not begun to eat when conversation continued, excited discussion about that evening's Assembly. She ate her flakey crusted fish pie, not feeling qualified to enter the chat. It was Daria who first became aware of Riana's silence.

"You are, of course, joining us at the Assembly, Riana. I will not hear no from you. Only this hour I sent appropriate garments to Susan. Once again, they are not new, but they have never been worn here in Whipford."

Riana felt warmth in her cheeks as she lowered her fork, "Beggars can't be choosers, can they? I am very grateful to you for everything. You have taken a stranger into your house, without question, and have provided more than just the necessities of life, and I thank you for it. I know very little about myself, and you know even less. You have been extremely generous to me."

Generva smiled and Aunt Fanny nodded her approval. Daria reached across the table and caught Riana's hand.

"It has been my great pleasure to have you, dearest. And," she gave a cheeky smile, "it is so interesting to watch Donaghmore. I have never seen him so taken with anyone before. We have all thought he would be a life-long bachelor, for no woman of our acquaintance has ever seemed to have caught his fancy. Yesterday when he brought you in, senseless, he was frantic, worried that your quarrel had been your undoing."

As if her words had conjured him, Kieran pushed into the room. He was in his paint splattered smock, causing Aunt Fanny to gasp in indignation, but his dark eyes were wildly searching, softening as they settled on Riana. He was still holding the door knob in his hands as he looked at her. His brow cleared and he almost smiled.

"You are well? Your colour is much improved." he noticed the other women and gave a belated, sketchy bow, "Ladies, please forgive me, I have interrupted your meal, but I was anxious to learn of Mrs.. Ingram's health. I could not find Susan." he finished lamely.

Daria and Generva smiled at one another across the round table, nodding as if they had had a discussion aloud. There was something secretive in that look, a look that their cousin, in his close examination of Riana, did not see. Aunt Fanny steepled her fingers under her chin, her eyes going from her nieces to the man at the door to the other woman who stared back at the man. She too, nodded, but did not look at anyone else in the room. She lowered her hand and picked up her fork.

"You will be joining us at the Assembly this evening, Donaghmore? Mrs.. Ingram has already promised to go and we should very much enjoy your company as well." Daria frowned as she spoke, "My husband did speak to you of this, did he not?"

He was still gripping the doorknob and the corner of his mouth quirked up in a significant smile, "He did speak of it, yes. And I did agree to accompany you." His eyes slid to Riana, "Are you feeling well enough, Mrs.. Ingram?"

"Oh, more than well enough, thank-you. It will be an experience for me, since I don't think I have ever been to one before."

Why had she ever agreed to this? Riana stood in the middle of the bedroom in her odd, bulky underwear, her hair twisted into papers with Susan kneeling to tie the embroidered garters above her knees. Already she had been bathed, creamed with Milk of Roses, fed miniscule amounts of food and laced even tighter into stays. The garters tied to her satisfaction, Susan gave Riana's knee a pat before rising again to her feet.

"Is this all really necessary?" Riana asked querulously.

Susan turned her to face the mirror again, "You shall be the most beautiful tonight, m....Riana."

"Even in my borrowed finery?"

Susan looked at her as if her words required no answer. Patiently, she steered Riana to the dressing table and began pulling out the curl papers. It was soothing to have someone else work on her hair, and she realized she had not spent nearly enough time with her Vancouver hairdresser. She closed her eyes, all but resting on Susan as she relaxed. Only when Susan moved away did Riana open her eyes to see her hair with green ribbon twisted through it, with pretty curls around her face.

The face was next, with a light layer of rouge, something that surprised her. Her brows darkened only slightly and a narrow line drawn around her eyes. My God, Riana thought, eyeliner! In this era. Susan's hand on her shoulder told her to get to her feet.

Riana stepped into a dress that Susan called Pomona Green, with darker green swags and rosettes around the hem and small sleeves layered to look like unfolding rose petals. With these went dark green slippers that laced up her ankles with satin ribbons, ivory gloves and a very pale green light shawl. She frowned as Susan handed it to her, hating the work that carrying a shawl entailed.

If Riana was not thrilled with the efforts of dressing to go out, she was truly unhappy to be riding in a carriage. The movies had made it look so pleasant, but the reality was less romantic. The four of them were jammed together in a landau that bounced along unpaved roads and without seatbelts they jostled one another with annoying frequency. The leather seats were uncomfortable, as the deep quilting of the backs prevented any kind of relaxation.

Her bones were aching when she finally saw lights through the trees. Daria sighed, leaning closer to her husband, that single motion telling Riana they were near their destination.

"My apologies, Mrs.. Ingram, I have neglected to tell you who is hosting this Assembly." Daria spoke with a raised voice to be heard over the din of the wheels, "Sir Winston MalMr.ose and his wife, Juliet. They have a son, Denby, who is a good enough sort, is just home from Cambridge."

The carriage came to an unexpectededly easy stop and a man in a dark blue coat and white gloves, opened the door and let down a set of clattering steps. Viscount Thorpe was the first to descend, reaching up a hand to help his wife. Lord Donaghmore was next, turning as he touched the ground to hold up a gloved hand to Riana, giving her an encouraging smile as she shook her way down the two steps, wishing she had Daria's grace.

They went up a tall flight of steps and found themselves in a line-up that reminded Riana of the receiving line at her wedding, and was surprised to find that that was exactly what it was. Still in mantles and caped cloaks, the four of them waited patiently until it was their turn. Sir Winston was a tall, portly man with a fringe of suspiciously orange hair and a welcoming countenance. His wife, Lady MalMr.ose was much shorter and as portly as her husband. She too, greeted them with warmth and hospitality. Their son, the Honourable Denby MalMr.ose was between his parents in height, in his early twenties and quite conscious of the fact he was exceptionally good-looking and dressed in what Riana thought was outrageous fashion.

Once their greetings were done, they walked up a set of stairs not as elaborate as Riverton Abbey to a cloakroom where they left their outerwear. Lord Donaghmore tucked her hand into his elbow as they followed Daria and her husband down to the ballroom.

"I believe young Denby will be asking you to sign your dance card." he teased.

"Dance card?" she echoed.

He flipped the thing dangling from her wrist, something the maid in the cloak room had slid over her hand. Riana looked at it, pulling out the little pencil to open it. On one side was a list of dances; quadrille, Roger de Coverley, cotillion, the reel. She looked at it, her heart sinking deeply into her stomach with dismay.

"I don't think I know how to dance. These words don't look familiar." she raised her eyes to his, "What do I do?"

He caught her hand, patting it with his gloved hand, "We will do something. Daria!" he called out, half-turning his head.

Daria paused to look back at them, her brows raised in wordless question. With a quick glance at her husband, she left him to hurry back. Her eyes went from one to the other.

"What is it, dearest?" she turned her question to Riana.

"This!" she thrust the card toward her friend, "I don't think I can dance." Panic raised the tone of her voice and Daria put her hand on Riana's arm.

"Did you not fall and hurt yourself on your walk this afternoon? Such a pity that you will not be able to participate in the dancing."

She spoke in a reasonable tone, as if it was something they all knew, turning her head back to her husband to make certain that he, too, understood. After a moment, he nodded agreement. Calmly, Kieran took the card still attached to Riana's wrist, closed it and tucked in the pencil before letting it drop.

"We are decided then." Daria said with finality.

After taking their proper places they started toward the stairs again. As they started down, Riana heard the faint sounds of a pianoforte, a violin and a cello; all instruments with which she was familiar. The tune they played was not, being an obvious dance tune and as the music got louder with their approach, so did the laughing voices of many people. Riana hung back a little, causing Kieran to look back at her anxiously as she unconsciously tugged at his arm.

"There is nothing to fear, Mrs. Ingram. Those are but people."

It amazed her that he so understood her hesitation. Smiling thankfully at him, she resumed her pace until all of them were in the squareish ballroom. The men found seats for the women away from the drafts of windows and doors, bowing before they left to fetch glasses of punch. For a moment, Riana watched with no little pleasure the black clad back of Donaghmore, enjoying the shape of his white-clad legs and the movement of his head on broad shoulders. No movie star came to her mind that was as appealing as that man. Daria's folded fan tapped Riana's wrist.

"He is a devilish handsome man, is he not?" she whispered.

Riana dragged her attention away, and laughed, embarrassed at being caught staring.

"Oh yes, you could say that!" she burst out without thought.

Daria simply raised her fine brows, not showing her slight confusion of the words. She said nothing more as her smiling attention was drawn upward.

"Mr. MalMr.ose." was all she said.

"Lady Ranleigh." he acknowledged before turning to Riana, "Mrs. Ingram, may I be permitted to sign your dance card for the next dance?"

Daria tapped his arm with her fan, "I am afraid Mrs. Ingram is rather indisposed. She fell this afternoon and injured herself. We are both disappointed that she will not be able to dance this evening."

"But I thank you, sir, for the honour." Riana was greatly shocked at the words that came out of her mouth.

He bowed, his eyes lingering on her bosom, revealed as it was but the uplifting stays and the low cut of the neckline. She felt like reaching up and smacking him with her own fan, but decided to not make a scene. She gave in a chilly smile and he departed.

"How horribly rude of him!" Daria declared, offended by the look, "I know he has been taught far better than that. Juliet has always been a stickler for decorum. He needs his ears boxed."

"He is young. He's feeling his oats."

"Who's feeing his oats?" was Kieran's question as he approached them with two silver cups in his hands.

"Young MalMr.ose. I fear he has the makings of a rake in him.

No further conversation on that subject was possible as a woman in her late teen or early twenties approached them, smiling widely and fluttering her fan. She looked at Daria, but it was obvious her attention was on Kieran who had passed Riana a cup of an over-sweet orange flavoured drink that needed an ice cube or two.

"Lady Ranleigh. How nice to see you again." she spoke breathlessly in a rather high voice.

"Althea." Daria recognized cooly, "How very lovely you are looking this evening. Are you come with your parents?"

The girl shifted, impatient with her parents, "They are in the card room. Mamma does so love *Vingt-et-Un*." she gave Riana a curious look.

Daria touched the back of Riana's hand, "I forget my manners. Mrs. Ingram, allow me to present Miss Althea Grindle. Miss Grindle lives closest to our home. Miss Grindle, please meet Mrs. Riana Ingram, our houseguest."

Miss Althea Grindle tipped her head in a charming manner and waved her fan more languidly.

"Are you the one everyone is talking about? The one who has entirely forgotten who she is?"

Riana recognized the cattiness of the tone, but simply smiled wider, "That's me. But things come back a bit at a time. I have enough memory to be able to function without seeming to be too unmannered."

Again, she frowned briefly as the words came from her mouth. Where had they come from? By the look on the girl's face, Riana's words at least had found their mark. Two more flaps of the fan passed before she spoke again.

"I do so look forward to meeting you again, Mrs. Ingram. I live but half an hour's walk from Riverton Abbey."

She spoke perfunctorily as she was turning toward Kieran, "Sir, would you sign my card for the cotillion?"

He bowed and set the cup on the chair beside Riana, "It would be my great pleasure." He told her without so much as an ounce of pleasure in his tone.

They watched the dancers as they chatted and sipped their punch. Lord Ranleigh had vanished into the card room but Kieran sat with the women. It was exhausting for Riana just watching the intricate movements, although some dances bore a striking resemblance to square dancing and there was not a waltz in sight. A supper bell rang and as they walked to it, they passed under one of the many chandeliers and Riana gasped in pain, her hand going to her shoulder. Kieran peered down at it with a frown.

"It is a drip of candlewax, Mrs.. Ingram. Allow me to assist you."

He brushed at her shoulder, tipping his gloved hand to show her a little blob of wax. *Where*, she thought with a silent giggle *were electric lights when you needed them?* Movies didn't show this kind of thing. She rubbed at the reddened spot and continued.

Supper was an amazing sight, spread on a long, cloth-covered table. Salmon in shrimp sauce, roast turkey, sliced ham, sweet breads, salads, cakes and pudding-like desserts. The array and colours were dazzling, the flavours sharp and defined to her 21st century palate. She sat with her hosts and Kieran at a small table, Lord Ranleigh monopolizing the conversation with his talk of his card prowess. At one point, feeling aggravated eyes on her, Riana looked up to see Miss Althea Grindle watching her with narrowed, irate eyes.

The supper finished, the four of them started toward where the music was beginning once again. As they passed the library that was now substituting for the games room, Lord Ranleigh stopped.

"Donaghmore, there's a fellow I should like you to meet. He's a squire here, living very close by."

He gave an apologetic bow to his wife and houseguest even as he was reaching to grasp Kieran's sleeve. Daria put her hand on Riana's arm, smiling as she watched her husband and cousin disappear.

"They will find us in the ballroom without a doubt. Card players at these assemblies take their card-playing much too seriously. I prefer the playful games we have at home."

They found chairs placed farther away from the orchestra, near the window where the cool air was welcome. Daria unfolded her fan and spoke to Riana about those dancing around. She did not gossip, instead giving names, where they lived, how many children they had and what were their strengths. They had been there only a few minutes when Ranleigh and Donaghmore returned, with another man between them. Oddly, Daria rose to her feet at their approach, a slight frown marring the perfection of her face. In her concern for Daria, Riana did not at first look too closely at the third man as she too, rose to her feet. Lord Ranleigh spoke.

"Daria, m'dear. You do remember my good friend?"

"Yes." She replied with astonishing shortness.

He continued as if he had not heard her tone, which, in fact he had not noticed.

"Mrs. Ingram, please allow me to present my friend, Mr. Regis Wigmore, he has land nearby and is the justice of the peace. Mr. Wigmore, please meet my houseguest, Mrs. Riana Wigmore."

Riana's gasp of shock was audible as she looked up at the man. He was taller than Lord Ranleigh but shorter than Lord

Donaghmore. He was dressed lazily; his stock loose, a yellowish food stain on his vest and a darker stain above the knee of his white breeches. One of his stockings was beginning to fall in folds around his thick ankles. But those were not the things that startled her, nor were the lines of dissipation around his eyes, it was that as she looked at him, she saw the identical twin to her youngest brother Brian, even to the small balding patch on the back of his head as he bowed to her. She was torn between repulsion and the urge to throw her arms around his neck. But the lascivious look he gave her from his bent position threw that urge right out of her mind.

She bowed her head as she had seen Daria do, tightening her grip on the fragile, carved ivory fan.

"Mr.. Wigmore." she acknowledged as with Daria's same coolness.

"A pleasure, Mrs. Ingram."

Even his voice sounded the same and she felt his finger stroke her palm, something that she guessed was not socially acceptable. She withdrew her hand effortlessly, resisting the urge to wipe her hand on her skirt. She was repulsed by him, yet he fascinated her. This was her many greats-grandfather, although how he managed to persuade some poor woman to marry him was beyond her. He was the reason for the family's bad luck. At least as far as she understood. She took a tiny step back from him, catching Lord Donaghmore's assessing gaze as she did so.

"Mr. Wigmore." she said in a low voice.

"Have you seen the charms of our countryside, Mrs. Ingram? I would be more than delighted to show you."

"And your wife, sir?"

He looked startled, "Madame, I have no wife." he bent his head closer, "But I am in search of one. Are you available? I have heard the gossip that says you are a widow."

Daria was aghast at the man's words and his impudence, inhaling sharply and laying a hand on Riana's arm. Donaghmore had taken an enraged step forward, stopped only by his good manners. Lord Ranleigh, however, was already shifting with annoyance from one foot to the other.

"Come along, Wigmore. Th'cards are calling."

Regis Wigmore ignored him with more than a touch distain. He continued to study Riana until she took another step back, wanting to get away from the stale sweat odour that emanated from him. Donaghmore moved this time, stepping forward to bend solicitously toward Riana who was now looking so pale he was afraid she might faint.

"Mrs. Ingram, are you ill?"

She swallowed and gave him a rather shaky smile, "I'm fine. I think I ate too much."

Daria gave a forced laugh, "As did we all. Ranleigh, play cards if you must." she laughed, but her tone was dismissing and he instantly obeyed.

Donaghmore moved closer to her as they watched the two men depart, and just as they left the room, Riana caught the icy glare of one of the dancers. It took a moment for her to recall the name. Oh, yes, Althea Grindle. And those eyes slid to the door from where Regis Wigmore was departing. Goodness, was Riana's immediate reaction, that girl knows him better than she should.

It was some time later as she and Daria, with Donaghmore between them, were strolling around the room that it happened. They must have ventured too close to the dancers, for an outflung arm, wearing a heavy bracelet of gold and rubies, struck her own arm above her glove and below her sleeve, tearing a bleeding gash in her flesh. At first, Riana did not notice it, but Donaghmore did, turning her to face him as his other hand pulled a handkerchief from his pocket to press staunch the blood.

"Riana!" Daria's voice was filled with horror, "You are bleeding! How could that be?"

She checked Donaghmore as he tied his handkerchief that was rapidly turning bloody. Already, their hostess was crossing the floor to them, a footman in her wake. With her body, she shielded Riana from curious stares.

"I will have Thomas here, take Mrs. Ingram upstairs where we can tend to her wound." Mrs. MalMr.ose spoke with swift efficiency.

Donaghmore had already swept her up into his arms, heedless of the blood that began to stain the bright white of his damask waistcoat.

"Show me the way, Mrs. MalMr.ose, if you please."

As she left the room in the unanticipated comfort of his arms, Riana looked over his shoulder and saw Althea Grindle, still in the middle of the dancers, smiling with triumph as she watched with glittering eyes.

Chapter 7

One day in bed was enough for a rather small cut. She had to get up. Never before had she been treated so extravagantly for such a small injury. Twice, Donaghmore had checked with Susan yesterday as to her condition, but she did not see him. But this morning she was going downstairs to have breakfast.

She knew her way now, to the breakfast room and found only Lord Donaghmore sipping coffee at the table. He jumped to his feet at her entry, giving a little bow and pulling out a chair for her.

"You are improved?" he asked formally.

"It is only a little scratch."

"But done most deliberately. Do you recall if Miss Grindle is of your acquaintance?"

Riana gave a small, humourless laugh, "I think I would have remembered someone like her. But," she hastened to add, recalling her 'amnesia', "you can never tell, can you? I wonder what I did to her to make her dislike me so much."

"May I fetch you some breakfast?" he removed his hand from the chair as she sat down, "Some people do not need an excuse to be unpleasant. One merely needs to be Irish." he finished ironically.

"Just coffee please, for the moment. I need to wake up a little."

Going to the sideboard, he took a cup and saucer and poured coffee from a silver pot.

"You are more awake than most in this house." He commented dryly as he handed the cup to her.

A voice spoke from the doorway, "And here I had planned to have my breakfast alone."

They both turned to see Daria's Aunt Fanny entering the room. She favoured them each with a rather pretty smile as she started directly to the breakfast sideboard.

"Are you always an early riser, Donaghmore? I have yet to be here before you, no matter my efforts." she looked at Riana, "And you my dear, how is your injury?"

"It's barely a scratch."

Fanny took a plate of kippers, eggs and sliced apples before choosing to sit facing Riana and Kieran. She beamed at each of them, something secretive in her pale blue eyes.

"Even as a child, Althea Grindle had a vicious bent. I am sorry, my dear, that she has chosen you."

She smiled up at Donaghmore as he set a cup of tea before her. She continued to watch Riana.

"I think I can handle myself." Riana told her and sipped the cooling coffee.

Fanny did not answer immediately, "She will find in you an admirable foe."

"Oh, I don't intend on being her 'foe'. I think she is best ignored."

Fanny looked at Kieran who had seated himself comfortably again, "She will not let you ignore her." she put a forkful of eggs in her mouth and chewed thoughtfully, "Ignoring her will not be the thing. I think she has set her cap for Donaghmore here."

He choked on his own food, then smiled at the older woman, "Me? Black Irish?"

"You. Handsome Black Irish. Rather rich Black Irish."

Riana turned to him, a teasing smile on her lips, "Are you rich, Lord Donaghmore? Had I but known."

Even as the words came from her mouth, she wondered where the archaic tone of them had come. It was not her usual speech pattern. Was it because of what was being spoken around her? He did not appear to notice as he returned her smile.

"What is rich?" he challenged.

Fanny's wise old eyes went from one to the other again and the understanding in them made Riana so uncomfortable she rose to go to the sideboard for her own breakfast. Just what was that woman seeing, anyway, she wondered?

"What are your plans for today, Donaghmore?" the older woman seemed to change the subject.

"I am hoping Mrs. Ingram is feeling well enough today for us to continue with her portrait. The weather is fine and there are no clouds in the sky."

"I'm feeling wonderful, thanks. If the bandage on my arm doesn't bother you, it won't bother me."

The afternoon was warm and Riana felt quite comfortable as she leaned against the chair. The warm breeze brushed her hair and she felt at peace as she watched him scowl with concentration, one hand dipping and swirling colour on his palette.

"Stop smiling, Mrs.. Ingram." he ordered somewhat absently, "Must you always smile?"

"Sorry." she replied without so much as a hint of repentance.

He looked at her suddenly, over the top of the canvas, his work temporarily forgotten.

"I have not given you a chance to rest, have I?"

She shrugged, not shifting her pose, "I don't mind. It's peaceful here."

Their attention was drawn away by the sound of hoof beats coming toward them. A rider on a dun coloured horse came across the glade, the rider bouncing rather uncomfortably on its back.

Riana glanced at the painter and saw his scowl of irritation as he watched.

"Mouse Dun." he muttered under his breath.

It was soon apparent that the rider was none other than her ancestor, Regis Wigmore and the swift trepidation she felt made her hold her breath and her hand tightly grip the chair back. As he neared the gazebo, the rider hauled back on the reins, jerking the horse's head back, making it dig its back hooves into the grass. With studied care, Donaghmore put down his brush and moved away from his painting. He did not like Regis Wigmore in the slightest, Riana decided.

"Mr.. Wigmore?" he spoke with careful dignity as if reminding the other man of their differing stations in life.

The reminder went unheeded as the man dismounted awkwardly, causing the horse to sidestep a little. He approached them, slapping his riding crop in his hand.

"Donaghmore! Ranleigh told me I might find you out here." he gave Riana a piercing look that made her skin crawl, "And Mrs.. Ingram, too."

He gave her a bow, his eyes giving her an insolent stare before he slowly turned to look at Lord Donaghmore.

"Ranleigh says that you sell horses. I do like the stallion you sold him. Do you have another? I will not haggle the price."

"As you can see, I am occupied and must work with the fleeing light. But to answer your question. No, I do not have another stallion that is ready for sale."

Wigmore had already lost interest in horses. He moved closer to the rail of the gazebo and hooked his arm over the top rail, the crop in his hand lightly striking the posts.

"Mrs.. Ingram, you enjoyed yourself at MalMr.ose's Assembly? It was most enjoyable, was it not?"

She forced herself to smile, "It was."

"I regret I did not dance with you. And you departed so early."

"I don't dance." she told him with as small a smile as she could manage.

She cast a desperate glance at Donaghmore who moved closer to her. Space still separated them, but she felt better for his presence. From the corner of her eye she was able to see the flutter of his smock.

"You must excuse us, Mr.. Wigmore, but I really must continue while the light is good. Perhaps in a day or so I will ride over and visit you and we can discuss horses then."

This time, the man understood his dismissal. He nodded curtly and swung away from them to grasp the hanging reins of his horse and mounting so badly that the horse shied again. He touched the crop to his hat brim and turned the horse sharply, digging spurs into the horse's flesh. Neither spoke or moved until the man was out of earshot.

"I'll be damned if I will sell any of my animals to that man. He's a threat to good horseflesh." Donaghmore said under his breath, then, "Mrs. Ingram, if you please. Would you take your place?"

Riana took her place at the chair again, her thoughts racing. He was still resettling himself, so she ventured to speak.

"Do you know Mr. Wigmore well?" she heard the hesitation in her own voice.

"Somewhat." he replied with absent shortness, "He is rather a hail fellow well met and he spends far too much time with cards. And," he finished under his breath, "with Ranleigh. He lives some distance from here at Stonemere, but he is very much a politician."

"A politician?" she echoed.

"As much as one can be. He is the justice of the peace and has aspirations to becoming the mayor of Whipford."

Riana recalled her brother Brian's political career, from starting as student council president in secondary school to sitting on several committees in Vancouver with an eye to running for city council. It was rather eerie, considering how much they looked like one another. Perhaps there was something to reincarnation.

"Are you ready, Mrs. Ingram?" his voice broke into her wandering thoughts.

She turned back to the chair and settled into position. While he painted with quick, experienced strokes, she reflected on the similarities between her brother and the man who had recently departed. Brian had never married, yet seemed to always have a girlfriend; none of which had ever lasted for any time. As far as she knew, their ancestor had no wife as yet. Whatever the circumstances of his eventual marriage, Riana realized she did not like the man and his slithery glances.

The light dimmed suddenly, making Riana forget her pose as she looked up into the sky to see dark clouds scudding across the sky. She jerked defensively as a clap of thunder roared into the glade.

"Damn!" Donaghmore hissed, glaring upwards as his concentration was broken, "We must hurry to the house before it rains. Come, Mrs. Ingram."

Warily, with another quick glance at the sky, he covered the canvas, before moving around the easel, holding his hand to her. She pulled the shawl up over her shoulders, tucking it tightly against herself before taking the paint-splattered hand. Anxiously, she looked back at the covered painting.

"My man will fetch it." he assured her with a grim smile.

Together they had all but reached the little bridge when the heavens opened up. Within moments, Riana was soaked to the skin, her eyes focused hopefully on the house that was barely visible through the pouring rain. Donaghmore pulled her to the shelter of the chestnut tree that had been the location of their previous and delicious encounter.

At first they merely stood side by side, peering out at the rain as if wishing would make it stop; instead the downpour increased with a roar of thunder and a flash of lightning. Unconsciously,

Riana leaned closer to him, her arm lying along his, their wet sleeves sliding together. Without his being aware of it, his arm slid away from hers to move upward and curve protectively around her shoulders, drawing him even closer to her. Another clap of thunder made her jump slightly and press to his side, for she had never liked thunder. He looked down at her, and her face raised to his.

He did not know what to do. He looked at the wet face framed in dripping tendrils of hair and gave himself over to his impulse. She was compliant when he turned to face her, her expression was expectant and willing. His mouth covered her cold, wet lips, warming them, and he felt her sigh of acceptance. He pulled away almost immediately, recalling their last encounter and his own boldness.

Riana grasped at the wet sleeves of his smock, startled by the sudden departure of his warming lips. His eyes were on her face, his mouth trying to form an apology. She could see the broad, darkened outlines of his chest under the smock and she wanted to run her hands over its expanse, wanting to feel the heat and texture of his skin, wanting to strip the garment from him and touch his bare flesh. Her breath quickened and he saw it, knowing the reason for it. He was startled and she smiled softly.

"I have been married." she reminded him in a low, throaty voice, her tone causing his blood to hammer through his veins.

"And now you are not."

These were all the words he was able to utter as his hands moved to cup her elbows.

She knew exactly why his eyes darkened as he took a step closer to her. They were all but touching and she turned her hands to grasp his wet sleeves, willing him to move even nearer. He released her elbows and caught her waist, urging her to him so that they were touching from breast to knee. Her hands slid up his back, her fingers feeling the hard ridges and his increasing intake of breath.

Her face was so close he felt warm breath touch his face when she spoke his name with a sigh.

"Kieran." another smiling sigh, then, "Kieran."

The sudden flare of lightning released inhibitions and their grips on each other became so tight that all awareness but themselves was gone, taken by the bright light. They pressed tightly, feeling wet outlines of bodies, warming each other with nearness and the rush of passion. Mouths pressed and kissed, hers opening to admit his probing tongue, relishing the taste of him, her body arching into his, feeling the rise of his desire that made her relish her power over him.

Still joined, they sank first to their knees before she lay back under him, her arms circling his shoulders, pulling even tighter. His hand brushed along one of her legs, pulling up her skirt, his fingers lingering momentarily on the garter on her knee before touching lightly in exploration. Her own fingers fumbled for buttons on his smock, finding only a few close to his neck. She made an inarticulate sound of frustration and his warmth and his hands came away from her to tug his smock over his head. He tossed it aside impatiently and her eyes finally saw what she needed to see; the perfectly sculpted chest, dusted with fine hair that narrowed toward his waist, tempting her to search further the bulge that stretched his breeches.

He let her touch him, let her hands smooth over is cooling skin, his own fingers on the flesh bared by the neckline of her gown. Slowly, he dipped his head to kiss the firm mounds that threatened to burst from the restraining fabric. He knew her hands were on the waist of his breeches, searching for an opening, just as he wanted to see what her gown was hiding from him. He began to help her, needing to be free even from his own restrictions, but a voice calling from the distance stilled them both.

"Lord Donaghmore! Lord Donaghmore! Are you about?"

Kieran hissed through clenched teeth and reluctantly took his hands from Riana, raising himself to his knees. Not saying a word, he searched for his smock and with some difficulty pulled it over his head. He looked down at Riana who had not moved and who still watched him expectantly. As he rose to his feet, he lowered her raised skirt before reaching out his hand to help her stand.

"Lord Donaghmore!" came the cry again.

"Damn!" he hissed under his breath, before calling out, "Here Ralston. Under the tree, seeking shelter."

He pushed aside the branches and waved an imperious, beckoning hand. He looked back at Riana who pulled her wet shawl around her.

"My apologies, madam." He muttered, sounding not the least apologetic.

"If you apologize again, Donaghmore, I will slap you." she told him fiercely.

He grinned, knowledge warming his eyes as he clasped his hands behind him like a recalcitrant schoolboy.

"We will finish this, you know." she told him suddenly, her new familiarity with him making her bolder.

He gave her a mocking bow, "Yes, madam, I believe we will."

They were standing quite apart from one another when Donaghmore's valet pushed through the branches, holding out an umbrella.

"My Lord, Lady Ranleigh is most concerned for your welfare."

He took the umbrella and opened it, holding aside the branches to let her into the rain, shielding her from it and his valet's eyes.

With the valet in the lead, they hurried toward the house, Riana's concentration on the house such that it was too late for her to realize where she was until the rush of sound and darkness overtook her.

Chapter 8

It was strange to wake up in her bed in her own time. Her last memory was the kisses and caresses under the tree in the rain. She lay very still, recalling the touch of Kieran and the fee and smell of him, longing to be back with him to finish what they had started. She had never wanted a man so badly; not even her husband at the beginnings of their relationship. She closed her eyes, smiling, all the better to bring back the breathless sensations. The recollections causing her blood to warm her. But reality was brought back with a light rap on her door.

"Riana?" her mother called out softly, "Are you awake?"

Riana heard the anxious note in her mother's voice and had to respond. Getting up from the bed, she went to the door, walking unsteadily, the simple motion causing her head to pound and her vision to blur. Blinking, she opened the door.

"I'm awake, Mom." she stood back to let her mother enter, wincing at even that slight movement.

Clare peered at her daughter, "You haven't taken your medication this morning, have you? I came by earlier and there was no answer. I was worried after the way you came in yesterday."

Riana released the door knob, letting the door close on its own as she watched her mother open pill bottles.

"Yesterday?" she echoed, resisting the urge to touch her forehead, "I've been in bed since yesterday?"

Clare turned to her bottle in one hand, cap in the other. A quick flash of fear crossed her face. Riana watched her swallow her fear.

"You came in around three yesterday afternoon. One of the chambermaids said you were walking like a zombie, looking only straight ahead and came straight here. I think you frightened her."

Riana did not answer for the space of several moments, "I don't remember. I know I was walking across the lawn," she lied, "and that's the last thing I do remember. I came back here on my own?"

Clare nodded, her fear making her unable to speak. Fear that Riana's tumour had increased more rapidly than the doctors had predicted, causing unexpected symptoms.

"You've been here ever since. I came here to get you for breakfast and when there was no response I got Arthur to let me in here and found you so asleep that I couldn't wake you. Are you hungry for lunch?"

At the word, Riana felt her stomach rumble, "I think I am. Can you wait for me to change?"

Clare's shaky laugh was from obvious relief, "Of course I can. Lunch is open for two hours. We have time. But first take your medication."

Riana was already making her way to gather up fresh clothes, "I'll take my food meds. There's no point in taking the others now. I've been in bed more than twenty hours?"

"Unusual for you. You had me worried. What is so fascinating about the back of this house? I've seen you go that way before."

Riana simply waved her hand dismissively as she entered the bathroom to begin dressing.

Jared joined them halfway through their lunch. He stood with polite anxiety at their table until Clare invited him to sit down. He pulled his chair closer to Riana, to peer at her closely.

"You're ill, Riana?"

She swallowed her mouthful and made a sad attempt at a laugh, sounding weak even to her own ears.

"Nothing for you to worry about."

He cupped his hand around her cheek and it warmed Clare's heart as she watched him bend nearer her daughter.

"One day I find you unconscious in the garden, the next day I hear from the staff that you were walking around all but senseless." he swallowed, "I care about you, Riana."

Dropping her fork, she turned in her chair to face him, feeling his fingers slide away from her skin.

"I am somewhat sick and it makes me sometimes do odd things. But there is really nothing for you to worry about, especially if I take my medication on a regular basis.....see, I'm taking another pill."

For effect, she popped a pill in her mouth and swallowed it with her cooling coffee. The concern in his face lessened as he caught her free hand and squeezed it between his two.

"Do you feel well enough to go for a drive later?"

Her swift smile eased the concerns of both him and Clare, "I'd love that. It looks like a perfect day for it. Where are we going?"

"A surprise for both you and your mother." teasing dimples appeared in his cheeks.

Clare spoke quickly, "I'm afraid my dears, that I need to have a nap. All this good food and English fresh air. You go without me. Please."

Clare left the table with a polite smile before Riana was finished, leaving her alone with Jared who did not move from his position close to her.

"I am very much looking forward to this," he told her, "for I have planned this all morning hoping your long sleep improved you."

Riana studied her plate, "Will I need a sweater?"

He looked a little confused, "Cardigan." she corrected.

He crossed his legs and grinned at her, "I believe not. If there is a chill in the air I will find a way to keep you warm."

"Nice!" she laughed.

When they left the house through the main entrance, a small red sports car with a tan-coloured rag top was parked, waiting. It was an old car, elongated so that the fenders and running boards formed and elegant curve. She looked up at him curiously and he ran a fond, possessive hand over the sharp extended hood.

"This is a 1953 MG. My grandfather bought it new, but didn't use it very often. It's been stored in the old stables for decades until I found it whilst I was trying to find my father's old hunting saddle."

She went to his side, her fingers lightly stroking the boot extension.

"It's beautiful." she breathed in awe, "I'm almost afraid to touch it."

He was folding down the tan top, "And it's all in original condition. I think my grandmother did not like it because my grandfather drove too fast. But I have been taking very good care of it."

Once the top was in place, he went to the passenger's door and opened it, reaching in to open the tiny glove box. From it he pulled a piece of thin, pale pink fabric and handed it to her with a flourish.

"I hope this is my grandmother's scarf. I found it in here. It will keep your hair tidy whilst we're driving."

Riana knew real silk when she slid the scarf through her fingers, relishing the feel of it before she dutifully tied it around her head. He gave a short nod of approval before standing aside to let her drop down the slightly cracked tan leather of the seat. In only moments, the engine was roaring to life following the line of the drive. She could not help laughing up at the blue sky with pure joy, not seeing Jared's quick glance that revealed his own sense of joy.

They entered Whipford from another road that the one Riana had ridden on her first day. These were much older buildings, terraced houses, most of which had been taken over by businesses and bed and breakfasts. The last of these old buildings right at a stop sign had a rather discrete sign that read, "Gould, Barristers and Solicitors since 1806".

Riana peered up at it, expecting to see evidence of modernization, but there was none.

"Wow! That's a long time to be in business."

He chuckled, "Not for England. We rather tend to stay with what we know. They have been our solicitors almost since its inception. I had rather hoped to join the firm, but I'm afraid I was not up to their standard."

"You're a lawyer?" she asked, surprised by his profession.

"Solicitor." he corrected, revving the engine before pulling away from the stop sign, "I'm the one who speaks to clients, but does not represent them in court."

"We have Barristers and solicitors in Canada."

"True, but there they can be a single person. In England it's impossible. But in any case, I was not a particularly good solicitor, so I decided on another profession. Telly production has its own rewards and a great deal of frustrations."

"But you enjoy it, don't you?"

He laughed, "Funnily enough, yes, I do."

They left the village and drove along a narrow road edged by stone walls, and Riana, watching the scenery pass by was not able to read the small sign at the roadside where Jared turned off the main road to another short dirt road. The road was well maintained, passing under the arching branches of oak trees that line the track.

"Where are we going?"

He gave her a cheeky grin, "You'll see soon enough."

She jiggled in the soft leather seat with impatience as the car paralleled the low stone wall that kept the trees from the road. And then, there is was, framed by an old oak, covered in fall foliage and an equally old apple tree, its branches all but bare of leaves, yet decorated with unharvested red apples. The house was square and stuccoed in bright white, four windows on the upper story and two windows separated by a small enclosed porch entry on the ground floor. The slate roof was steep, broKen by the protuberance of two small dormer windows and a set of chimneys that jutted out of the middle of the roofline. There was little landscaping here, but for the leaf-dotted lawn that edged the gravel drive. Jared stopped the car and draped his arm over the steering wheel as he grinned at her.

"Here we are." he said rather unnecessarily.

"*Where* are we?" she shot back.

He raised his brows in mock surprise, "Why Mrs. Ingram, I would have thought you might have recognized your ancestral home."

She raised her head to look closer at the building, "My what? I didn't realize we had an ancestral home."

"Well," he admitted slowly, "technically it is no longer your ancestral home. The Wigmores lost it long ago, in the early 1800's, in a game of loo at a club in London. It has, of course, passed through many hands since then, but presently it is a bed and breakfast and the owners have done their best to present it as it was during the Regency era. There is, I believe, some rather historic papers from that time as well. Care for a boo inside?"

"Would I? Try to stop me!"

In her eagerness to get out of the car, working the unfamiliar handle, she broke a nail to the quick, breathless with wanting to see inside. As Jared closed the car door, the door of the house opened revealing an average sized woman in old jeans and a big, striped sweater with a silk scarf tied attractively around her head to hold back a long mane of curly dark hair.

"Jared!" she called out happily, "How good of you to visit."

He came around the car to Riana's side and hooked an arm around her shoulders.

"I have brought someone special, Adela, from Canada. She's a descendent of the original Wigmores."

The woman rushed forward, hands outstretched, "Welcome! I thought the last of the Wigmores left long ago."

Jared had not forgotten his manners, moving aside with an amused expression as the owner grasped Riana's hands.

"Riana, please meet my very good friend, Adela Marston. Adela, my guest from Canada, Mrs. Riana Ingram."

"This is exciting, meeting both a Wigmore descendant and a Canadian. We seldom get Canadians here. We don't really have any exciting historical happenings here in Whipford. Well, we do have the Fairy Festival, but I suppose Jared has already spoken of it."

"Riana makes dolls and we have sold some of them during the Festival and we have some in the shop even now."

"Dolls, is it? How exciting."

Riana smiled as she felt Jared's hand on her back, urging her forward.

"Yes, most of the time it is."

Adela waved her hand, motioning them to come inside, "Please, please come in. I should think you would be most anxious to see the house."

The door inside the little outside alcove was dark and thick with old paint, leading to a well-worn stone entry hall, featuring a substantial old and battered wooden table and an equally old and battered hall coat rack. She led them to the first door on the right and into a big room with a high dark beamed ceiling and cozy, floral printed couches, not new tables and light floral drapes that let sun into the room from two walls. Riana stopped three paces into the room, smiling with delight.

"Oh! But this is so lovely. And so cosy."

Adela stood proudly off to one side, clasping her hands loosely in front of herself.

"We like to make this as comfortable as possible for our guests. Rather shabby chic, wouldn't you say? We don't pretend to be as elegant as Riverton Abbey."

She slid a teasing glance toward Jared, who smiled with her, enjoying her sly humour. She briskly walked several more paces into the room, going to a door on the inside wall farthest from the door. She twisted the knob and gave the stubborn door a little push.

"I think this will be more interesting for you. This was the study, quite small, actually, but it has all the papers from the house. We found them in the attic when we were trying to reorganize things. I'm afraid I have not yet completed organizing it all, but there is enough to peak your interest."

It was a small room, brightened with a single window with plastic Venetian blinds, decorated with a rather cheap desk and wooden chair. She recognized the Ikea shelving on which had been placed cardboard boxes labelled in Magic Marker with dates going back as far as 1789. Riana did not even try to stop her feet as they went to the loaded shelves. Her hand hovered uncertainly near the shelves and their contents.

"My family?" she breathed in awe.

"Mostly accounts and lists. Rather mundane, boring stuff. Here, 'tho, is a miniature of Regis Wigmore, painted for his wife."

The painting style was rather simplistic, but Riana was able to recognize the man she had seen, although he was a little older and a little more jaded looking.

"Yes......" she started, then bit her lip, for in this life she had never met him, of course.

"He looks like my brother Brian. He's a politician wanna-be. He was married?"

"None too happily. He kept a journal and from the sound of it, his wife was a bit of a harridan. They had ten children, but only three lived to adulthood."

"You have his journals? He wrote journals?"

Adela smiled gently, "Most people in the Regency era kept journal. All of them were inveterate writers; letters, journals, bad poetry, decent doggerel.....not that his were decent, mundane ramblings. All that, sorry to say, is your ancestor. And of course his loss of the house was not his fault. He was cheated out of it." she finished slyly, "And that is the reason only two generations of Wigmores lived in this house; the man who built it and his son who lost it."

Riana felt Jared's hand on her back, comforting and supportive. She turned her head a little to smile at him, liking the warmth in his returning smile.

"May I see one of his journals?"

"But of course. I have them in a special box, but you are his descendent, so you have every right to see it. Was it your mother or your father who was a Wigmore?"

"My father." Riana answered as Adela pulled a metal box from a desk drawer, "Daniel Wigmore."

Adela clutched the old journal compulsively to her chest, "Your father was Danny Wigmore? He was an old school mate of my father's. So your mother is Clare Wigmore. Dad said he would have married her if Danny hadn't got to her first."

Riana did not control the chortle of laughter that burst forth, "I never thought of my father as a Danny! He was always so stern and uptight. Only mother was able to control him."

Adela handed over the journal and Riana opened it, to squint and peer at the small, crabbed, yet elaborate handwriting, unable to distinguish a single word.

"My God! How can anybody read this?"

"There's a man I know in London that is an expert in both the Regency period and their letters and journals. For him, this would be as easy as any font on a computer. I can take it to him and have him transcribe it, if you like." Jared offered suddenly.

Both women looked at him as if he was some kind of saviour, both speaking at once.

"Could you? It would be lovely to show it to my guests."

"You can do that? I'd love to see what he has to say. The old reprobate." Riana finished under her breath.

"Why do you say that?" Jared asked, being the only one who had heard her words.

Damn! Caught! She swallowed, trying to think quickly. She looked down at the miniature on the desk.

"He looks like he would have been one, don't you think?" she winced at the false note in her voice.

He did not appear to notice, murmuring only, "Hmmm." as he too looked down at the painting. Adela glanced between the two of them, a corner of her mouth turning up in a knowledgeable smile.

"Would you like lunch? It is just now being made."

Jared's hand slid up Riana's back to her neck. He held it in a rather proprietary manner.

"Thank-you, Adela, but I'm taking her to the 'Ass and Crown', her first real English pub. Yes?" he dipped his head to look at her.

"Yes. There are the ones in Vancouver, 'tho."

Both Jared and Adela chuckled, but Jared replied, "Yes, but they are not English pubs in England. A different thing altogether."

"It's a lovely place." Adela affirmed, "Very old and historic. Older, I think, than even Riverton Abbey."

"Parts of the Abbey." he grinned.

The Ass and Crown was very old, set a block back from the main street through Whipford. It was low and rather dark inside, reached through a rather short, solid door. Dark, old wood formed the walls and the bar itself had been modernized with a favourable eye to its origins. Three men were playing darts in a quiet corner and a stout, sassy barmaid of middle age bounced from one of the round, scarred tables to another. Several people nodded silently in recognition as they entered, but none spoke. Jared led her to a table with two chairs in the bow window that looked out onto the street.

"This is the first place my father brought me when I became of legal age. It's always been my favourite. The pubs in London can't touch this one."

She was looking around with interest, her eyes lighting on the horse brasses by the huge fireplace, to photographs of men with horses, to a shelf of old and battered books, to an incongruous flat screen television perched high in a corner. The floor was old wood, worn over the years, yet kept well enough. She hitched her chair closer to the table.

"This is wonderful! Thank-you for bringing me here. It is everything I thought a pub might be."

The bar maid was approaching, "Jared, love, what'll you be having this fine day? And who is your lady friend?"

"Emma!" he rose to his feet to bend and kiss her cheek, "This is Riana Ingram, from Canada. Her father was Danny Wigmore."

She put her hands on her hips, tipping her back a little as she looked down at Riana.

"You're Danny's girl? Well, I'll be! Fancy that! Where's your Mum? Clare Pickett she was."

It was Jared who answered, "They're guest as the Abbey. Mrs. Wigmore is having a lie down."

Emma laughed loud, throwing back her head, "Best friends we was in school. You tell your Mum to hie herself over here so we can catch up." she cupped Riana's chin and gave it a little shake, "You're a lovely thing, aren't you now? Must introduce you to my eldest son Tony."

"I will be keeping Mrs. Ingram busy for the next few days."

Emma did not release Riana's chin, "So you married? Pity."

Riana smiled, gently pulling her chin from the gripping hand, "I'm a widow. As is my mother."

"Danny's dead, then? Oh, dear, what a pity. He was handsome as the devil, that one. Give my condolences to your Mum. And to you, dear. We are all widows, although you should not be at your age." she tipped her head toward Jared, "So you will be keeping her busy, will you? Good. But watch out for my Tony, I'm pointing him in her direction, lad. But it's passed time you both settled.

He laughed; it was loud, full of the fondness of familiarity and caught her elbow in his hand briefly, "You have been trying to marry off both of us for as long as I can remember. How is Tony?"

"Still a mechanic, always fixing motors and coming home filthy. But he's a good lad for all that. Now," she became professional again, "what can I get you for lunch?"

Chapter 9

Riana felt, looking back at the end of the day, that this had been one of the best days yet here in this country of her ancestry. They had had a wonderful lunch of Cornish pasties, mushy peas and French fries…..chips she had to remember to call them, all washed down with a shandy; this being a combination of ginger ale and beer, for Emma would let them drink nothing less. She returned to their table when she had a moment to talk about the past and Riana's parents, regretting aloud that she had not kept in touch, but admitting she had been angered by Clare's emigration to Canada.

"Without so much as a by-your-leave, they were up and gone. 'Course Danny'd lost another job and your Mum was preggers, so I guess they did what they could. Did they make out alright, there in Canada? They never wrote, not so much as a Christmas card."

Riana was feeling good, her stomach was full and she felt oddly at home in this place.

"They did very well. Dad had a building company; he went into the construction just before Jacob was born……he's the baby Mom was pregnant with…. and eventually bought out his employer. Jake is now the company President, but my brother Brian is a computer geek and sometime politician."

"And you, pet? What do you do?"

Riana swallowed suddenly, feeling the beginnings of an unwelcome, yet familiar headache. She touched light fingers to her temple, quickly dropping her hand as she realized just what she was doing. Jared bent his head and put a light hand on the curve of her shoulder, his face tight with concern.

"Did you forget to take your tablets?" he asked the question in a low voice, but Emma heard him, nevertheless.

"You're ill, my dear?" she asked breathlessly.

Riana was already opening her purse to dig out the pill container she diligently filled every night.

"Only if I forget to take my medication." She popped the pills into her mouth and washed them down with her shandy.

"Should you be taking those with alcohol?" Emma cupped Riana's chin again to peer anxiously into her face.

"It's pretty diluted with ginger ale. I'll be okay in a minute." she looked from one to the other, "I will. Honestly!" smiling as Emma released her.

Jared's hand was shaking as he took a deep swallow of his own drink, and within moments, the threatening headache was gone.

"In answer to your question," Riana spoke as Jared set his glass on the table, "I make porcelain dolls. I'm good with my hands." she finished rather lamely.

"Dolls? Like Raggedy Ann and Andy, or baby dolls?"

It was Jared who replied quickly, and odd pride tingeing his tone, "No, she makes those fancy dolls that we sell at the Abbey during the Fairy Festival."

"You mean those ones that are so dear, only you can afford them?"

Riana's laughter joined with Emma's as Jared tried to find an answer to Emma's question.

"Yes," Riana tried to catch her breath as she spoke, "those would be the ones."

"Emma!" a man's voice called out suddenly, "Y'got thirsty customers!"

"Don't get your knickers in an uproar Tom Snead! I'm comin' in me own time." she called over her shoulder as she clambered to her feet, "And you girl, tell your Mum about me. I was Emma Davies, but now Emma Blake. Tell'er to pop in, she knows the way, lord knows she spent enough time here in her day."

Riana clasped the woman's hand as she started to leave, "Thank-you. I'm very pleased to have met you."

She gave an embarrassed wave of her hand, "Oh, pish! I just like to talk! Cheerio, and you," she pointed a thick arthritic finger at Jared, "remember, I'm sending my Tony after her."

The sky had darkened with clouds when they left the pub, threatening rain. They stood side-by-side at the low car looking up at the threatening sky. Riana shivered a little as a chill breeze blew across her bare arms. She tipped her head in a teasing way.

"I thought this was going to be a nice day."

Jared was already beginning to put up the top, he paused to grin back at her.

"Best laid plans, my dear, best laid plans. So much for a stroll in the gardens before tea. I wanted to show you the old stables. They're as old as the house, and better than most people's homes. Dad and I have been thinking of turning them into extra guest suites with small kitchens."

"That sounds like a great idea, if you don't mind all the extra people on your property."

She crossed her arms to ward off the chill, watching as he secured the top. He looked at her from his bent-over position.

"Would you mind extra people hanging around?"

Riana gave a fleeting look at the menacing sky, "If I owned that house, I would keep it all to myself. I wouldn't like strangers traipsing through it."

He opened the passenger door, "But the economics of the place is that we have to have guests or sell it. The older those houses get, the more it costs to keep them up. The Abbey is my home and it's been in the family for hundreds of years, so we can't lose it now. If having strangers poking into every nook and cranny is the price we have to pay to keep it in the family, that's the price we pay."

She nodded in agreement as she slid down to the seat, "You're right of course. I just find it kind of awful that that is what you have to do."

Once settled in her seat, she watched him walk around to the driver's side and get in. He draped his arm across the wheel as he turned to look at her.

"I do too. But this is the legacy that will be passed on to the next generation."

She gave him a teasing chuckle, "Well, you'd better get busy on that little project."

He slid his hand from the wheel and turned on the engine, looking at her, his head dipped mischievously.

"That's just what I'm trying to do, Mrs.. Ingram. I *am* trying."

The unspoken meaning in his tone made her catch her breath and she felt heat in her cheeks. Silently she chided herself for letting the light conversation go just a bit too far, for she understood the tone of his words and the intense look on his face. Just as she knew it could never be.

The ride back to Riverton Abbey was neither silent nor uncomfortable, Jared saw to that. They took a different road back and he played travel guide, pointing out friend's homes, historic sites, what had been grown in now harvested fields and a pretty brick and stone church that he promised to show her in the next day or so. She clutched at the arMr.est as the little car bounced along rough, paved roads.

Rain started spattering the windshield just as the car pulled into the gravelled parking area in front of the house. Jared clicked his tongue with annoyance, turning to look at her, his hand resting on the key in the ignition.

"I don't want to leave this in the rain. Care to come with me to the mews? I like to keep this where the old carriages were put away. Then, if it's not raining too hard, we can slip over to the stables."

She tied the lovely silk scarf around her hair, "Sounds good. I'm from Vancouver, remember, so I'm not afraid of a little rain."

He gave a little chuckle and turned on the engine, "That's m'girl!"

Riana wasn't quite sure what a mews was, but once the car had been driven through a set of old, wide doors, she understood that this was the place where carriages had been stored, for there was still a couple in place and Jared pointed them out for her; a high-wheeled curricle for two passengers and a landau that held four people and a coachman, both with their folding, convertible-like tops up revealing the cracked old leather. She ran her hand along the black side of the landau. There was something very familiar about it, although the leather interior was faded and nearly grey with age.

"These are lovely. Imagine riding in one of these."

He touched her shoulder lightly, "They shake your bones out of place, I swear! The curricle was their version of a fast motor. There were a good deal of deaths caused by racing those things. We pull them out for the Fairy Festival, and Dad waves from the safety of the landau and I put on a show in Regency costume driving the curricle with an old horse that is deaf, but has an even temper."

"You must look wonderful."

He caught her hand and dragged her across the old brick floor to a wall on which hung several framed photographs. With a flick of a wrist he turned on the lights that brought the photographs into more prominence. They were pictures of decades of the carriages in present day use. Sliding her hand from his, she bent to peer more closely at them until she found him grinning from a high seat, long whip in hand, dressed in a manner with which she was now familiar; a blue coat with gold buttons, a red brocade waistcoat, buff trousers tucked into leather boots that all but reached his knees. A bright yellow watch fob hung from his waist and on his head was a grey hat with a wide, flat brim and flat crown, similar to ones she had seen in that other life on men strolling about the grounds. She decided that she would not comment on his clothing, seeing inconsistencies.

"You used that horrible whip on that poor horse?"

"Of course not! Rolly is much too old and placid for me to do that. It's all for show. D'you like my costume? It's left over from one of the many Jane Austin films that the BBC seems fond of producing. The costume designer has won awards for her wardrobes."

"Anybody famous wore it?"

He raised his eyebrows a little, "I am too large for most of the stars. Colin Firth came closest, but no, this is a combination of extras costuming. Sorry." he switched off the light, "Shall we wander over to the stables?"

She nodded eagerly and followed him through a side door to an open area paved with the same bricks as the carriage house. The stable was a long low building, roofed in slate and sided with red brick. The white-painted doors here were smaller than the carriage house, to which they were attached in an L-shape, the stables being the longest leg of the L. The rain was pouring a little harder now and she stopped dead when she saw a familiar figure and the far end of the stables, all but hidden by the falling rain. He was leaning on his walking stick as he always did on his initial appearance, his head down in sorrow. Her head started pounding and without thought, she put her hand to her chest as if trying to slow it down.

"Riana?" Jared peered down at her apprehensively, "Are you feeling unwell?" he looked up at the sky, "This rain cannot be good for you. Let's go inside."

He took her back into the carriage house and fumbled around until he found an old, black umbrella, opening it over the two of them as they stepped through the door. She looked nervously toward where she had seen that other man, but he was gone as she knew he would be, just as she knew she had to go and find him as soon as possible.

The umbrella was a little more protection from the rain as Jared hurried her to the door that led to the kitchen and service area. The floor here was tiled in old slate, the hallway dark and narrow. He closed the umbrella and hurried into the kitchen for towels, leaving Riana standing alone. The urge to go outside overwhelmed her and she quietly went back the way she had come, closing the door softly behind her.

She wished she had thought to bring the umbrella as she ventured across the paved area between the kitchen and the stables, but she needed to find him again and now she knew where to go. Passed the stables, along the old brick wall and across the lawn to the arching bridge, where she hurried without hesitation, for she saw him there under the protection of the tree branches. He watched her as she rushed up to him, the same sad smile barely creasing his face.

"Riana!" he breathed and she could swear she felt his moist breath on her face.

"I'm here." was all she was able to say.

"My dear, I am sorry that I must do this to you. But you can take some measure of satisfaction that I have been permitted to tell you that you will find happiness with that man."

Riana stopped dead in her tracks; her eagerness to see Kieran once again momentarily paused.

"Kieran?"

Slowly, he shook his head, and then gave her an unexpected grin, Kieran's grin, one that warmed her suddenly.

"He is your destiny. And but for my own curse, the other one would have been your love as well. You are the most fortunate of women."

Somehow those words struck her to her soul. How could she be the most fortunate of women? She clenched her fists at her side and taking a defensive stance, looked up in to the face that was once again gloomy. She said the words that she had not planned to say to either of these men.

"How can I be fortunate? I'm dying. I have a brain tumour. I have only a few months to live."

He took a deep breath, tightening his waistcoat, "The fault for that, again, is mine. Often we do not think of the consequences of our thoughtless words. I wish I could tell you that all will be well, but that knowledge is not for me to give. I am content to know that you will be able to change the destiny of your family."

"But I will still die?"

"You will die. We all die, Riana, and some of us must linger to correct terrible mistakes we have made. I am long weary of this existence and desire to achieve the next level."

Her heart bled for him, for his torment and his weariness. She knew he was a ghost, but he was so different from Hollywood's version; any Hollywood version. She touched the gloved hand that curved over the head of his walking stick.

"Well then, it is best that we try to change things for you, isn't it?"

He looked away from her and looking up, she admired the sharp outline of his features. She liked the sharp nose and square jaw, the deep-set eyes and the perfect forehead that was edged by thick straight brows that was turned away in contemplation. This was not the Kieran she knew, but another man on whom his conscience sat heavily. As if the motion pained him, his head turned in a jerky action to look at her again.

"You will do this thing?"

"Haven't you asked me this before? Yes, for both your sake and for mine, I will do all that I can." she held a hand out in the direction she knew they had to go, knowing the pain it would cause her, "Let's go."

Perhaps it was because her body was becoming more accustomed to the transition, but barely had the headache formed than she was opening her eyes to Kieran's face anxiously bent over her. This was the face of the man who swelled her heart. She reached up to touch his cheek, and saw that she was wearing the yellow gloves.

"Kieran?" her voice sounded raspy even to her own ears.

His fine brow was wrinkled with concern as he bent closer, "You have fainted once again. Luckily this time you were out only minutes. I did not want to take you back until the rain stopped and it now has, so here we are. Shall I carry you?"

"Oh, no!" she said in horror as she struggled to get herself upright.

Effortlessly he raised her to her feet, and with his arm around her waist, held her with her back to his chest, so that she felt his warmth and his breathing. Slowly, she turned in his light grip, sliding her hand up to touch his face, watching the change in his eyes as she pressed herself closer to him.

"Mrs. Ingram….." he began, his voice raspy.

She placed her fingers on his mouth, "Shhhhh! Hasn't anybody told you that you talk too much?"

He smiled under her fingers, "No, that has never before been a criticism. The most frequent is that I am too silent."

"You're talking." she told him with a smile.

"What then, do you want from me?" there was fun in his tone.

She slid her hand from his mouth, standing on her toes in order to curve her hand around his head, drawing it down to hers. He came willingly, his hands tightening on her back, urging her against him. This time there was no hesitation, his lips pressed to hers, kissing her as if her mouth was the only nourishment for a starving man and she welcomed his probing tongue with joy. She felt the strength in the body that pulled her even more tightly to him, she felt the sudden, pulsing length of him, familiar, yet so different from what she had known with her husband. He sought the wildness in her, unexpectedly letting go of his own wildness.

One of his hands moved up her back, pressing to feel her bare skin above the neckline of her gown, stoking slowly over the damp smoothness of her skin. She embraced him with her soul, with her entire being until there was only him in her senses. Waves started at the pit of her stomach, undulating downward to the very core of her; a core she had all but forgotten in the misery of her widowhood. She felt his own light gasps filling her mouth, knowing his need mirrored her own.

Kieran kisses changed even as the hardness against her stomach increased, but she grasped as his smock, unwilling to let go of him. He gave her several light kisses on her mouth, his hand in her hair as he slowly pulled back his head.

"This is not what I wish. Not this way, Riana. Not rolling around on the wet ground like some rutting animal."

She went very still, "You don't want me?" she asked in a low, breathless voice.

He raised his head to laugh mirthlessly at the tree above them, "Want you? I doubt I have wanted anything so much. I am frightened of you Riana, for I think one time will not be enough. Forever will not be enough. But I want it to be something we will both remember with delight, something that will be long and lasting….." he broke off as if searching for more and proper words.

She understood and raised herself on her toes again, to put her lips to his so that the simple motion of her speaking lips against his sent more hot surges through him.

"Tonight then? Come to my room?"

His eyes were intent on her face, yet he did not answer immediately, "The gentleman in me wants to say no….."

"…but the wild Irishman wants to say yes?"

He chuckled, taking the fingers of the hand at his face, and kissing them lightly.

"The wild Irishman is screaming 'yes, you bloody fool, what are you waiting for?'"

She laughed gently and took a step back from him, "I think I'm going to like the wild Irishman."

He lowered her hand so they might walk hand in hand to the house. She went with him, her lips still tingling from the pressure from his, her smile up at him warm and promising. They were halfway to the house when he squeezed her fingers before tucking her hand more courteously into his elbow, his head bent solicitously to her, his smile reflecting her own expectations

"Are we expecting company this evening?" he asked in an affable manner as they walked up the steps that led to the lawn and before the house.

"I don't think so, but it is Daria's business and she does not confide in me."

He opened the door that led into the damp and green conservatory, letting her lead the way.

"I pray not. This is one evening that must not drag on so long." He closed the door before he spoke again, his boot heels loud on the marble floor tile, "Are you regretting anything, Mrs. Ingram?"

She turned to face him, a soft smile on her face as she pulled the shawl more tightly around her shoulders. It was a nervous gesture, she knew, for she was already to warm.

"I regret nothing, Lord Donaghmore. In fact, I am more than eager for this."

Chapter 10

As it turned out, there was company this evening. Daria met them as they came from the conservatory, her face tight with flustered concern, something not usual for her.

"We have a very important guest. The Marquess of Didsbury, Brice Chilton. And this day Mrs. Peasland and Agnes have also chosen to visit. And you know Mrs. Peasland. Oh, dear this is dreadful, Mrs. Peasland will be dangling after him for Agnes, as he is not married nor betrothed."

Kieran was smiling with delight, "Didsbury is here? How delightful! I have not seen him these past five years. He does fly to the time of day, so I doubt he will be easily led, he's a regular out and outer, almost a rake. Do not get yourself into a dudgeon, dearest cousin; all will be well, unless of course," he grinned cheekily, "he chooses to be caught."

Daria gave him a light smack on his arm, her stiff posture relaxing, "You are the very devil, Donaghmore. You do vex me sometimes."

Riana looked from one to the other as they spoke. They were speaking English, and oddly enough, she understood the meaning of the odd display of words; the Marquess was wise to the world, nearly a man of vices, so do not get upset. How did she know that, she wondered, for taken by themselves, they made no sense? It was like listening to the words of rap music. Only those in the know understood.

Kieran patted the hand Daria still had on his arm, "Do not fret. All will be well. Perhaps Mrs. Peasland is due for a comeuppance and perhaps this is the night."

Daria shook her head, "She is a very trying woman."

Kieran forced himself to keep from looking at Riana, afraid his perceptive cousin would see something in the glance.

"You speak truer words than you know." was all he said in a low voice.

Daria visibly relaxed, "They are for dinner as well and that should go easily enough if we forestall as much of Mrs. Peasland's conversation as possible."

"You worry, my dear. We are at your service, are we not, Mrs. Ingram?"

Riana nodded, "We most certainly are."

That crisis solved, Daria looked at Riana's damp gown, "I must have Susan clean your gown. You were caught in the rain? Yes, of course you were, even Donaghmore here is wet. Did you not make use of the umbrella I sent out? No mind. Mrs. Ingram, I have sent another gown to your room, for we do have a special guest this evening."

"Thank-you, My Lady for all your attention to me, but would it not be preferable for me to wear what I have already?"

Daria laughed and patted Riana's cheek, "Of course it is not. For your meeting with the Marquess you will outshine, Agnes Peasland, with no difficulty."

"However will I be able to pay you back for all your kindness?"

There was a fond smile on Daria's face as she reached up and touched Kieran's cheek.

"Marry my cousin and all will be well." she said with more than a little amusement.

Riana felt Kieran's fingertips on her back and forced herself to have no visible reaction. The fingers did not linger as the intention was simply to remind her that he had heard his cousin's words. Daria caught Riana's cold, damp arm and tugged her away from him.

"Come along, my dear, before you catch a chill. It would not do for you to sneeze in the face of a Marquess, would it?"

The Marquess of Didsbury was an average looking man; average height, average, pleasant features, light brown eyes and a friendly smile and manner. It was his hair, however, that kept him from being completely average. He had a head of thick, wavy light blond hair brushed forward in a studied wild tangle of curls, accented by thick sideburns. He dress with flair; dark blue coat with, lighter blue breeches and a heavily embroidered white satin waistcoat from which hung two red watch fobs.

He was standing with Kieran, talking with great animation as Riana approached, turning away from the Irishman, he gave her a wide, welcoming smile. Nervously, she smoothed her hands down the sea-green and gold pattern weave gown, letting her hands brush lightly over the embroidery of sequins and bead, drawing her pale green shawl over her wrists.

"Hello." he said simply, showing small teeth in a bright smile.

For the briefest of seconds, Riana saw the fire in Kieran's eyes as he watched her come toward them. He held out a hand to her, a hand that was simply friendly, but she chose not to take it, fearing her own reaction.

"Didsbury, meet my cousin's houseguest, Mrs. Riana Ingram. Mrs. Ingram, it is my pleasure to introduce you to Brice Chilton, the Marquess of Didsbury."

He clicked his heels together and gave her a deep bow, "My extreme pleasure, Mrs. Ingram. I did not know my hosts had another guest."

It was Kieran who answered in a rather sour tone, "Didsbury has already had the pleasure of the Peaslands. I do believe, Didsbury that you will find Mrs. Ingram much more pleasant."

"And your husband, Mrs. Ingram? Are we to have the pleasure?"

"Mrs. Ingram is a widow, sir." Kieran told him rather stiffly.

There was a slight change in the other man's expression, one she might not have seen had she not watched so many movies. He took half a step toward her, coming slightly ahead of Kieran. Awkwardly, Riana held out a gloved hand to him, and he took it, nonchalantly brushing his lips across her covered knuckles. She heard Kieran's swift intake of offended breath but did not look at him.

"I am pleased to meet you......" she hesitated, not knowing what exactly to name him.

Kieran shifted from one foot to the other, "Lord Didsbury." he supplied softly.

She gave him a quick smile of thanks, "Lord Didsbury."

That man gave another small bow, "Madame."

Daria came toward them at that moment, looking more relaxed than earlier in the day, holding out a hand to them.

"Come along into the drawing room. The others are waiting."

They were waiting, Mrs. Peasland's face brightening at the entrance of the Marques, not seeing either Riana or Kieran. She sat very straight on the sofa, tugging at her daughter's arm as she did so. At first, Lord Didsbury did not notice them as he smiled back at Riana and Kieran who had followed him into the room. Daria moved easily around them, stepping closer to the two seated women.

"Lord Didsbury, please allow me to introduce my close neighbours, Mrs. Arthur Peasland, their daughter Miss Agnes Peasland, and Mrs. Riana Ingram, whom I believe you have met."

Lord Didsbury strode immediately to the sofa and bent over the older woman's hand, raising it only a little as she offered it to him.

"Mrs. Peasland."

He did the same to her daughter, taking only the tips of the fingers, his eyes brushing the eager face that turned up to him. With a polite bow, he released the hand.

Mrs.. Peasland gave her daughter a quick, satisfied nod as she watched the man return Riana and Lord Donaghmore. Riana had been observing the manoeuvring with more than a little interest and felt the slight touch of Kieran's reassuring hand on her back.

She took a chair close to the Peaslands, the one she most favoured in the room and Kieran pulled another close to her, forcing Lord Didsbury to take the chair closest to Agnes Peasland. Riana saw the brief flash of humour that crossed Kieran's face at the seating arrangement. It was Lord Didsbury who started the conversation; a discussion that did not at all please the Peasland women, judging from their sour expressions.

"So Napoleon has mired himself in Russia. I visited Moscow several years ago and I think the French will have no easy time of it. Russians can be very fierce."

Lord Ranleigh leaned forward eagerly from his seat on another sofa.

"But you must remember, sir, that Napoleon has been successful in Europe, thus far, when it is he who leads the way. It is my belief that we are victorious in Spain because he is not there."

"Our soldiers are doing well because they are well trained and are English. The English will not be defeated." Lord Ranleigh announced in a dull, satisfied tone.

Without hesitation, Kieran crossed his legs and spoke, "It is my thought that the English will not be successful in America. There have been too few victories there. And did they not lose the Colonies in any case?"

"So speaks an Irish bog trotter." came the teasing response from the same man.

The air was suddenly thick with shock. That a host should speak so to a man who was a relative to the Baron, openly criticising his heritage. Riana's eyes went to Kieran's face, surprised to see that he did not show anger or insult. Instead, he leaned back in his chair and crossed his arms over his chest, regarding the other man with something close to pity.

"One cannot deny what is in fact, truth. It is the leaders of men who in the end, lead to victory. Wellington is one of those men. It is he who will take England to a successful conclusion."

Daria rose easily from her seat beside her husband, her eyes on the door,

"I believe that dinner is ready. Shall we?"

It amazed Riana at how easily everyone found their proper places as their hosts led them to the dining room. She was beginning to understand that there was an order; hostess and honoured guest first, Lord Didsbury held his arm to Daria. Lord Ranleigh and Mrs. Peasland, Riana and Lord Donaghmore, with Mrs. Peasland and her daughter in the rear, in order of precedence, as they crossed the entry to the other room.

There was a little awkward juggling, but Riana found herself seated between Kieran and Agnes, who faced Lord Didsbury across the table. Riana was so pleased to be seated next to Kieran, that she paid little attention to the effects of the others; Mrs. Peasland seated next to Lord Didsbury. The meal began, and after a few moments, Daria opened a discussion on the latest gossip from London, in order to keep tempers from rising about the wars in which England was presently fighting.

"Have you read the latest book, *Sense and Sensibility, A Novel by a Lady*? I have lately finished it. I greatly enjoyed it, especially having no sisters, I found the relations between them fascinating." Daria began.

"I never read novels," Agnes declared, straightening her back as if offended, "I find them too insipid. I take great enjoyment in history."

Lord Didsbury dipped his head at her, "Then you should be most interested in the exciting period in which we now live."

"My Lord," Agnes replied with a smothered titter in her voice, "a lady does not take too much interest in war. It is not done."

Looking for the first time at the man across the table, Riana sensed that Lord Didsbury had, in the vernacular of her time, set up Miss Peasland to expose her ignorance to others. But Miss Peasland's mother nodded in agreement with her.

"It is most unladylike to discuss such an appalling thing as war." Her mother nodded, "That is best left to the gentlemen over their cigars and brandy. Not at all fit for mixed company."

Lord Didsbury shifted his eyes toward Riana, "Mrs. Ingram, what is your opinion of the wars in which England finds herself?"

Riana did not hesitate, "*All* war, no matter where, is vicious and a useless waste of men and money. It seems to me that the cost if not worth the victory."

He gave her a silent clap, grinning widely, "Well spoke, Mrs. Ingram. Well spoke! But," he pretended to glower at her, "not the most popular of opinions."

"You will find, sir," Kieran spoke in a light tone, "that Mrs. Ingram is not afraid to speak her mind."

"It is remarkable what can be recalled by someone who claims to have lost her memory." Mrs. Peasland murmured in a low voice.

Riana felt Kieran grasp her hand under the table and give it a light squeeze. She smiled but did not look at him, turning instead to Agnes beside her who was looking at Lord Didsbury under her eyelashes, her lower lip between her teeth. She slipped her hand from Kieran's and picked up her soup spoon.

"Yes, it always amazes me at the things I say without thought. The Countess has been very kind in not taking offence by what sometimes comes out of my mouth."

"Mrs. Ingram has been a joy of a houseguest and I must declare that I am not looking too hard to discover who she truly is. I do not wish her to leave. Nor, I think, does my cousin."

The remainder of the meal continued to be uncomfortable with Mrs. Peasland's sly insinuations and Agnes' simpering Lord Ranleigh did as he always did; ate with total concentration, all but ignoring his guest, speaking only to utter words not connected with the talk at the table. Only Kieran and Lord Didsbury held conversation with Daria and Riana, politely including the Peaslands when possible.

After dinner, the women retired to the drawing room for tea and the men stayed in the dining room for cigars and brandy. The dining room conversation more comfortable than what was in the drawing room. The women sat uneasily on chairs and sofa around the room, holding tea cups as a table for cards was being set up.

"Where is your lovely sister, Lady Lynch, Lady Ranleigh?"

Daria sipped her tea, delaying her answer, "My dear Generva has long since returned to Templedown. She greatly missed her children. We are expecting them here for Christmas. I do so adore her little ones, and Shelby enjoys the company of children closer to his age."

"Does your son not have the company of that ragamuffin of Wigmore's. Such a scandal that was, his wife dying in childbirth."

"Why should that be a scandal?" Riana could not help but ask.

"Oh," Mrs. Peasland leaned closer as if sharing a dark secret, "every one knows he mistreated her so that the child was born early."

Daria caught the corner of her lip between her teeth and looked down at the floor, her body stiff with anger. Riana could not stop herself from speaking.

"And how do you know this?"

The reply was rather spiteful, "Servants talk to one another and some pass on information."

The door opened just then and the women looked at the entering men with relief.

"Oh!" Agnes exclaimed, "Here are the gentlemen. Lord Didsbury, do come sit beside me!"

Kieran moved to take the chair beside Riana, leaning close to speak, "I fear I have been supplanted, my dear. Who would want a mere Baron, and an Irish one at that, when one can have a Marquess?"

She tilted her head to reply, "I would."

She caught his gaze then, smiling when she saw the ardour flicker in his eyes. She turned her look to where Agnes was flirting with Lord Didsbury over the top of her fan.

"You are wearing a lovely gown, Miss Peasland."

Agnes did not look at her, instead smiled at Lord Didsbury, "I take great pride in dressing well and dressing up to the mark." she finally looked at Riana, giving her an appraising study, "It is a woman's duty to be always perfectly groomed in order to be a credit to the man who supports her."

The satirical curve of the man's smile told Riana that he was very familiar with the angling of marriageable women.

"In truth, that is what my sister and mother often declare when I am paying their dressmaker's bills. I would that they were more discreet in their enthusiasm for their gowns and fripperies."

"Mrs. Ingram," Daria's voice was raised, "Will you do the honour to play for us this evening. My cousin, I am certain, will be more than happy to assist you."

For Riana, the evening dragged on, Kieran's closeness as she played a torture, for his scent surrounded her, a constant reminder of what the night was going to offer her. The Peaslands were in no hurry to go home and Lord Didsbury played to the family's eagerness to marry off their daughter, enjoying their obvious enthusiasm.

It was nearly midnight when Mrs. Peasland rose to her feet, "My dear, we must take leave of our hosts. It is a long journey home."

Riana almost smiled at the speed at which Daria ushered out her guests. She stood in the open doorway, waving as the carriage rolled away from the house, and as Smith closed the door, she spoke.

"Smith, from now on when those people come without an invitation, we will not be home for them. I have never seen such atrocious manners! I was so embarrassed in front of my houseguests that I cannot bear to be so again." She turned to Riana and caught her hands, "I do so apologize, Mrs. Ingram, that you were a target of Mrs. Peasland's spite. You took her words with amazing grace."

Riana laughed, feeling the tips of Kieran's fingers on her back as she tightened her grip on Daria's hands.

"It was almost funny, you know? She was so obvious I was a little embarrassed for her. And now, I must say good-night and thank you for the delicious meal."

As her husband began to thump up the stairs, followed by Lord Didsbury, Daria bent to kiss Riana's cheek.

"Sleep well, my dear."

Riana had to force herself to not look at Kieran, "Oh, I believe I will."

In her room, she readied herself for bed, trying to speed Susan, who liked to do things in her own order, so that not too soon, Riana found herself finally in her bed and under the warmed covers with only a single candle lighting the room. Susan bid her good night and quietly closed the door behind her. She was waiting eagerly, yet Kieran did not come, and she felt weak with fear that he would not. She was dozing when she heard the door open so quietly at first that she thought she had misheard, but she saw to door move and rushed to go to him.

He was in a red tartan garment that looked like a loose robe with wide sleeves but without fasteners, and lined with dark green silk. He was still wearing shoes, breeches and shirt, but no neckcloth and the shirt's top two buttons were undone. He stopped with his hand still on the knob, watching her with eyes that glittered in the candle light, as she approached him.

"Riana!" he said in a mere breath of the name.

She stood before him, feeling overdressed in the long-sleeved, high-necked nightgown. She heard, rather than saw, his hand fall from the knob to reach for her and she met him by taking another step closer, and another until she was able to reach out and lay her hand flat on his chest, on his heart, feeling it beat through the layers of clothing he wore. There was a whisper of silk as she slid her hand across to the opening of his robe where she felt the heat coming from his body.

"You came!" was all she was able to say, for her heart was beating as rapidly as his.

His hand curved over her bent elbow as he tilted his head to look at her. He gave her a smile that trembled a little.

"Nothing would have stopped me......well servants roaming the halls delayed me somewhat."

A small laugh escaped her and she was taken aback by it, for her feelings were so intense at that moment, all she was aware of was him. That he had a sense of humour at that moment was endearing. Her fingers moved to the fine hair at his throat that peeked out from the opening of his shirt and there was a warm pulse there. As she felt his hand slid lightly along her arm, she wished her nightgown was off so their skin was touching, but that momentary thought vanished as his head came slowly closer to her face, his eyes intense on hers, willing her to meet his mouth. Yet, as she followed his lead, his head halted, so close that their hair was touching and she trembled with wanting him to do what he started.

"I love you, Riana Ingram." he told her in a harsh whisper.

That he had said those words and the way he spoke them made her curl her fingers against his skin, her nails slightly scratching.

"And how I love you!" her own voice was impatient with longing.

He obliged her then, at first lightly brushing her lips, then as if wanting more, pressed harder, yet with wondering tenderness. She rose on her toes to reach him, both hands now encircling his neck, so that her fingers were able to feel the warm texture of his hair. His hands came to grasp her waist, pulling her tighter to him, making her feel his need of her. She was not close enough, so his grip tightened and he lifted her off her feet, and felt joy as her small giggle of delight filled his opening mouth.

Her tongue joined his as her arms gripped his shoulders possessively and her now painful breasts pressed to his hard chest, seeking relief. There was only Kieran in the world now, all else had vanished leaving only the overwhelming need to have him surround her with his warm, bare skin, still she was unable to pull away from the mouth that was heating her core. His lips moved to trail light kisses along her cheek to her ear, where the sound of his breathing only added to her longing.

"We are both wearing too many clothes." he whispered, his words sounding like a breeze in her ear.

He lifted her in his arms, startling her with the rapidity of the motion, causing another titter of gladness. She slanted a wide-eyed look at him as he took her toward the bed, her smile meeting his as she thought of how unexpected a lover he was becoming. Carefully he lowered her on to the exposed sheets, and straightened to fling back his robe with grand impatience, letting it fall on the floor in a messy heap.

From her place on the mattress, Riana could see his arousal, the sight of it adding to her own even as she had to see it completely exposed to her eyes. He stood very still, watching her, waiting for her to make the next move. She pulled herself into a kneeling position and reached for the buttoned flap of his breeches, fumbling a little in her eagerness. The exposed buttons let the flap drop, but then there were unforeseen inner buttons that caused her to pause, looking up at the face suffused with passion.

"More buttons? Really?"

He gave a little frown and a small movement of his head, "What were you expecting?"

Her fingers were already undoing the buttons, so she did not answer and in any case, how could she answer. When the last one was undone, she pushed aside the opening, not knowing what next to expect. He was already opening the buttons on the ruffled cuffs of his shirt, and when those were done, he pulled at the body of his shirt, exposing bare skin and the beginning of a growth of dark hair close to her eyes.

"No underwear?"

She did not wait for an answer as she pressed her fingertips to the hot skin exposed by the opening of his breeches. She looked up then as he pulled his shirt over his head, for the buttoned opening of the shirt ended close to his waist. She gave him a wicked smile as his head disappeared into the voluminous white lawn of his shirt and reached inside his breeches to feel his burning, pulsing length. He gasped aloud at her touch, then as he tossed his shirt behind him, his hips thrust forward in invitation. She was just grasping him when his hands brushed hers on their way to removing the now offending breeches.

He sprang forth in her grip, proudly aloft, impatient, wanting. Leaning forward, she touched her tongue to the tip of him, circling it, tasting it's salty flavour. His hand curved into her hair as his hips involuntarily moved to her.

"God, Riana!" he gasped aloud.

She gave him a long, leisurely stroke as she raised up her face to him.

"God has been very kind to you." she teased.

She released him and gathered up the bottom of her nightgown, lifting it above her knees, but he forestalled her with a light hand.

"Let me." he told her, with a passion-harsh voice.

She unbuttoned the cuffs on her wrists, and went backwards on the mattress to accommodate him. He cupped both of her covered breasts, lifting them as if feeling their weight and for the first time she wished she was better endowed, the thought quickly vanishing as his thumb brushed her already peaked nipples, making her breath come faster. He kissed her as his hands moved to the bunched fabric around her knees and raised it slowly, letting the backs of his fingers trail along her skin. And once he freed her arms, she raised them, even as the long kiss continued, to the heat of the bare skin that covered his horseman's chest, curving into the fine hair that spread across it.

She did not care where her nightgown went once he had removed it as she lay back on the mattress, making room for him beside her. Kieran did not stretch out beside her as she expected, going instead to the foot of the bed, to crawl along her, his mouth kissing, his tongue tasting from her knees to her breasts, all but ignoring the core of her that screamed for his touch. He gripped and loosened his hold on her breasts, using his hands to raise them to his lips, and reaching down between them, her own hands cradled and teased him, trying to get him where she wanted him, yet he resisted and she felt his smile on her skin.

"You're the devil!" she managed amid her straining demands.

He did not lift his head as he released her nipple and as he spoke, his unshaven jaw caused more delight.

"You are too impatient, my delight."

She tried to move her legs, begging for the next level, but the strength of a single arm kept her trapped as he wanted her.

"You're too slow."

He chuckled, lifting his head so that the impassioned look in his dark eyes seared her soul.

"Slow is what you need, is it not? I have a need to learn about you."

She loved the passionate and raspy sound of his voice, for he was so different from Ken, who never spoke, never lingered at

Kieran was doing. She grabbed his hair, giving his head a little shake.

"Now, Kieran." She insisted.

His cheeky smile did not change, "Soon. I have waited too long to hurry."

"And I have been a widow for more than three years."

He gave her a teasing laugh and went back to kissing her, raising himself again to cover her mouth and she melted, letting him do as he wished for it felt so good. Finally, when she thought she would die from wanting him, he raised himself up on his elbows, shifting his body higher so that she could feel his pointed heat drag along her burning skin.

"Now?" he rasped at her.

Joyously, she moved to let him in, feeling his hard length slide into the core of her, filling her, making her feel as if they two were the only people in the world. She dug her nails into his hips, urging more from him, but he resisted, slowly teasing her, his grin slowly faded as his own body took over from his mind.

Never had Riana had such a night; she felt deliciously sore and replete. Was the man able to go on forever? A gentle snore from beside her answered that question, and he turned in his sleep, his hand curving more protectively around her waist. He was close enough to her that it was easy to turn her face into the sweaty skin of his chest and deeply inhale the scent of him. There was an uncontrollable tingling that vied with the wonderful pain and as her hand hovered over that part of him that had given her so much bliss, she decided to let him sleep a little longer.

She watched his sleeping face, feeling a love so intense that it stopped her breath. How was she going to live without this man? She knew that it was only a matter of time before she would be permanently back in her own time and then would have to spend the rest of her life alone. Tears trickled down her cheeks already mourning his loss as he slept in exhaustion beside her. And what of her leaving? She could not let him think she had abandoned him and all they had shared; she knew that experience and the wrenching ache of it.

It was then and that memory of loss, that decided her. She had to tell him, had to convince him that she was from his future and that she was probably required to return permanently.

"Please, God," her mind yelled, "let me have a long time with him. You gave me this man, don't take me away from him too soon. Or if I still have to die, let it be with him."

"Riana?"

Kieran's sleep smoky voice drew her from her thoughts as his finger wiped a tear on her cheek.

"Misgivings?" for the first time, she heard fear in his voice.

She smiled and cupped her hand around the sharp edge of his jaw, kissing him lightly.

"Never! Oh, God, never! I have never had a night......I've never...." she could not find the words to tell him of her unexpected happiness, of the memories created that would never be forgotten.

He understood, moving over his pillow to press his lips to hers, his hand shifting toward her breast. She caught his hand, forcing it to flatten on her skin.

"Kieran, there is something you don't know about me. It's something I have to tell you even if I have to lose you because of it."

His hand relaxed under hers and he kissed her again, his mouth warm and dry.

"I cannot see how that will happen. From this position right now," he grinned proudly as he looked down at their naked bodies pressed so intimately together, "I think I will need a lifetime of this."

The words were blurted out without her forming them, "Your lifetime or mine?"

He became still, his face lifting from the pillow, followed by his shoulders as he bent over her.

"That makes little sense, my love. We will share a lifetime."

She was blinded by hateful tears that did not let her see the face so close to her. She lifted her hand again to his cheek and turning his head, he kissed her palm.

"I have lied to all of you. A terrible lie. I have forgotten nothing of my past; I remember all of it. I'm from Canada...."

"I hear it is a beautiful, unspoiled country.....England is fighting a war over it, if you recall..."

"Not from where I come from. That place does not exist yet."

"Victoria? I knew that."

"Vancouver," she corrected softly "and it will not come into existence until the middle of this century."

His eyes clouded as he became still, "I do not understand. Vancouver was a great explorer, in spite of the trouble he had. I do not recall a city named after him."

"A good deal of places will be named after him."

"'*Will be*'?" he echoed, raising an eyebrow.

"For one thing, a whole island that is about a third of the size of England."

There was a long silence as he watched her face, "How do you know this, Riana?"

Oh God, she thought. Just how much of the future should she tell him. Explain who she was and from where. Would giving him just a little information change the future and her own place in that future. Would the future be radically different from what it was right now? She took a deep breath and hurried on with her answer.

"I'm from the future, more than two hundred years in the future."

He reared back from her, dragging himself into a sitting position, "Impossible! There can be no such thing. How could you get here?"

She looked up at him, feeling her heart break, "You brought me here."

Chapter 11

He did not reply as he rolled over to the other side of the bed and rolled out, walking naked to pick up his robe, a garment he called a banyan and dragged it on. Riana sat up and dragged the covers with her, pulling them up to her neck as protection, her head turning to follow his movements.

"Impossible! Unnatural!" he muttered to himself as he crossed to the window.

He stood at the window, a bracing arm holding back the draperies as he looked out at the early morning. Her eyes traced the width of his shoulders under the red silk tartan, recalling delicious images of the night before, trying to reconcile them with the stiff back she was watching. Morning was here, an end to the night's fantasy and all she knew now was how much she loved him; a love so new and so intense she would never have another like it. She cried silent tears of grief at the loss of it, knowing now she should have kept silent.

"Can you prove any of what you say?" his voice echoed off the glass.

Her voice trembled with her tears, "I know that Napoleon will lose the war fairly soon, but don't ask how or where, probably because of Russia, just as I know more than a hundred years later another dictator will try the same thing and he too, will be badly defeated by the Russian winter and the Russians. He will be exiled and return months later to be defeated finally by Wellington."

"That can be construed as conjecture, lies or pure fantasy."

He turned to her, his face looking as miserable as her own felt, his face, too, streaked with tears. His expression was still and waiting.

She hitched the bed clothes higher on her chin, "I know that you will involve yourself in a duel with Regis Wigmore and he will kill you." she told him in a voice so low he had to strain to hear her.

He straightened suddenly, "How can you possibly know that? I dislike the man, but I would never……never," he hissed through his teeth, "duel with him. Duelling is illegal and there is nothing between us that would end in such a manner?"

"You told me….or rather, your ghost told me. He has been haunting Riverton Abbey since that day……."

"My ghost? What day? When? This is all foolishness" he interrupted sharply.

"I don't know the exact day, but it will be soon, I think. You cursed his family and you deeply regretted it and that's why you haunted this place. I am here to try to change things."

"Haunted! What nonsense! Have you been reading gothic novels? Only silly girls read such foolishness. I expected better from you."

She rested her chin on her knees, trying to find the words to convince him.

"Ever since that curse, the Wigmores have failed at anything they attempt here in Whipford. They are successful only if they leave the country. My own parents left here in the 1970's and my father became a very successful builder in Canada, until he and my husband were on a fishing trip when he crashed his plane.."

"Plane?" he snapped out, "What is a plane?"

"They were once called flying ships because they fly through the air. It takes about ten hours to fly from Vancouver to London."

"Impossible! The air will not support a ship, and nor can anything travel so fast as to take less than several weeks to go that distance."

"Nevertheless, in less than a hundred years from now the first attempts will begin." She stopped to take another deep breath, "Your spirit wants rest and it wants to repair the damage your curse caused."

He was diverted by her words, "Why ever would I fight with that man?"

"That I'm not certain of.....something to do with a woman I have heard, although not from you.....your ghost."

"You do not know a great deal, do you?" came the snide question.

"How about this? Lord Thorpe is broke. He's lost all his money gambling and on horses and he will commit suicide. His son, Shelby will eventually restore the fortune so that Riverton Abbey still remains in the family. I am visiting the Abbey."

He jerked his head, "How do you know of his finances?"

"His many greats-grandson told me. I have seen the portraits you did of them. And those of horses you painted. You really should have put your name on those......."

"I do not name my paintings." He said in a hard voice.

"Oh, I know and in the future there is a great deal of speculation as to the artist. They are worth a great deal of money now and they still hang in the house."

He gave her an odd smile, "How do you know this?"

"When I faint, I return to my time. And when I'm there you always bring me back." she rubbed her chin across her knees, "I'm very ill there, so maybe this is all a result of my brain tumour. Maybe you don't really exist; maybe you are just the fantasy of a diseased brain."

He was very still then, swallowing rapidly.

"And how do you know you have a diseased brain?"

She laid her cheek on her knees, "Tests. Brain scans. Brain surgery. All bad news."

He was across the room in three strides, grabbing her shoulders and drawing her up to him, kissing her with a fierce, angry passion. Her hands gripped his solid arms as she fervently accepted whatever he chose to give her. He dragged his mouth from hers, giving her a tiny shake.

"Does feel like a fantasy? Does it?" he demanded.

His eyes were so close that she watched the movement of his pupils before she replied.

"No. But if I am dying, Kieran, how can I tell truth from fantasy?"

His brows drew severely over his eyes, "You will not die on me, Riana. You will not die! Not now." He finished in a lower voice.

She gave a bitter laugh, "How can I stop it? Even with all the advances of medicine, nothing can be done to stop the growth of tumours."

He released his grip on her shoulders and hugged her ardently to the solid trunk of his body, his cheek resting on the hair badly matted from the night's exertions. She smelled the dried sweat on his skin and revelled in his closeness.

"Ashley's dibs are definitely not in tune. He asked me for a loan only yesterday. I returned the money for the horses. But what of you?"

Gradually, he eased away from her, turning to go across the room to the chair by the fireplace and sat down.

"I will never stop loving you, Riana, but what you have told me is far beyond reason. Ghosts and flying ships, Napoleon captured. I do not think I could live with a woman of such imagination. I want children with you, but how could I trust how you raise them?"

"I would never tell them about what was to come. It might change the future too much....which could not, sometimes, be such a bad thing."

The idea of children with this man swelled her heart and halted her breath, making her heart beat faster.

Kieran clasped his hands together and rested his chin on them, "You speak in such an odd mixture of daydream and logic. I cannot help but believe you, yet my head tells me, and loudly, that all you have said are lies, that you are deceiving me for reasons known only to you. Deceiving not only me but those in my family that I hold very dear."

"Have my deceptions been so terrible? I must protect myself."

"You have me for that now." He muttered, as if against his own will.

"Do I Kieran? Do I? I have told you my most costly secret, a secret that could mean my life, at the very least."

He watched her for a very long time, his face expressionless and he rubbed his hands together as if having made a decision. He pushed himself out of the chair and went back to the window. Feeling a little more secure now, Riana reached down and picked her nightgown off the floor by the bed. She struggled it over her head and arms, needing the protection of the billows of soft lawn. She waited for him to speak, waiting fearfully for his next words, watching his back, following the way his hair flowed over the collar-less banyan. He shifted suddenly as if startled.

"Who is that man out there in the park? It is not Ashley, nor is it Lord Didsbury. He is just standing there under the tree."

Riana hurried from her seat on the bed, going to him to peer around the width of his body. She did not have to search the grounds for her gaze seemed to be drawn immediately. Lightly, she put her hand on the arm that was braced on the window frame.

"Why," she said in a voice filled with wonder, "it's you. Strange....."

And she knew. She pushed away from him and ran to the door, pulling it open without care. She had to go to that figure below, she had to find him. She ran barefoot down the dimly lit passage, down the stairs and outside. Her instinct told her where he was and she followed that instinct. From behind her, she barely heard Kieran call out her name, first in alarm, then in anger.

Down the stone steps and across the gravel, not feeling the little stones cut into her bare feet. The wet grass soothed her feet as she ran, using her hands to lift the gown away from her knees in order to run faster. She was running so fast that when she reached the waiting figure, she skidded to a stop, all but falling in her haste. She looked up at the waiting face.

"Kieran, why here?"

"It is coming soon, but first you must return to your own time to find a way to convince him that you speak the truth."

"But I don't want to leave him now. I can't leave him now."

"It will be difficult, but it will not be for long. He will barely notice that you have gone. You are well aware of how time passes. Shall we return?"

He held out his hand and she took it, so that together they crossed the pretty bridge to go toward the grove. The familiar headache began and her vision was silvering, so she held her breath in expectation of the pain.

Chapter 12

"Bloody hell, Riana, why didn't you stay inside if you were feeling ill. You scared the shit out of me."

Rainwater cascaded down her cheeks as she looked up at Jared where he squatted over her in the kitchen yard, struggling to open the umbrella. She felt too lethargic to attempt to sit up and it was rather funny watching him twist himself and the umbrella against the wind.

"Sorry. I thought I forgot your mother's scarf."

He relaxed his shoulders as the umbrella finally popped open, providing little protection from the slanting rain.

"My dear girl, it's still on your head."

With his free hand, he caught her arm to help her to her feet. She wobbled as she gained her footing and he slid his arm around her waist to steady her. The solidity of his body was so comforting she relaxed into it and he waited only a moment before urging them toward the warmth of the house.

"Do you need your tablets?"

She shook her head, "Not right now. But I am thirsty."

He pushed open the door, letting her enter before him while he shook the water off the umbrella and closed it. They were almost at the kitchen when Clare hurried around the corner, her hands outstretched.

"Riana! My God, I saw you from the upstairs window! Are you alright?"

"I'm fine....."

But Clare had already swung to face Jared, anger twisting her face, "You know she's ill, yet you take her out into the rain! How could you be so thoughtless? Are you trying to hurry her death? Are you trying to kill her?"

The umbrella dropped from Jared's hand as his head swivelled between Riana and her mother. There was a sinking feeling in the pit of Riana's stomach as she realized that she had to tell another man of her condition.

"Riana.....?" he began, swallowing her name.

Clare had already forgotten him as she turned her wrath on her daughter.

"And you! You know you have to take care, you let him do this to you."

Riana reached out and caught her mother's arm to give it a little shake, trying to smile enough to minimize Clare's fearful anger.

"We were in the mews and it's not so far away. I was hardly in the rain very long, and look at this. I have this lovely scarf Jared lent me, so at least my head is dry."

Clare glared at Jared who was standing very still in shock, "At least he had sense enough for that. But you know...."

Riana squeezed her mother's arm so tightly that her words were stopped, and gave Clare a slight shake of her head.

"It doesn't matter Mom, does it?"

"What doesn't matter?" Jared was finally able to speak.

Riana looked up at him and saw with no little surprise, the stunned shock in his face. He had, she realized, only partially understood Clare's angry words. She took her hand from her mother and laid it on his forearm. He twisted his arm to be able to grasp her hand. She looked up at him, but spoke to Clare.

"Mom, everything is fine, go back to your room. I guess I need to talk to Jared. Is there a place we can go?"

With a quick, perceptive glance between the two of them, Clare stroked Riana's arm and with a little jiggle of her fingers, did as Riana suggested. He watched Clare's departure for a moment before looking back at Riana.

"My rooms." he gave her a small, twisting smile," In there none of the guest will hear me yell, for I fear I shall be yelling. Come along."

As they passed through the house, he all but ignored the people they met as he tugged her along behind him, his pace was such that she had trouble keeping up with him. They took back stairs and seldom-used passages until they were in the corridor outside his suite, where he stopped to look down at her again. He lifted a hand and tugged on the ends of the damp scarf on her head and pulled it off, placing it carelessly on a table beside him.

"It's wet. Your mother will have my head if you catch a chill."

Reaching behind himself, he opened the door, pushing it back to let her enter before him. Immediately, he went to the little cart that held the decanters of alcohol.

"Sit down. I think I'm going to need a drink."

She obeyed him, but as she sat, she looked at the painting of the black horse that hung beside the fireplace, and Kieran's face came clearly into her mind.

"Coke, Riana?" Jared asked, still holding one of the decanters.

"No thank-you. It's a little too cold."

"Shall I ring for tea? Or coffee?"

Wordlessly, she shook her head. He took a deep draft of whatever he had in his glass and moved to the fireplace. Placing the glass on the marble mantle, he squatted before the firebox and lit the paper and wood inside it. In only a moment, the wood began to burn satisfactorily. Lifting his glass again, he moved to sit beside her, this time only sipping from his drink. He shifted in his seat and put his arm along the back of the sofa.

"Now tell me. Why are you ill? It's something terrible, isn't it?"

She gave him only a short, sharp nod, not wanting to tell him specifics, remembering Kieran's reaction. Jared, at least, would have a better understanding.

"I had a brain tumour and surgery, but my doctor said there is a good chance it might return." she finally managed through lips that trembled with threatening tears.

He went very stiff and still, only his eyes moved as he searched her face. Very carefully, he placed his glass on the coffee table and it was forgotten.

"You are very certain? Can it be a mistake?" he asked very quietly.

She shook her head as she looked down at her hands that lay loose in her lap.

"No mistake. Not after test after test after test. I've seen it on X-rays and brain scans. There are parts of it that couldn't be removed."

She was shocked to see unshed tears in his eyes as he brushed her cheek with the back of his hand. She tipped her head into his hand, closing her eyes as she welcomed the tenderness of it.

"D'you know I love you, Riana?" his voice was so low she barely heard him.

She forced a smile, "How could I? I barely know you."

He ignored her words, misery rising in him, "How long?"

"A month, a year, ten years. Who knows?"

"Yet you travel here?"

"My mother has always wanted to show me her home; this seemed to be the best time, since she did not want to come in the heat of tourist season. We thought the weather might be more conducive, because I struggle now with the heat."

Jared took a slow deep breath, raising his head to stare blindly at the plaster decorations on the ceiling. His hand moved to cup her cheek, but his fingers were stiff and cool.

"Why didn't they remove all of it?"

"It was in a bad spot and removing it all would have turned me into a vegetable and I didn't want that."

"But you would live." He said softly, still speaking to the ceiling.

"That is not a life, Jared. That is only for my family, not for me, I will not be a burden on anyone and I have already made sure I will not be resuscitated."

"Shit! Bloody damned hell." he muttered, "Had you come sooner, we should have had more time together."

"How would I have known that, Jared?"

He looked at her at long last, "Right now, I am not thinking logic."

"Maybe you should." she suggested with the tiniest of smiles.

He moved so suddenly, he caught her unaware. He jerked her tightly to him, pressing his face into her neck as his arms gripped her ever tighter. She slid her arms around him as she felt his tears damp on the skin of her neck. That they were silent tears seemed to be worse than the yelling he had suggested earlier. She felt his back heave under her arms and felt the painful grip of his fingers in her flesh tighten with each moment.

Somehow, after long minutes, they found themselves stretched out together on the sofa, taking comfort in the crowded closeness of their intertwined limbs. Riana let her hand drift between them, seeking to give Jared an age-old kind of solace. She stroked him lightly, hesitantly until she felt movement shift where she wanted it. Briefly, he fought her, attempting to shift away from her hand, but the confines of the sofa would not let him and he gave in to her touch. Neither looked at the other, each pretending that nothing was happening, not even the slide of his zipper changed that odd displacement.

She freed him, and he let one of his hands flow down her side the hem of her short skirt. His hand rested there a moment as if asking permission and when she did not release his grip on him, the hand pulled it up to the edge of her panties, one finger dipping under the fabric. He raised his head from her neck, his lips in search of hers and finding them, kissed her so tenderly she thought her heart might break.

She released her hold on his and felt the denial on his mouth, the sudden stiffness in his back, and the slow acquiescence when she fumbled with his belt buckle and button on his jeans. He removed the hand that had been caressing her to mindlessness, to help her remove his encumbering clothes. She cupped him immediately, feeling, touching, weighing, and he in his place, all but shredded her panties in his own impatience to have them gone.

As he shifted his position, moving one of her legs to accommodate himself, she closed her eyes, letting the sensation of his hands, his mouth and his tongue engulf her. On their own, her hands made their way up his back, her nails digging into his flesh, her gasps of ecstasy caught in his kisses. He filled her slowly, hesitantly as if expecting rejection and once fully where he wanted to be, he became still, rejoicing in the sensation and the scent of her. One of her hands came to rest on his buttocks, urging him on, wanting more, wanting completion.

Their mutual explosion came too soon for both of them and for a time, they lay crammed, one on top of the other, on the narrow sofa, letting their breathing go back to normalcy. Finally, Riana opened her eyes to look up at him, finding him watching her with awe and wonder. She freed one of her trapped hands to brush her fingertips over his sweaty face.

"Jared!" she breathed up at him, "Who knew?"

He chuckled and she felt him slide from her, "Damn!" he muttered with frustration. But there were no more words and he shoved himself off the sofa, bending in one motion to lift her up, his mouth probing for hers again. He knew where he was going and she did not care where he was taking her, as she unbuttoned his shirt, spreading the edges to allow access to her hands. His hairless chest was well-muscled and still slightly damp with sweat.

She kissed his breast bone, "You work out." she murmured on his skin.

He was struggling to open a door so did not answer, and in several long strides, he was wrenching back bed clothes and placing her on a firm mattress. She looked up at him as he tossed aside his shirt, his now naked body showing her he was not yet finished with her. She began to remove her skirt, but his impatience was such that he did it for her, drawing her t-shirt up over her head when he had finished his first task, ignoring her bra completely as he stretched out beside her again. He curved his arm over her head as he pulled her to him.

"This time we go slow." his voice was soft with a scratchy edge to it.

Riana awoke to the sound of Jared's sobs; deep raw crying that cut her deep to her core. Wordlessly, she gathered him to her, but after a moment he shoved her away with such fury she all but fell from the bed.

"Go away, Riana! Just go away." he told her through gritted teeth.

With tears stinging her own eyes, she dropped from the mattress to the floor, bending to retrieve her clothes. She was searching for her discarded bra when he spoke again.

"Why did you let it get this far?" he questioned with a fury that shocked her.

She knew what he was asking and fought to keep her temper, asking calmly, "Was I alone in this?"

"You could have stopped me." came truculently.

She had to smile, turning to face him, holding her t-shirt to her breasts as protection from his ire.

"But I didn't want to."

He raised himself up on one elbow, bracing himself with his free hand, "You should have," he insisted, "because now I will always remember this and know it is what I have lost."

"You haven't known me long enough to say that."

His smile was brief and cold, "I have seen nearly every inch of you."

"And that," she said in a tone almost as cold as his, "is entirely beside the point. There will be plenty of other women, especially in the business you're in. You are a good-looking man, Jared, and rich and a Lord and you live in this great big mausoleum of a house. You practically walk around with a sign, "Good Prospect" tattooed on your forehead."

His laugh was so unexpected that it caught her off-guard.

"Christ, Riana, you do call a spade a spade, don't you?" he held out a welcoming hand to her, "Come back to bed. We have to make damned good use of the time we have."

"That's what you want, Jared?" she asked carefully.

"What I want, my darling girl, is to marry you, now; tomorrow or the day after in our own chapel."

His words stunned her to thoughtless silence and she watched a slow, satisfied smile cross his face as he realized her total confusion. There was power over her now and he was going to take advantage of it.

"Come here." he beckoned with one finger.

And she went, dropping the collection of her clothes, eagerly returning to the bed. She reached for him again, but this time, he held her off, dropping a teasing kiss on her nose.

"There'll be no more of that until you agree to marry me. Until you say yes," he stroked her teasingly, feeling her surge toward him, "nothing more is to be done."

This time it was she who moved away, "Why do you want to do this?"

"Because I love you and I want to spend as much time as I can with you. I want....no, I need to be your husband."

"You want to sit by my bed and watch me die?" she asked viscously, trying to negate the happiness his words caused.

He didn't flinch, "Yes. I *need* to be sitting at your bedside."

She reached out to touch his chest at his heart, "This will not be easy for you. Think, Jared. It would be better for you if I was at home....."

"This can be your home." he interjected.

"...at home," she continued stubbornly, "in Vancouver. That way you will not have all that in your memory, you will just know I have gone. It will be much easier for you, less pain."

"Don't you see, my darling girl, that I want all that? I want all the time with you I can get."

"And my mother? My brothers? What about them?"

His answer was immediate, "They can come here. I won't have you in hospital, this will be your home."

Riana cried then, bursting into deep and loud tears, the first time since her diagnosis, in a rage that at this time in her life, when it was nearly over, that she should find the love of two magnificent men, even if one was probably a figment of her sick brain, and there was going to be so little time for happiness. Jared drew her into the warmth and strength of his body, wrapping his arms and legs around her, his hands still on her, his face pressed to her, letting go again of his own tears.

Chapter 13

They spent the rest of the day and the night together, talking and planning and crying. Only Jared got out of the bed to retrieve Riana's medication and to bring up food on a tray. While the food was being prepared, Jared grew impatient with the smiling, knowing glances from the kitchen staff and realized he had forgotten something important. He made his way to Clare's room and knocked on the door. She opened it, her face wary.

"Lord Thorpe?"

He controlled a wince brought on by her incorrect usage, and put his hands behind his back.

"May I speak with you, Mrs. Wigmore?"

"Of course." She stood aside to let him enter, signalling him to take a chair, which he refused, "Is Riana alright? Where is she? I must see her."

The smile he gave her had a trace of wickedness, "Riana is fine, very fine, I believe. I have her medication and will take it to her." he paused, "I left her asleep....in my bed."

Instead of shock or indignation, he was relieved to see Clare's smile of delight. She cupped her hands over her mouth, her eyes dancing.

"She is happy?" her question echoed in her hands.

"More than happy, I should think." even he heard the trace of self-satisfaction in his voice, "She will be staying the night. I have come with a request, Mrs. Wigmore."

"I will pack up her clothes. It will be my pleasure."

"Oh, no, not that. They are already being packed up. No. I am here to ask permission to marry your daughter as soon as can be arranged."

Clare was speechless, for she had not expected this. She had hoped for a lovely romance between them, but given Riana's illness, never thought of marriage. She frowned in consternation and let her hands drop to her sides.

"Lord Thorpe, do you know, has she told you..?"

"About her condition? Yes. I have already begun to make arrangements for her medical records to be transferred here and preparations for her treatment here."

"Away from us?" she wailed.

"Of course not," he told her softly, "that would be the worst thing for her now. I want every second I can have with her and I would not deny you and her brothers the very same thing. God knows this house can hold the three of you."

There was a long silence, "I don't know what to say."

He bent toward her, "Say you will give permission. I will take very good care of her."

"She hardly needs my permission. She has always been headstrong."

He laughed, "I have noticed that about her. But, *I* need your permission."

She laughed too, "Then, of course, you have it. When do you plan to be married?"

"Well, it will have to be at least three weeks, since she is not a resident of the UK. I am hoping to be able to get permission from the Home Secretary to marry earlier, given her condition. My solicitor is already working on it, but told me not to get my hopes up."

Tears filled Clare's eyes and she grasped Jared's hands, "Thank-you for this. She has been so lonely since Ken." she broke off, embarrassed, "I wanted her to find some kind of happiness, and you, my dear boy, have given it to her."

"As she has given me. I only regret," he searched for the words and she squeezed his hands again.

"There is never enough time, even fifty years Jared, for some people, is not enough. Make the very best of what you have."

"I will."

"Now you must get back to her. Will I see you for dinner?"

Another wicked smile, "Maybe breakfast, if it's late enough. I'll ring you when we are on our way down."

She gave him a teasing push, "Be off with you!"

The night had been full; they were learning about one another, trying new things that she had never dared before, talking, planning and once again, giving in to the cravings of their bodies. They awoke to bright sun and flesh raw with over usage, and as she lay beside Jared, she wondered that the soreness of that other time had not carried over to this. But then the symptoms of her tumour were not evident there.

Jared was already leaning over her, covering her face in light kisses. Her hand slid across his flat belly and he laughed on the skin of her face.

"I am done for pet, you have used me hard. We must get up now and face the smirks of the staff. And there is a great deal that I must show you."

"Like what?"

"Oh, the secret places of the house where we can make love..."

"Jared!" she burst out with a giggle.

"....the attics where we can see all the hidden, untold things of my family's past..."

"There is a past to this house?"

"Naturally, any good family house in England has an undisclosed history. For example, did you know we have a ghost?"

"Yes, actually, I did."

"Really? None of us know for certain who he or she is, or why we are being haunted. But at least we have one ghost to brag about to our guests."

"Have you ever seen him?"

He raised his head a little away from her, "Him? What makes you think it's a man?"

Oops, she thought, mistake. Keep it light.

"Is there a book about the history of the house?"

"Not really. Just old diaries and journals and old lists of people and animals, but it would be interesting to put one together."

"Maybe I could do that." She said speculatively.

"Are you sure you are up to it?"

"Yes, if I start now."

He lay back on the bed, his arm raised above his head, "I can see it now. *A History of Riverton Abbey*, by Riana Thorpe, Viscountess Whipford. It's bound to be a best seller, especially to Abbey guests."

She sat up, stunned by his declaration, "Viscountess? Me?"

He looked up at her amused by her words and tone, "Of course. I am the son of the Earl of Ranleigh, and my title is Viscount Whipford. When my father is gone, I become the Earl of Ranleigh and my son becomes the Viscount Whipford."

"You have a title?"

"Yes. You have heard me called 'Lord'."

"But I didn't think....I didn't know."

"Well, my darling girl, get used to being a Viscountess, it comes with me."

She gave him a sad smile, "I doubt I will have enough time to get used to it, or to even like it."

"Most of the time, you forget about it. Sometimes you will be called Lady Thorpe. Not so bad, you know. C'mon now, future Lady Thorpe, we have things to do today."

And there were knowing smirks as Jared predicted. They sat in the dining room for breakfast with Clare who laughed with delight when Jared told her of Riana's ignorance of his title. It had never occurred to Clare to explain it to her. They were relaxing with their coffee when Riana spoke as she looked into her cup.

"You have a family cemetery?"

"Of course. We're all buried there, as I will and you...." he broke off, confused by what had come unbidden, out of his mouth.

"And I will be." she finished for him, covering the curled fist on the table between them, "I would like to see it after breakfast."

"If you like. Not my favourite place, but it is attached to the chapel and you might want to look at it to see if you want to be married in it. Most of my ancestors have been."

"Then as far as I'm concerned, so will we. The venue doesn't matter."

"And what about your gown?" Clare asked, relived that for the first time Riana was talking about the wedding.

"Oh, I'll find something. Maybe we can go to London, or maybe I'll just make it myself."

"Yourself? Can you do that?"

"I design and make the clothes for my dolls. I have the mass produced clothes sourced out to a clothing manufacturer. But I do know how to sew."

"She makes a lot of her own clothes." Clare offered eagerly.

"Then, Riana, my love, we shall really have to make a trip to the attics. Marianne always said there was a treasure trove of material up there, but it wasn't her style. I don't know what shape it's in, but you can look." he looked out the window, "Time we got moving, the weather is fine out there and it would be a shame to waste it."

He led her through the black-painted iron gate into the cemetery, but she did not at first look at the lichen speckled grave stones, rather at the lovely stained glass window of the chapel. She grasped Jared's wrist as she traced the stained glass heraldic symbol that was the centre of the window.

"Jared, that is so beautiful."

He put hand in his pocket and looked up at it as if seeing it for the first time.

"Yes, I suppose it is." he shifted his shoulders, "If we marry here in the late afternoon, the sun will be shining through that window."

She flung her arms around his neck and hugged him tightly, "Can we? That would be so perfect!"

He bent his face into her neck and she felt his breath on her skin.

"Wanna quickie in the vestibule?" he whispered into her ear.

She smacked at him, feeling a freedom she never had with Ken, "Jared! What a thing to say, or even to think! Shame on you."

He shrugged as if giving in, "Ready to visit all those old buggers?"

"Have some respect for your family!" she hissed as she followed his lead.

Most of those in the family gallery were there, the older head stones had names and dates nearly weathered away. When she found Daria's and Shelby's graves, she felt like crying, for they were still fresh in her memory, Ashley, she wanted to kick over, but was shocked when she saw the date of his death.

"He was so young. But how could he have done that to his wife and son?" she bit her lip to keep from repeating what she already knew.

He gave her an odd look, "No, he took the coward's way out. He gambled away all his money and committed suicide, leaving his wife and son destitute. Only when she turned the house into a finishing school for girls was she able to survive and keep Riverton

Abbey in the family. Her son brought back their fortune years later. We have had some black sheep, you know."

"Who's this? Caroline. Why no date."

"Daria was pregnant when her husband killed himself. Caroline was a still birth."

"How terrible for her, to lose a child has to be the worst thing. Maybe second worst." she looked up at Jared sadly, "Not being able to have one to have one with the man you love is the worst. Jared, you will marry after I'm gone. I think you would make a fabulous father."

He studied her face for a moment, "Absolutely not. The men in my family only marry once. Look at my father. No, darling girl, I will not marry again."

"But what about your family?"

"At present, Marianne's oldest son David is my official heir. I am content for him to remain that way."

She put her hand flat on his chest, "Consider it at least. You should be married and a father."

"No, Riana, I will not." he gave her a smile that was a mere lift of one corner of his mouth, "I will forever be the playboy widower. Didn't say I would not take what will be offered."

She gave his chest a thump and continued on without him while he was content to watch her without following. And that was when she found a small tombstone all but hidden by an overgrown rose bush that had, even this late in the year a single overblown yellow rose that was a beacon amid dead leaves and dry brown branches. With her foot, she pushed the brittle branches aside to read the engraving on it.

"Kieran Daire Oran Gilmartin, 3rd Baron of Donaghmore
Born May 10, 1781
Killed Most Foul
October 29 in the Year of Our Lord 1812"

As she looked down, she felt the air move around her face and her face heat until she thought she might faint. So here it was;

he had been a living person. She closed her eyes feeling his warm touch on her, oddly not concerned at that moment for the man who was still watching her, the man she was going to marry. Her stillness forced Jared to rush to her side, fearing another fainting spell. From behind, he circled his arms around her and held her tightly to warm her.

"Riana? You want to return to the house?" he asked in her ear.

She shook her head, her hair brushing his shirt, "Who is this? His name is different from the others."

"Oh, old man Donaghmore? Dunno, really, but he was the artist who painted some of the horse paintings in the house, there's not much more of a record of him and nobody was interested enough to find out. But that was in the time of Daria of the lost diaries. I'd bet that he'd be in one of them."

She was finally able to breathe normally. The shock of seeing his headstone, knowing his bones lay beneath her feet made her want to wail and mourn his death. She closed her eyes, recalling that only days ago she was embracing him and kissing him, feeling the heat of his skin, the damp pressure of his mouth and the knowledgeable touch of his hands. It was easy to summon up the look in his eyes as he held her and the sweaty scent of his skin.

"He wasn't that old; only thirty-one." she told him through stiff lips.

Her body moved with his as he twisted to closer examine the headstone.

"Oh! He was younger than I am now. I've always thought of his as old man Donaghmore. I first found this when I was twelve and it became a week-long obsession to find out who he had been. Dad said he did the same thing at my age. C'mon, let's go back to the house. I don't want you to catch a chill."

She turned in the circle of his arms, loving the warmth of his body and the warmth of the smile he was giving her. Standing on her toes, she brushed his lips, her feeling of loss receding.

"Please don't treat me like a china doll, I'm no different than I was yesterday before I told you. Please, Jared."

He gave her a little shake of his head, "I can only promise to try, love. You will have to excuse me if I sometimes get carried away."

"Good God, Jared, I don't speak to you for a week and you get yourself engaged." a new male voice broke into their embrace.

Turning their heads, they looked at the distinguished looking man of average height who grasped the iron pickets of the fence to lean toward them, only a few feet distance. He was grinning with delight, his pale blue eyes going from one face to the other. Jared slid his arms from Riana and she stepped away guiltily.

"Dad!" Jared burst out, "I wasn't expecting you!"

David Thorpe, the Earl of Ranleigh straightened and shoved one hand his pocket, a gesture in common with his son.

"What? You ring me to tell me you're getting married in less than a month and you expect me to sit on my hands until the event? If you think that, you don't know your old Dad very well, do you?"

They embraced over the low iron fence, and with his hands still on his father's arms, Jared glanced back at Riana before speaking.

"Oh, I knew you'd come, if only to check her out. But I expected it might take a couple of days, not hours. Is Marianne and her tribe on the way as well?"

"But of course. We had a rather long discussion about this last night."

His eyes were on Riana as he spoke, silently assessing and Riana guessed that he might be a good business man who carefully studied those he met. He continued to watch her as Jared drew her to his side.

"Dad, please meet my fiancée, Mrs. Riana....God Riana, I don't know your middle name. I'm embarrassed." he gave a nervous laugh.

She took the hand his father extended, "Riana Clare." She offered to Jared even as she smiled at his father, "I'm very pleased to meet you, do I call you My Lord?"

He laughed, "Good Lord, no. Dad seems most appropriate. You have a last name, girl?"

"Ingram."

He continued to hold her hand, "Jared did say 'Mrs.'. You are still married?"

Jared put his arm around her and drew her close, "Riana is a widow. She's a guest at the Abbey with her mother. Her mother is Mrs. Wigmore, Daniel Wigmore's widow."

"Danny Wigmore? I've downed more than a pint or two with him until he saw fit to move to Canada." he paused, frowning, "How did he do there?"

She now knew why he was asking, "He did very well, sir. But he was killed in a plane crash, along with my husband, three years ago. It was his own company plane."

He nodded slowly, "Yes, of course. He was at sixes and sevens here. And how is your mother? I had a small crush on her at one time."

"She's well and pleased to be back here again."

"Her mother worked at the Abbey once, yes?"

"Yes, but Mom had never been inside so she took the opportunity when she found it."

"And what do you think of that great pile of old stone?"

"It's beautiful."

"Well, at least the bits the public sees." his smile vanished, "And now the granddaughter of one of our maids is marrying my son. How is that?"

"I love her Dad." Jared interjected.

"Ah, but does she love you or Riverton Abbey?"

Riana stiffened with indignation, but Jared drew her closer to his side and she felt swift resentment in him.

"She loves me Dad, I have no doubt of it. None at all."

"Well, my boy, you must excuse me if I have many. Only a week ago, you were dating that little actress."

Riana looked up at Jared with shock and he gave her a rueful shrug before turning his attention again to his father.

"It came as rather a shock to me, too, Dad, but there you have it. I had to convince her to marry me."

"Could have been a ruse."

"It could have, but she has more reasons for not marrying me than for marrying me."

Riana had seen that sceptical brow lift on Jared's face, "Really? Well, Mrs. Ingram, you are going to have to convince me as well. And worse, his over-protective sister, Marianne."

"And if you do not want me to marry Jared, you are both going to have to convince *me*." She retorted, instantly regretting her words.

But Lord Ranleigh smiled slightly, "Bravo, Mrs. Ingram. I did not see that coming." he gave two rather cynical claps of his hands.

"Dad, I have to take Riana back to the house. I don't want her to catch a chill," Jared told his father in a cool tone, "so If you will excuse us for now, I will talk to you later in your study."

The older man nodded and stepped back from the fence, but Riana felt his eyes on them as they made their way back to the house.

Jared had insisted that she take a nap, battling her resistance by kissing her back into his bed. She gave herself up to his touch and his kisses then fell asleep snuggled into his back, smiling and complete as she surrendered to sleep. Her dreams were a jumble of faces and sensations; fear, anger, confusion, Jared and his father, Kieran and Daria, her mother and Ken. There was love, too. The intense love for Kieran that made her body pulse, the warm love for Jared that made her wish for children, love she had had for Ken that did not come even close to what she felt for the other two men, and whose face was fading. She struggled to wake, not wanting these unfettered dreams.

Chapter 14

Riana woke suddenly to the sound of thunder and rain spattering on the windows. The day that had started so beautifully had degenerated into a rainstorm. For a quick moment, she wanted her mother; she wanted to be at home in her own house in Vancouver, away from this place that had changed her life and her thoughts. She wanted to die in peace, wanted to not have to think about a wedding, or the men, or live in a different country and her death in a different country.

But the moments of self-pity were quickly gone as she knew she had things that must be done and she got out of bed and gathered her clothes off the floor to dress. She was brushing her hair when Jared came in to check on her and he looked annoyed to see her out of bed. He opened his mouth to speak, but she shook her hair brush at him.

"Don't say it." she threatened, "Nothing will get done if I stay in bed all day and besides, I don't like staying in bed, there will be enough of that too soon."

His shoulders relaxed and he grinned, "You just don't like being alone in bed." he retorted, then more seriously, "I had a long talk with Dad. He is convinced now that you don't want me for just my house."

She regarded him calmly enough, "You told him, didn't you?"

"I had to, Riana. He will be your family, too, you know. It is his right. Marianne and her husband, Drew will also have to be told."

"Does everybody have to know?" she demanded of the ceiling.

"Those that need to know, yes." he crossed the room to her and gathered her to him, kissing first her forehead then her nose, "I've come to take you to the attics. Dad said he didn't know exactly where the boxes were, but there is what he calls 'fancy material' up there somewhere. He's very pleased that you are at least willing to look at what there is. He likes your dolls as well. In fact he was very impressed with them."

"Guess he thinks I'm not after your money?" she teased.

"You wouldn't be after much then, would you? His exact words were, 'well at least she knows how to work' and suggested that you can take one end of the mews to set up a workshop."

"Really?" she gasped, "How nice of him."

He jiggled the arms that held her, "You are accepted. I think he likes you. For myself, I love you."

She kissed his stubbled chin, wondering just when he had last shaved.

The attics of Riverton Abbey had been fitted with electricity, but the bare bulbs that hung from the ceiling were old incandescent, a couple of which had burned out. But the many windows made up for the lack of light bulbs. Jared turned on a switch that did give plenty of light. Riana stood by the stairs, looking around in silent wonder at all the things stored there. Jared had told her there was a lot of old junk, but it was so much more; old furniture, some of it broken some discarded for being out of fashion, boxes upon boxes upon boxes, paintings covered with old sheets, some not, old toys, old bicycles, old trunks. One wall was taken over with filing cabinets that spanned hundreds of years, wooden cabinets and metal cabinets, each drawer meticulously labelled. There were a dozen armoires spanning decades upon decades, some in good repair, some not that vied for space with hat racks, several ratty stuffed animals or their heads, vases and dusty porcelain figurines.

"Riana." Jared's voice put her in motion, "Over here, a box labelled 'Material'."

He saw the expression on her face and sat back on his heels, his features softening, "You need to explore a little?"

"May I?"

"I have spent so many hours up here that I know where almost everything is. Tell me what you'd like to see."

"Why would you spend so much time up here?"

He gave her a little snigger, "I was a very skinny and spotty teenager. Kids didn't care who my father was, or that I had a title. I was just that skinny, geeky Thorpe kid who wore thick spectacles and couldn't speak to a girl without stuttering."

"Wow, you have changed, haven't you?"

"The business I'm in helps a good deal as well." He continued, "Now, tell me what you fancy."

She answered immediately, "Paintings."

He spread his arms to encompass all within sight, "Paintings. I have paintings."

He crossed the floor to the first standing pile of covered paintings, "So what are you looking for?"

She knew she couldn't tell him that she was looking for paintings with the single letter 'K'.

"Something from the 1800's I guess." she paused to distract him from any questions, "There is so much stuff up here."

He was peeking under a dusty sheet, "Its generations and generations of Thorpe junk. We used a good deal of it when we were preparing to open this as a B and B, all the guest rooms have genuine Thorpe antiques. It was my mother's project and she was very proud of what she accomplished. She wanted all the staterooms to have antiques rather than more modern furniture."

"She was right, wasn't she?"

"Dead on. Look, here we are, nineteenth century."

She crossed the floor to where he was kneeling, "How do you know that?"

"Simple. When Mum was choosing antiques, she had a museum curator come and date the paintings as best he could, just in case she needed to use some more. Early or late?"

"Early." She told him from her spot behind him.

"Righto."

He flipped through the elaborate frames, without comment, and she watched, seeing more landscapes than she ever wanted to see again, until she stopped him at a landscape of the arching bridge and the familiar grove beyond, with just a bare hint of the gazebo.

"That one."

He pulled it out and first looked at the painting, the turned it over to quickly assess the back.

"No artist name on this one. Oh wait. If you squint your eyes, you can see a faint 'K' in this bed of flowers."

Riana held her breath. Kieran's work. He had breathed on that old cracked paint, had carefully applied each stroke of paint.

"There's a landscape in your room with the same signature." She commented, hoping he heard nothing in her voice.

"Not bad, either. Shall I take it out? You can have it where you like."

"No. I was just curious. Isn't it the same bridge that's outside?"

"It's been renovated several times, but yes, it's the same bridge. You can see it from my sitting room."

"I know."

He was once again rifling through the paintings, and stopped, his back going very stiff.

"What the bloody hell!" he burst out in a low voice.

"Jared?"

Without answering, he pulled out an unframed and unfinished painting, turning it to get more light on the surface.

"God, Riana, this looks just like you."

For a moment she thought she might faint and on shaky legs she went closer to see what he was holding. It was her, she knew without question, just as she knew the raised lace collar of the yellow and white gown was scratchy on her neck and the yellow gloves were a little too tight. The figure was complete, although there was a vaguely frightened expression on the face, but it was her face, even to the odd way one of her eyebrows lifted at the end, but the background gazebo and the fall-coloured leaves were barely sketched. Looking closer, she saw the faint 'K' becoming part of the folds of the lace-covered skirt. It saddened her to see it had never been finished. Jared balanced it against another stack.

"I'm keeping this one. I can't believe how much it looks like you. Like you sat for it just yesterday. Doesn't say who painted it, 'tho."

Somehow she was relieved to know he had not seen the initial incorporated into the lace overdress. As he returned to his task, Riana was thankful that he was not watching her until her breathing returned to normal. Blindly she chose a painting of two horses with the bridge and glade in the background.

"I like that." She pointed.

He pulled it out and looked at the back, "Shelby Thorpe. He painted? I never knew that. And here's a date '1853'."

"He had talent. Are there more of his?"

The check was done quickly, "None here anyway, but I can keep looking."

She was too ill at ease to continue, "No, not right now." she put her hand on his shoulder, "The fabric is more important right now and you have already found the box."

This was a box of extraordinary fabrics in long lengths. She found delicate laces in three different colours, several lengths of old-fashioned brocade and some pretty pale blue crepe embroidered with darker blue dainty flowers. A smaller piece was blue Alencon lace embroidered with sequins and pearls and this she pulled out to measure on herself.

"I love this. And this."

A paler darker blue taffeta that seemed to change colour with the shifting of the light, once called watered taffeta. Jared tugged out the embroidered crepe.

"This for Gracie."

"Gracie?" she asked, catching it as he handed it to her.

"My niece. Marianne's daughter. She's going to be a flower girl, yes?"

"Seriously?" she chided, "Flower girl? Ring bearer too?"

"David, of course, Charlie is barely walking so he won't do."

"Jared, I've had a huge wedding....."

"But I have not and I want one now."

"Please no. I wanted something quiet with just us and close family." She looked around blindly, "I need to talk to my mother."

"She went into the village to have lunch with Emma. She said she'd be back later in the afternoon. You don't think she is going to agree with you about the wedding? She's very excited about it."

"I know. You were at breakfast with her. Did she once stop talking about the wedding?"

He laughed as he rose to his feet, "No, she didn't, but I got a few ideas from her. Like this."

He reached into his pocket and pulled out a small box, the velvet worn with age. He had to struggle to open the lid and as he did so, he gave her a wicked, secretive glance. In a moment, he was holding a ring out to her.

"Hope you don't mind a family relic. If you don't like it, I will buy you one that you do like. It belonged to my great-great-great grandmother Julia."

It had been well worn; a band of beautifully intricate bright gold, carved with leaves and flowers that accented five pointed medallions holding perfect, pink topazes, the points worn smooth by usage. He caught her hand and slid the ring on her finger, tsking impatiently.

"Too big."

"But beautiful. I love old things like this."

"So your mother told me while you were having a nap. But if you don't like it."

She snatched her hand away from his light grip, covering it protectively with her other one.

"Don't you dare." She threatened with a happy smile as she held it up to the light.

"No diamonds?"

"No diamonds." She affirmed.

"Riana Ingram, will you marry me? I'll get down on this dirty floor if you like."

She reached up to kiss him, "You took your time asking. Did you just assume I would marry you?"

He gave her a long, deep kiss and when he raised his head, his eyes were cloudy with desire, "I hoped you would, especially after we started planning, and I told my whole family, but I thought I should make it official. You haven't said yes." He reminded her.

She threw her arms around his neck and rained little kisses on his throat and chin, "Yes, yes, oh, yes!"

She pulled slowly away from him and went to a round, dusty window to more closely examine her ring, smiling as the five stones glimmered in the rain-dark light. As she turned her hand, she caught a movement out of the corner of her eye and looking down, saw the too-familiar figure standing on the arching bridge. The head lifted and she could feel unseen eyes on her beckoning silently. Holding her breath in anticipation of the usual pain, she looked over at Jared to see him retrieving the fabric she had dropped in her surprise at the presentation of her new ring. She had to leave. She knew the past was rushing forward.

"Jared, I have to go." She said breathlessly.

He folded the fabric over his arm, "Go where?"

She said the first thing that came into her mind, "To the bathroom."

Chapter 15

Kieran was bending over her anxiously. She was lying on a bench in the kitchen area, a kitchen far different from what it would be in the future. The bench was at right angles to the huge fireplace and it warmed her, drying the nightgown that was still damp in places. She struggled to sit up, but he held her down.

"Why must you always to out to that place, and in the rain? You are wet to the skin."

She looked up at him, "I thought I saw somebody..." she paused searching for a plausible explanation, "digging in the park."

The explanations sounded lame to her ears, but the others seemed to accept it.

"No doubt a poacher digging a trap." Kieran told her, "He might have hurt you. Damned cheek digging close enough to the house to be seen."

He was carelessly dressed, as if he had simply covered himself to leave the bedroom. His shirt was open halfway down his chest, the cuffs unbuttoned and hanging loose from the sleeves of his banyan. His breeches were wrinkled from their time spent in a careless pile on the floor, and the knee button on his left leg was completely gone. His dark, curling hair was in a jumble all over his head, from his exertions in the night, falling close to his eyes.

Watching her, he curved his hand around her hip, caressing the covered flesh. It warmed her soul but she still shivered from chill.

"You must return to your room. May I assist you?"

Smith hurried forward with a rough wool cloak and draped it around Riana's shoulders as she rose from the bench.

"Ye must be decent, Miss." she said to Riana, eyeing her with silent censure, "Shall I have some tea and bread sent up?"

"Thank-you Smith, that would be wonderful."

"You will take to your bed for the entire day." Kieran announced as they started toward the door.

"Alone!" Smith called after them.

Riana slept for most of the day, feeling the beginnings of a cold threaten. She knew Susan checked in on her from time to time, but for the most part she was left alone, for which she was grateful as she escaped the realities of her existence here in sleep.

It was dark and she was wide awake, yet trying to sleep when Kieran slipped into her room carrying a bottle of wine and two glasses, dressed as he had been the night before, except that his breeches were black. He put the glasses and wine on the table by the fire and poured the glasses full, only glancing at her as he poured, watching to see her struggle to a sitting position.

He joined her, putting the full glasses on the bedside table and fluffing a pillow to make a backrest as he sat on the bed beside her. He passed her one of the glasses and she tasted the red wine, loving the flavour of it.

"We must speak of this." he told her before sipping his own, "I have given this much thought. I do not necessarily believe all you have said, but much of it has a ring of truth, and I am willing to believe because," he looked down at her to make sure she was looking at him, "I love you and need to believe you or I will go insane from the madness of it."

"Consider my side of it." She said in a voice she fought to keep calm.

"I have tried. It is so; you are from a time in the future, so I have been long in my grave, yet feel this."

Without warning, he reached over and pinched her shoulder. She reacted by drawing away from him and spilling a little of her wine.

"Ow! Why did you do that? It hurt!"

"To convince you and to convince myself that we are here and we are in this time."

"I *know* I'm in this time. I *know* I am out of place. Surely you must have seen that. I'm lost here, Kieran. I'm lost and I want to go home where I'm dying, yet I want to, no I need to stay here with you." his marvellous eyes were silently watching her, waiting, "But sometimes we have no choices in our lives."

"You said I brought you here. How did that happen?"

She did not answer right away, "I saw your grave. You were buried in the churchyard here at Riverton Abbey. You died on October 29th. 'Murdered Most Foul' your headstone says. Somebody planted a yellow rose bush on your grave. And your portrait of me is still in the attic here, but you never finished it."

"Here? Not Ireland? Murdered?" there was a thoughtful silence, "The 29th? That is only two days from now." another silence, but one where he watched her closely, "Yet I brought you here?"

"Your ghost, Kieran. You have been haunting Riverton Abbey, yet nobody knew who was haunting, man or woman. But I saw you. I saw you the day I arrived, standing in the trees looking so... so sad. Something made me go to you....I think it was the fact you were signalling me. Anyway, I went and found myself here, still at Riverton Abbey, in this time and with you."

He looked up to the darkness of the ceiling, "One finds it difficult to think of the actuality of one's grave."

"Well, seeing it nearly killed me. And there is a man there who loves me...."

"I love you." he told her tersely, "Does he wish to marry you?"

It was a minute before she answered, "Yes and soon, since I have little time left there."

She saw his Adam's apple bob several times as he swallowed, "Do you love him?"

She did not hesitate or lie, "Yes, I do. He's a different man in a different time and he's a good man."

"Who is he?"

"The son of the 10th Earl of Ranleigh. He is Jared Thorpe, the Viscount of Whipford."

"So you will be marrying a man far richer than I."

Amusement sparkled in her eyes as she studied him, "In truth, I am richer than he. I have a world wide business."

He looked more than a little skeptical, "Doing what?"

"I make dolls. Very special dolls, for which people pay a lot of money."

Kieran jerked his head, "So he marries you for your money."

"He docs not know, yet. He's marrying me because he loves me."

Kieran uncharacteristically, caught the corner of his lip and chewed on it for a time. The ticking of the clock was the only sound in the room.

"I would marry you if you promise to stay."

The eyes that looked down at her again, were oddly shy as if expecting rejection. She smiled up at him, sipped her wine and put her free hand on his waist.

"I wish I could promise. But you have to promise not to die in two days and be the cause of ruined lives. That's why you, or rather, your dead self brought me here. A Wigmore to prevent a Wigmore curse, brought upon by you. In effect, you need me to save you from cursing my family."

"It is too much to fathom, Riana. But god, I love you so much I am willing to believe anything that comes out of your mouth."

"And I want you to live."

"Would you take me over him?"

She did not give it a second thought, "Yes. But I can do that only if you don't fight that stupid, idiotic duel. Who ever thought that was a good way to settle a dispute, anyway?"

He took a long swallow of his wine, "Duelling is illegal in England."

She raised her glass to her mouth, but did not drink, "So you have already told me. Not that it made any difference at all. You duelled and you died."

The horror of the thought of it dried her throat and she too took a long swallow of the wine.

"Please don't do it, Kieran."

"I cannot see any reason that I would duel with a mere squire, and even less reason to duel with a drunken sot."

It was hardly the answer she wanted, but she did not wish to argue further with him. He was here in her bed, sitting comfortably, drinking wine with her. A hundred other more pleasurable possibilities crossed her mind and the way his foot was touching her foot that was still under the covers, was deliciously insinuating. But his next words cooled the rising warmth within her.

"Has Donaghmore survived? I would hate for it to be lost."

"I don't know. I don't even know where Donaghmore is."

He lifted an eyebrow, "Ireland." the corner of his mouth curved in a half smile, "Donegal. Fifteen miles from the town of Donegal. Donaghmore is on Donegal bay."

"You miss home?"

"A great deal. I would very much like you to see it. No, to be there, with me." he looked up at the ceiling, "It's not as grand as Riverton Abbey, but t'is a large house, with plenty of room for children. I have my breeding stock there, and I make a fine living raising my horses. You would want for nothing, Riana. And I promise to adore you for the rest of my life."

The hand she had lifted to take another sip of wine began to tremble so much that he gently took the glass from her fingers, setting it on the night table beside him. She was unable to take her eyes off his face as he did that simple task.

"What are you saying, Kieran."

He placed his own glass on the table and slid down on the bed until they were face to face. The rustling, sliding sound of silk filled her ears as his face filled her vision. He was so close to her she smelled the wine on his breath. His calloused fingers stroked her face

"I want to marry you and take you home to Ireland. I do not want to even wait to marry in Ireland. I want to marry you as soon as is legal to do so here."

"Holy crap!" she breathed, unable to think of any other comment.

He chuckled, "Holy crap? That is your reply to my effort to make an honest woman of you?"

Her expression was much more serious as she stroked the tips of her fingers along the rough stubble on his cheek.

"You just told me what you wanted, that's all."

He rolled his head partially away from her, looking up at the ceiling again.

"I have never done this before, Riana, so forgive me if I lack propriety. Perhaps this will do."

He caught her in his arms and rolled until he was off the bed and she barely on it. He threw back the covers and let her sit on the edge of the mattress, and while she was struggling with the nightgown to sit, he was buttoning his shirt very properly and smoothing the tangles of curls back from his face. She was smiling down at him, her hands resting on the mattress as he moved himself into a kneeling position. He took one of her hands and enveloped it between his own.

"Mrs. Riana Ingram, will you do me the very great honour of becoming my wife? I promise I will love you more each day and love you to the end of my life." He opened his hands like a clam shell and kissed the back of her hand before closing them together again.

The face that turned up to her was half-smiling and expectant. She sat with his warm hands in her lap, her heart pounding so hard she heard it in her own ears. Her mouth was so dry she was certain she would never speak again.

The single word that she managed to produced shocked them both.

"Why?"

"Why?" he repeated, dumfounded.

She swallowed, wishing she could have another mouthful of wine, "Why do you want to marry me? You think I'm a little crazy, don't you? Are you forgetting that I told you I'm from the future, are you forgetting you don't really believe me." he opened his mouth, but she held up her free hand, "Oh, I know you said you believed everything I said, but even to my own ears it sounds like a pack of lies, and I'm living it."

She slid off the bed until she was knee to knee with him, pulling her hand from his grasp so that she could place a hand on either side of his face.

"I love you Kieran. I love you!" she repeated fiercely, "And that is why I want you to be certain that in the future you will never have cause to regret anything. Kieran, I am not completely certain that you are not something my brain has conjured up to cope with my illness. How horrible would that make God if that is what's happening!"

His lips drew back from his teeth as he shook her hands off his face, "I am as real as you are. Look, cut me and I will bleed, burn me and I will blister..."

"Shoot you and you will die. Either way, Kieran, you will be gone. You will die the day after tomorrow and you will be lost to me no matter what."

He flattened his hands on the tops of his thighs, dropping his head so that they were forehead to forehead.

"If I do not die in two days, you would marry me?"

She saw his eyes so close, the pupils large from the dim light, "If you survive until October 30th....Halloween at home...I will marry you. I will marry you and stay here in this time with you, always."

Kieran lifted his hands to curve around her shoulders, drawing her close for his warm and tender kiss. As she leaned into him, wanting more, he rose suddenly and easily, putting a space between them.

"I will now become a gentleman. I will stay out of your bed.... and you out of mine...until we are properly married. I will not dally with you until them."

She gave a choke of laughter, "Dally?"

He smiled with joy, "Dally. And I will not do it."

"Is that so?"

She reached for him, for the buttons on his breeches, feeling under the fabric a stirring, but he caught her wrists, holding them behind her back as he placed his face close to her.

"You will not tempt me, wicked woman, for I am resolved. But," he allowed himself a brief peck on her lips, "keep in mind what is in store for you on our wedding night."

His low, intimate tone sent shivers down her back and he stepped away from her, sliding insinuating fingers along her hips as he released her. He left her, the wine and the half-empty glasses as he sauntered to the door. He opened the door and gave her a jaunty salute before leaving the room entirely. She felt like throwing something after him, but refrained.

As Susan dressed her the next day, she spotted the wine and the glasses on the night table and gave Riana a sly, knowing look as she tied the embroidered garters snugly to Riana's legs.

"Drinkin' alone, Mu'um? Not a good thing t'be doin'."

"Don't play dumb with me, Susan. You probably knew what was going on before I did."

Susan did not lift her head, but Riana saw her cheek plump in a smile.

"Lord Donaghmore is very clear." she lowered Riana's skirt and petticoat, and rose, "It be a terrible day, so there will be not paintin' done t'day."

"It's not much of an answer, Susan."

"But all y'll get from me."

The day was drizzly, of that there was no doubt, yet despite feeling the onset of a cold, Riana felt the need to escape the house. Wearing a warm pelisse of scarlet Merino wool and a scarlet hat with a turned up brim, and half-boots on her feet, Riana tucked her hands into a white fur muff and left the house. Her thoughts were confused; Kieran's disbelief and his proposal, her own desire to live in two places at once with two different men, her entire confusion about the lives she was unwittingly living. She walked with her head down along a walking path most used by the family and wished her mother was here to consult with her. But what would her mother say about this confusing state in which she found herself? Could she have changed any of it? Perhaps not fallen in love with either or both men? She felt most guilty about Jared, for it was with him she knew their time was limited. But would staying here with Kieran change the length of time on this earth?

So concentrated on her own thoughts was she that she did not hear the sound of approaching hooves until a horse was dragged to a stop before her. She looked up in bewilderment to see Regis Wigmore leering down at her from his saddle. He put one arm across the pommel, his fingers tapping the skirt, his long, thick-lipped face waiting.

"Well, well, if it is not the guest without a memory. Is that the truth? Come, Madam, you can tell me, for I would love a secret such as yours. Who are you in truth?"

She stepped two paces back from him and his jittery roan horse, "I am Mrs. Riana Ingram, and you are in my way. Please move aside to let me pass."

He simply smiled, revealing square yellowed teeth that had hints of decay, and were rather intimidating, but she stood her ground, not taking her eyes off him, not trusting him, her own ancestor. He kneed the horse closer to her so that it's shoulder touched hers. Still watching her, he dismounted, and she still did not shy away from him as he walked under the animal's head toward her, stopping to stand over her, slapping the reins across the palm of one gloved hand.

"Together, we two can accomplish more. I do not know just what is your game, but I do know you have one. There is nobody in this district who knows you, nobody is missing you, as you claim. So there is no other explanation. But know this, Madam," he raised a gloved finger, "there is nothing in that house that is for you. There is no money. Ashley Thorpe...Lord," he lifted his lip in a sneer, "Ranleigh has not a sixpence to scratch with, so you'll get nothing there. And that sod-kicking Irish paddy is no better off, I have no doubt. We two should join and bring down our fine, high lord, if you are not too mawkish about the lot of them now."

Riana was appalled to the point of silence by the words coming from the man's mouth. Ancestor or no ancestor, he was a ghastly man, and as he reached out to her, she pulled one hand from her muff and hit him with all her might, not knocking him down, but at least causing him to stumble backwards a few paces. He moved quickly, his face twisted in fury and his own hand automatically striking out at her. She fell backwards on to the gravel path, at the same time hearing an incoherent shout of pure rage and the sound of running feet on gravel.

She was struggling to lift herself to her elbows in time to see Kieran, his face darkened and twisted by his wrath, strike at Wigmore with all his might, knocking the man flat on his back. He watched only briefly to make sure his foe was down, before turning to Riana with a still heaving chest, to lift her to her feet. His mistake was turning his back on an enemy; an enemy who jumped to his feet and walloped him over the head with the butt of a pistol. Kieran staggered, almost dropping Riana back to the ground, before swinging to face his attacker, knees bent in a kind of assault mode, fists clenched.

Riana at first scrambled out of the way, then paused waiting as the men circled each other warily.

"I will kill you for that." Kieran hissed between clenched teeth.

It was happening, she realized suddenly. She was the reason for the stupid duel, she was the reason for the curse and the haunting. From the corner of her eye she saw Lord Ranleigh running toward them, followed by Daria and by the butler, but for the moment she had no interest in any of them. Kieran was her sole focus, Kieran and the man with whom he danced a fighting dance.

She snagged the tail of Kieran's coat as he moved passed her, the fabric slid from her fingers, but distracted him, so that when Wigmore lashed out at him with a small dagger, it caught the side of his hand, cutting him deeply. Kieran did not so much as wince, ignoring or not feeling the blood that began to drip.

"You strike a woman! A woman? And my woman!" Kieran hissed, still circling.

Wigmore gave him a rather feral smile, "You believe she is yours? D'you know anything about her? She is in league with me."

"No!" both Kieran and Riana shouted together.

The circling stopped abruptly as Kieran stood still at his full height, "I challenge you, sir, with pistols at tomorrow's first light."

"No!" Riana shouted at him, feeling on the periphery of the strange battle, "You can't Kieran. You can't."

He gave no indication that he heard her voice, so focused was he on the other man.

Ashley reached them after too long a time and Riana held out beseeching hands to him.

"He can't fight this man! It will ruin him. Please stop it."

For all that the man was a fool, he nevertheless assessed the situation, and even thought, or perhaps because of the great amounts of money he owed the man, he raised his own pistol and calmly shot Regis Wigmore through the back of his calf. The man dropped like a stone, and for the first time, Riana feared for her own existence. Regis Wigmore could not die childless or she would not be born. In a rage, Kieran swung toward his cousin's husband, breathing heavily, hands still clenched into fists.

"Ranleigh! My business!" he shouted.

The fallen Regis Wigmore was in pain but not vanquished. He lifted himself up slightly, grinning wolfishly through his pain.

"Sir, I accept your challenge. I will meet you on the morrow at the glade. Shall we have pistols at first light?"

His words galvanized Riana and she went to Kieran and grabbed the lapels of his coat, shaking him sharply once.

"Kieran!" she hissed in a low voice.

"He will kill you! You know he will, and all of this will be useless."

He was shamed by her words. His only thought had been to protect her, and in doing so he had endangered himself and the future. His shoulders relaxed and he bent his head to her forehead.

"He was hurting you."

"He will kill you." She reminded him.

She flung her arms around him, holding him tightly, "Apologise. Run away in the night. Murder him....no, don't do that or I will never be born and all this will be a waste of time.. Do anything to live, Kieran. You have to live...for me."

"There is no honour in running away, Riana. I love you, you have the life I want now, but I cannot run away."

For only the second time in her life, Riana struck another man, causing him to stagger only a little and not fall.

"I hate you, Kieran Gilmartin, for getting yourself killed." She spat at him before turning and running to the house.

She did not sleep that night and she locked her door against the one man she most wanted to see, but she could not face his morning duel and the loss of him. God, why did men have such fragile egos that they felt honour bound to get themselves killed for such a stupid thing? It might have been talked away, maybe even the exchange of one of Donaghmore's famous horses might be used to salve honour. Late in the night, she felt the knob rattle on the door, but she dug herself deeper into her covers, pulling the pillow over her head in order to be deaf to everything around her. She did not want to hear the moment of the death of her great love. She did not want to know when the joy of her life was taken from her. For a brief moment during that night, she blamed herself for not being stronger in her desire to keep him from fighting. Maybe if she had let him into her bed he might have forgotten what he was about to do, and now it was too late. As much as she tried to stay awake all night, sleep overcame her and she slept without waking and with terrible dreams.

The sun was shining in her eyes and she woke to the sound of wagon wheels across cobblestones. Gasping aloud, almost a scream, she tossed herself out of the bed, catching up her robe as she crossed the room to the door, fright coursing through every vein of her body. She flung open the door and all but ran into Kieran who was leaning against the opposite wall, fully dressed with arms crossed, smiling at her.

"His wound was infected and he called off the duel. He will recover, no doubt, since you are still here with me. Are you ready to go back to Ireland with me?"

She was speechless as she flung herself at him, lifting her face to the descending kiss he was offering.

Epilogue

Clare left her bedroom, her eyes now dry knowing she must now focus on her three year old grandson Carver and his father Jared. She knew she should be happy that Riana's partial tumour had miraculously shrunk somewhat, enough to give her a life and a child with Jared. But when the tumour started growing again, it grew with a vengeance. Three weeks from when it had begun growing again to the death of her.

She halted in the passage long enough for a deep breath that helped dull the pain, for after two weeks it continued unabated. Running footsteps made her smile and the shouting three year old voice called out.

"Nana, where are you?"

The voice filled her with joy. She still had a part of her daughter left, and she loved the man for giving him to both of them. Carver flew around the corner and nearly knocked her over in his race. She caught him up in her arms and kissed him roundly, seeing his mother's eyes in his father's face.

"Nana, I looked an' looked." he complained loudly.

"I'm sorry, my love, I was having a lie-down."

"Daddy went to his room 'gain. He hurted himse'f I think."

Yes, of course, Clare thought, he is hurt, much more deeply than she would have expected from a proper English aristocrat. He had expected Riana to live but a few months and when those months extended into years, he had relaxed, thinking, hoping that all would be well. Truth be told, she had hoped the same herself. Riana had stopped taking pills and chemotherapy when she discovered she was pregnant, and painful as it was, gave birth to a remarkably healthy baby boy. Now she was suddenly gone and he was bereft.

"Let's take a ride around the mews on your pony, shall we. I think he might be feeling lonely too."

Carver nodded enthusiastically, his tight blond curls bobbing around his face. He took his grandmother's hand and walked only a few paces before stopping.

"Nana, can we go see Mumma in the gall'ry?"

She did not want to see Riana's painted, happy face, but if Carver needed to see her, then she must go. It was a short distance in measure, but much farther from her own desire to see it. And the gallery had been Carver's favorite room from the time he was barely walking.

She pushed open the door and switched on the lights, glancing quickly at the small, unfinished portrait by the door, painted in the Regency Era, of an unknown woman who looked remarkably like Riana. It had been Riana's favorite. Hand in hand, she walked to the end of the gallery with the little boy until it was he who halted. There sat Riana in regal glory in a flowing nude coloured chiffon evening gown spread around her feet, with a modest v-neck, an embellished waist and set off by a hundred and twenty-year-old necklace of pink diamonds with matching dangle earrings. Carver was leaning against her knee as so many of his ancestors before him, but unlike them, Carver was barely two then, dressed, oddly enough in a miniature uniform of the Peninsular War. Riana, far more than Jared, had been anxious for this portrait to be done, and had had David, her father-in-law as a staunch ally in this endeavor. Jared had yet to have his portrait painted.

After a few minutes of gazing at his mother, Carver was on the move again, hurrying down the stairs leaving his grandmother behind, excited at the prospect of riding his pony. As they came to the entry hall, Arthur McGrath hurried across the floor to them holding a package. She smiled at him for they now had an unexpected fondness for one another, often having to pretend they had not spent a passionate night together.

"Clare! A package came for you from a solicitor in the village, you know, the old one, Gould's."

She gave him a curious look as she turned the package over in her hands, seeing inside a large plastic bag with a white label stating her name and Riverton Abbey, the crackling, very yellowed paper-wrapped package, tied with old string and a wax seal, faded now to a dull brown with the scrawling, faded to near invisibility, hand writing on it.

"To:
Mrs. Clare Wigmore
@ Riverton Abbey,
To be delivered on the death of Riana, Viscountess of Whipford"

"What is this?" she demanded of her sometime lover.

"I don't know, and neither do they. The man that delivered it said it has been in the office so long that it was only by accident that he found it when he was shifting old filing cabinets in a storage room. He brought it straight away. Are you going to open it?"

"Not immediately. I promised Carver a ride on his pony."

Despite her protest, Arthur was able to see the sudden anxiety on Clare's face and put his hand on her arm.

"I'll take the lad out. You go into my office and open it." He told her kindly.

Slowly Clare made her way to Arthur's office, smoothing her hand over the plastic as she denied herself the pleasure of opening it immediately. She entered the office and sat at the guest's side of the desk and opened the plastic bag. She pulled out the squarish package, mindful of the dry paper, not wanting to damage it, her mind swirling and whirling with curiosity and just a little fear. It was very old, but just how old was unknown, but certainly far older than Riana. The theme song to an old television series, 'Twilight Zone' flashed through her head as she tugged gently at the string. The old hemp pulled apart in her fingers.

She was more careful with the paper as she separated the edges of the wrappings, hissing a little with the paper separated at a crease. After a few minutes, she was looking down at a page on which the faded handwriting was so familiar she felt tears fill her eyes. Tenderly, she put the tips of her fingers on the old paper, fearing her mere touch would destroy the words written on it before she had a chance to read them. Hitching her chair closer to the desk, and blinking back the threatening tears, she began reading starting with the engraved printing on the top of the heavy linen paper.

"Riana Gilmartin, Baroness of Donaghmore
Donaghmore House
Derrybeg, County Donegal
Ireland"
"July 23, 1856

"Dear Mom,

Hope this does not come too far out of the blue that it causes you a heart attack, but yes, this is me, your own daughter, Riana Clare Wigmore Ingram Gilmartin and yes I have made no mistake about the date. I am now seventy-two a mother and grandmother many times over, and have been extremely happy in my life with a man I have loved to distraction for most of it.

"I am dying now and I think it's my old brain thing come back, for it does feel like it, but in this time it is not so easily diagnosed. My husband, Kieran grieves already and seldom now lets me out of his sight. He cannot understand that I am not afraid for I have been given a second chance at a life I had never expected.

"By the time you read this, I will have long passed on, and I do know that I did marry Jared before I died, although I know no details, nor, I think, would I have wanted to know. But Jared did make me happy before we married and I am grateful for it.

"But Kieran Gilmartin was my life and my soul. We were married in the chapel at Riverton Abbey before going to Ireland in November of 1812 and I was already pregnant with our first child, Eamon Dahey who was born in July 1813.

Daragh Connal followed him in December 1814. Kieran finally got his daughter in May of 1816, Cliona Aideen. Then we had a break of three years before the twins came along, in October of 1819, Aiden Finn and his identical twin Aengus Garrick, both little hellions from birth. And finally another girl, although by this time, Cliona was well able to look after herself by this time, being the middle of four brothers, but she was happy to welcome Neave Oona in September of 1825.

"Did you know there was a curse on the Wigmore family? If history has changed, as I hope it had, you probably will not know, but there had been a curse, and the Wigmore family did not thrive in England. It was only after you moved to Canada that you and Dad become very well off and I pray that came to pass. I hope most things that were promised to me in your time actually happened.

"My wonderful Kieran died cursing the Wigmore family and regretted it, spending two hundred years haunting Riverton Abbey in the hope of finding a Wigmore descendent to break the curse. Typical British haunting. And as much as I loved Jared, I loved Kieran more and decided to stay in his time with him after the curse was lifted, but I was promised I would continue life in my own time as well. Don't ask how that worked.....I can't answer you now anyway, but I have been very happy living here in the wilds of Donegal, overlooking the ocean. My children are, for the most part, in good health and happy.

"So now comes to the reason for this letter, sent so long ago. I would very much like you to go to Donaghmore House in Donegal, just outside the village of Derrybeg. At the present time we raise fine Irish horses, and I now know more about horses than I ever wanted to know and I hope that tradition has continued after my death and Kieran's death and those of my children. And any of my thirty grandchildren.

"I would like you to know that my life with my wild Irishman has been extremely happy, and, obviously extremely fruitful. And there was more to my life besides my husband, children and horses. As well, there is something very special I would very much like you to see.

"My husband was also a very talented artist. His paintings of horses are quite famous, but he also painted a few portraits. Did the one he did of me in a yellow gown survive? I know it was still there in that other reality. Kieran has always said it was his best work, even if he didn't complete it. Enclosed in this package are a few paintings he made just for your, for just this time now and they are very like us, nearly photograph quality.

"Mom, please go to Donaghmore House, you may find it will soothe your soul as it did mine.

All My Love
Riana"

Clare dropped her hands, still holding the letter, to the desk, not knowing how to react to this old letter. Should she believe it was real? In that case, everything she believed was no longer true. She flopped back into the upholstered chair, lifting her head to look up at the plastered ceiling, incredulity swirling in her brain, yet with a little bit of faith in its truth. That somehow Riana had escaped death as she escaped her own time period was something out of a rather bad movie. That she was able to also live out her shortened life here was even more incredulous.

As she lowered her eyes to the desk again, the letter still held in her hands, she saw the inside package also wrapped in brown paper and string and she arched toward it gently setting aside the letter. The string on this package was not so fragile and when she separated the paper, a faint whiff of oil paint drifted to her nose from the pile of painted canvases that measured about eight inches by twelve inches each before her.

She did not hesitate in lifting the first. It was Riana and a very striking man with curly medium brown hair and large, striking hazel eyes; eyes that looked at her and not the artist. It was the same Riana of the unfinished portrait, a happy smile on her face as her hand reached up to cover the man's hand as it rested on her shoulder. He was dressed rather informally in a painter's smock that was loosely tied at the neck and she was in a white satin, high-waisted gown with elbow-length sleeves and swags of ribbons and roses at the hem. Her hair was drawn away from her face, leaving only little wisps of curls, held in place with fine white ribbon, and it was obvious she was pregnant. In the corner of the painting, in glaring white on the dark brown of his trousers was the single word, 'Gilmartin'. The next five were paintings of children; all of Riana's children, although the twins were in a single painting, all seemingly painted on or near their thirteenth birthdays, all beautiful children that made her smile proudly. Each painting had the name painted on the bottom left corner so she was able to put a face now to each name, and 'Gilmartin' was a bare scratch on the right corner. Not one of them even remotely resembled the grandson she knew; her precious, motherless Carver.

Carefully, she folded the paper and put the letter between two of the paintings and carried them up to her room. Once there, she placed them around the room, focusing her attention on Riana and the man who watched her so lovingly. The artist was so skillful that Riana seemed to glow with happiness.

A sound at her door made her turn away from the paintings and she was in time to see a letter slide under her door. She reacted immediately and retrieved the letter, gasping as she saw Riana's handwriting on the envelope. She tore it open, not taking the care she had with the much older paper. There was no date on the letter and the handwriting was rather shaky.

"Hi Mom,

Hope the first letter wasn't too much of a shock for you, but I hope it was informative. I hope you are not in Stonemere visiting with Uncle Rufus and Auntie Kathleen, but this letter will still get to you.

Did I have a good life in Ireland? I'm positive I did, for Kieran Gilmartin was a good man, and in all honesty, he was the love of my life, both in Ireland and here. I do love Jared, I can't imagine a life without him...not that it will ever be a problem at this date, he is everything to me, but Kieran has had my heart since that first day we arrived at Riverton Abbey when he was a ghost looking for redemption. OMG! I can't believe I actually wrote those words...ghost looking for redemption...

Well, he got it, he did not kill our horrible, smelly nasty ancestor, so the Wigmores for the most part were fairly successful here in the UK although you and Dad did succeed in the better life for which you hoped. I was promised the best in each world and that is what I got. A wonderful man here who loved me, a lovely child, my career. Life.

But I know my life was in Ireland with Kieran, so therefore, I would really like you to go there, to wherever I lived and hopefully see what my life was there. I will never know what it was, but it would give me some ease if you knew it. I only hope there is something left for you to see.

All My Love
Riana"

There was a knock on the door and Clare opened it to a freshly showered Jared, who nevertheless was dressed rather carelessly without a belt on his pants or shoes on his and his shirt only partially tucked in. Still, he looked better than he had it days. She stood back to let him in.

"You look well, Jared." She commented with a smile.

But his attention was taken by the small paintings she had forgotten she had around the room. He walked around, starting with Naeve, who even at thirteen was startlingly beautiful and ended with the portrait of Riana and her Kieran. He came to an abrupt halt when he saw it and shoved his hands into his pockets.

"My God, she looks like Riana...." he hesitated, "and like that portrait in the gallery Riana liked so much. Same woman, d'you think? Where did you get it, and those?"

"They were delivered here this morning from Gould's. Apparently it's been in their office for quite some time waiting to be delivered. So here they are." she spread her hands to encompass them.

"I love this one with the woman, it's beautiful in itself. Are there any dates on these?"

"I haven't looked." She answered honestly.

"What are you going to do with them?"

"Keep them. They might be quite valuable as a complete set. And the artist had a good deal of skill, wouldn't you say?"

"Skill?" Jared swung toward her, "The man was a fucking genius. What's this name?" he peered closely at the painted signature, "Gilmartin? Never heard of him, but god, genius! I think you're right about keeping them together. Hey, d'you notice they all kind of look like each other. Parents and children?"

"That's what I was thinking."

She watched Jared as he walked around more closely examining each small portrait. Then it came to her, and impulsively she spoke.

"Jared, I hope you don't mind, but I need to get away, just to clear my mind."

He did not look away from the paintings, "I think that's a good idea, Mum. You worked hard at the end. Let me pay for it, it's the least I can do." He looked around suddenly, "Where's Carver? He's usually with you."

"He's out with Arthur riding his pony around the stable."

"Time you made an honest man out him, you know." he said absently.

Heat flared in her cheeks, for she was familiar with his rather absent tones. It was his way of telling he knew secrets. For this time she chose to ignore him, knowing that the subject would come up again. Right now she was not prepared for that discussion. Yes, she would go to Ireland and try to find any trace she could of her daughter and that mysterious family. And she would go without doing any research beforehand; she was looking forward to pleasant surprises.

She walked to the chapel, wanting the cool peace there. Riana's fresh grave was behind the chapel, the front being filled with much older graves, but Clare swerved off the old path to walk into this part of the cemetery. She spent the better part on an hour looking, but the grave of Lord Donaghmore was not there. She smiled with satisfaction and continued on the path to the chapel.

Clare stopped the car on the verge and looked down at the town as it spread before her. She had a moment of hesitation, fearing that Donaghmore House was gone and the Gilmartin name was a long distant memory. Yet she had to forge on, because even if the house and farm was gone, she could use the internet to find what she was seeking.

To her relief she drove less than ten miles before seeing a large sign on the road, "Historic Donaghmore House Farm and Bed and Breakfast 20 miles". Hope soared through her. It was still there, and she just might be able to sleep in the house where Riana had lived happily with her husband and brood of children. She turned back onto the road, she had to check often her speeding in her eagerness to be there.

A rather discreet sign announced her arrival at Donaghmore house, a black on white painted sign close to tall stone pillars that held black iron gates that were invitingly open. Her little rented car bounced over the cattle guard and she found herself on a well-graded gravel road that curved leisurely toward an old stone house that was outlined by a stormy ocean behind it. The grounds were all one expected of a house on the Irish coast; the lawns a bright emerald green with beds and boxes and pots of bright pansies, petunias, marigolds and spicy geraniums in all possible colours

Behind white painted rail fences several horses grazed and played and ran for the joy of it. Farther passed that were sheep on a low hill, and ducks, geese and swans floated on a pretty lake surrounded by tall, luxuriant willow trees and she saw in the distance a gazebo, similar to the one at Riverton Abbey, that also had an arching foot bridge. The beauty and peace of it charmed her as she slowed to a stop before the wide old oak door.

Slowly she got out of her car, looking up at the house. It was not as large as Riverton Abbey, nor as spectacular, but it looked and felt like someone's home, down to the pairs of wellington boots that lay here and there in the little porch at the door. A woman opened the door, plump, rosy-faced with a wide, open smile, she held a broom in her hand, and looked at Clare with friendly blue eyes, standing the broom by holding its handle.

"Can I help you?"

Clare forced her eyes away from a further examination of the house. She had been planning this moment since she left England.

"I'm hoping you have a room as I have no reservation, I'm afraid." she closed her car door carefully.

"There be little traffic at this time of year."

Clare took a deep breath, "My daughter suggested I come here, and I never really found the time to do it."

The smile didn't waver, "And now you found the time."

"My daughter recently passed away and I had a need to come here. She always insisted I come."

"Was she one of our guests?"

God, Clare thought, how do I answer that question?

"I don't think she was a guest, but perhaps a visitor? In any case she loved it here."

The broom was propped against the wall and the jumble of boots slid aside with one foot. She wiped her hands on her big white apron.

"Then you are welcome and sorry I am for the loss of you daughter. Will you come in?" she opened the door and let Clare wander into a dark passage with a very old and worn stone floor, "Donaghmore House isn't fancy as some, but it's clean and we serve good, plain Irish food. Oh, and this is a family house so don't be surprised to see children everywhere, the owners have seven children, but they do not go into the guest wing."

Clare was following her down the passage that ended in a wide bright room that faced the ocean.

"So you aren't the owner?"

"Lord no! I'm the housekeeper." was spoken with a deep, joyful laugh, "The owners have taken two horses to their new owners, and I'm here with those hooligans."

"Seven children! I had trouble enough with three."

The housekeeper was pulling a ledger from the drawer of a secretary desk. She set it on the drop down table and flipped it open.

"This family has always had lots of children, as far back as the early eighteen hundreds. Most of 'em's turned out well. But there's always black sheep in any family."

"I would like to read a history of them if you have one."

"We have two fine books about Donaghmore House, one is a history written by the grandfather of the present owner and the other a diary written by Riana Gilmartin, the Baroness of Donaghmore. It covers the years from 1812 until six months before her death, and very good reading it is, too. The tariff for is one hundred and fifty Euros per night, breakfast is served from seven am until ten am. It's a full breakfast, no yoghurt, no dry cereals, unless you want to fight the children for it. We have our own dairy so our milk, butter, cheese and cream are all made on site to exacting standards. And because we are rather remote, you are most welcome to join the family for tea. If you are worried about calories, this is not the place for you. We do take Visa and Mastercard. Have a look around whilst I do the paperwork. We take pride in our paintings of horses, for Riana's husband was a great artist and he is well known for them, but I think the painting of his family are by far his best."

Clare handed the housekeeper her credit card and began to walk around. As she wandered around the room, she saw her grandchildren growing, saw to her delight Daria and Shelby, but no Ashley until she remembered that Ashley had committed suicide. Daria appeared only once, but she saw Shelby grow as the oldest in several groups of children. She saw her grandchildren with their own children, saw her daughter and her handsome husband age, then the family portraits abruptly stopped. The walls of the entire room were a monument to Riana and her family.

"Are these all of the same family? Are there more?"

"No, I'm afraid not. When the Baroness Riana died, Kieran... did I tell you his name was Kieran Gilmartin...stopped painting and refused to do any more. His paints and brushes are in the little museum down the lane, with some of the family's possessions from that time. Would you like to see your room?"

"Before I do that, is it possible to buy those two books? I am a widow so must read myself to sleep."

"Of course, shall I add them to your bill?"

Clare took back her credit card and was unable to resist asking, "These are beautiful children, aren't they? All of them."

The woman's face softened, "All the Gilmartin children are beautiful even to the present day. And every generation has one stunning beauty, beginning with Naeve," which she pronounced 'neev', "but these ones here are still too young for that decision yet. Here's your books."

The paper work completed, Clare was shown around the grounds by a very proud housekeeper, it was interesting and informative, but Clare was anxious to get alone in her room and read Riana's words, to find out about Riana's life so distance in time from what she had known. She had to know it all.

Dedication

For my first reader, my late mother and avid supporter, Hazel Kathleen Bond Palmer. You pushed and pushed and finally I gave. Thanks Mummy.

Manufactured by Amazon.ca
Bolton, ON